THE BREAK

by

Rebecca Xibalba and Tim Greaves

(from an original idea by Rebecca Xibalba)

The Break
Copyright © 2021 Rebecca Xibalba and Tim Greaves

All rights reserved.

This is a work of fiction. None of it is real. All names and events (and some places) are the products of the authors' imagination. Any relation to any real persons (living, dead, inebriated, mutilated, poisoned, drowned or electrocuted), organisations or events within the story are purely coincidental, and should not be construed as being real.

No part of this work may be used or reproduced in any form, except as allowable under "fair use" with the express written permission of the authors. Violators will be sent to the island.

PRINCIPAL CHARACTERS

Carl Banks (an ex-army officer) (45)

The Hazelwood Family
Jamie Trot (31)
Vicky Hazelwood (30)
Billie-Jo Hazelwood (16)
Bobbi-Leigh Hazelwood (14)

The Mason Family
Nick Mason (45)
Kirsty Mason (42)
Charlie Mason (14)

The Kinley Family
Grant Kinley (29)
Jenny Kinley (32)
Jordan Kinley (11)
Jack Kinley (7)

The Page Family
Warren Page (46)
Lisa Page (36)
Caine Page (17)
Hollie Page (14)

Terence Hallam (CEO of Hallam Holidays) (61)

Caroline Smart (Hallam's PA) (40)

SUBSIDIARY CHARACTERS

Kabir Baddi (a shopkeeper)
Little Moz (a Churchill Hamlets teenager)
Malik (a Manchester postman)
Kevin Smart (Caroline's disabled husband)
Dimitri (a Greek minibus driver)

ΜΑΣΤΙΓΑ

CHAPTER 1

Carl Banks was feeling inordinately pleased with himself. He'd not only finished what he'd been contracted to do, he had achieved damned impressive results a week ahead of schedule and Mr H was sure going to be delighted. There might even be a nice bonus in it for him.

Withdrawing the half-smoked Woodbine from between his lips, he sat back on the threadbare swivel chair on which he was perched in front of his laptop, stretched and absent-mindedly ran a hand back and forth across the ridges on his depilated scalp.

Picking up a can of Special Brew from the table he drained the last few mouthfuls, crunched the can in one of his large fists and hurled it over towards the metal waste bin beside the door. It missed, bounced off the wall and clattered to the floor alongside several others, all discarded with equal disregard for tidiness.

He stubbed out the cigarette in a saucer filled with several days' worth of half-used butts and, without taking his eyes off the laptop screen, he reached out and felt for the carton on the desk. It was empty.

Frowning, he coughed violently, spattering the laptop keyboard with globs of yellow mucus. He quickly wiped off the mess with the side of his hand, screwed up the empty carton and tossed it across the room. It hit the wall and dropped neatly into the bin.

He grinned and triumphantly punched the air. 'He shoots, he scores!'

Standing up, he crossed to the door – cobwebbed and peeling paint, giving it the appearance of something from the set of a 1930s horror picture – where a camouflage jacket dangled limply from a rusted hook. As he felt around for his smokes, the jacket brushed against the door and a little more paint flaked off and fluttered to the floor. With a relieved smile he withdrew a fresh carton of cigarettes from the breast pocket. While his fingers fumbled to remove the cellophane wrap, he walked back to the table, dropped heavily onto the chair – barely able to support his bulk – and returned his attention to the screen. Yes indeed, job well done.

Attending to a sudden itch, he thrust his hand down the front of his shorts and scratched fervently at the prickling skin behind his testicles. He withdrew his hand and there beneath his nails were the telltale flecks of eczema. A grimace flashed across his face as he made a mental note to speak to a doctor the following morning.

Lighting a fresh Woodbine, he inhaled deeply and exhaled a thin plume of smoke. He watched it drifting upwards and becoming one with the thin fug that hung below the nicotine-stained ceiling, mottled with mildew. He stared up at a brown moth, no bigger than a penny piece, flitting in lazy circles, drawn to the yellow glow of a naked light bulb so dim that it barely illuminated the shabby attic bedsit.

Banks glanced at his watch: just approaching ten. Another two minutes then. Precision was Mr H's watchword and if he told you to call at ten o'clock that had better be when you called; not a minute before, not a minute after. Ten o'clock on the dot.

He didn't like his employer very much. He'd never actually met the man and their conversations over the phone had always been cordial, if not exactly amicable. But there was something in the way the man spoke to him that indicated he considered Banks beneath him and dispensable, a minion expected to obey orders. He knew he'd only got the assignment because he was prepared to work cheap, but surely that should have earned him a word or two of gratitude by now, not the indignity of feeling he was being spoken to like a child being kept in line. It didn't really matter of course – their association was, after all, purely business – and his suspicions might have been unfounded anyway. But every time they spoke Banks felt disrespected and it irked him.

Regardless, whatever he may or may not think of his employer, he was grateful enough for the work. His departure from the armed forces under a cloud of shame had been unexpectedly abrupt and at first he'd been at a complete loss for what to do with himself. But an old contact had put him in touch with Mr H and... well, long story short, things had worked out very nicely.

The deafening scream of a train tearing past outside startled him – how did they always appear so suddenly out of nowhere? The whole room and its contents shuddered in response as it thundered by.

He stood up, squeezed past the bed covered with stained and crumpled sheets that looked as if they hadn't been changed in weeks, moved to the window and peered out into the darkness. To his right he could see the little glittering lights of the train receding swiftly into the distance. Struggling with the latch, he pulled up the window and took a deep breath that filled his lungs with cool night air. It caught at the back of his throat and made him cough again, this time more aggressively, and for a moment he struggled to catch a breath.

Composing himself, he looked at his watch. One more minute. He felt the familiar twitch in his stomach, that little surge of adrenalin that always kicked in when he spoke with Mr H.

Closing the window, he scratched nervously at the three days' worth of stubble on his chin, walked back to the table and sat down.

He quickly extinguished the cigarette and glanced up at the tattered movie poster for *The Dirty Dozen*, which was pinned, slightly askew, to the wall. In vivid colours it depicted a montage of action scenes from the film, and there leaping out from the centre, brandishing a blazing machine-gun, was a particularly rugged-looking Lee Marvin as the iconic Major Reisman.

'Here we go then, Major.' Banks wiped his hand across his brow, which was suddenly beaded with sweat, picked up his mobile phone, looked at his watch again – 22:00 exactly – and then tapped in the number that he'd called twice a week, every week for the past month. He cleared his throat and wiped a trace of sputum from his lips as he listened for the ringing sound, thinking about the phone at the other end that was about to burst into life. It might be five miles away or it might be five hundred. Banks had no idea where

Mr H was. He didn't need to know and frankly, as long as he received his money, he didn't care.

The ringing ceased and the now familiar voice came on the line. 'Banks.'

'Yes sir, Mr Hallam,' Banks said with a subconscious hint of deference.

'Update.'

'The website is complete. Exactly as per your specifications. And a week sooner than promised.' Banks paused, waiting for a response. The line was silent. 'A week early, sir,' he repeated. If he'd been expecting a word of gratuitude, there wasn't one.

Hallam spoke quietly. 'There are delegators and there are the delegated, Mr Banks.' There it was right there, that superior tone. Banks bristled. Hallam continued. 'I, being the former, can assure you that I would never have granted you – the latter – an assignment of such vital importance were I not one hundred percent certain you could deliver.'

'Of course, Mr Hallam. And I believe I have. I've sorted out the bug on the mobile phone link and your artwork is ready.' Banks looked at the laptop screen which was displaying the colourful logo he'd painstakingly deliberated over to get just right. 'I think you'll be pleased.'

'Email it to me for approval immediately. You can forward all the links and passwords for the website tomorrow. Encrypted as discussed.'

'I will. I...'

'The agreed date for completion was the 31st of the month. I trust you understand that finishing early will earn you neither brownie points nor additional remuneration.'

What about a thank you, Banks thought. 'Since you've mentioned payment, sir, my rent's due and I could really use...'

'Your fee will be deposited into your bank account on the 31st.'

'Of course, Mr...'

Hallam stopped him. 'What about the island?'

'Running to schedule, sir. I spoke to Shaquille this morning. Everything you requested should be completed exactly as specificed within the next three weeks.'

'I would hope so.'

'I know Shaquille and his three men personally from my army days, sir. They're all top-tier.'

'Nothing less than I'd expect. What about the social media?'

'Oh, yes, of course. I can saturate all the platforms we discussed at the touch of a button, sir. You just have to give the word.'

There was a moment's silence. 'The word is given.'

'Tonight, sir?'

Another moment's silence.

'Monday. Pending approval of the website.'

Banks nodded. 'Consider it done, Mr Hallam. I...'

The click on the end of the line abruptly ended the conversation.

Banks laid his phone down on the table and looked up at the poster. 'Well, fuck him, eh Major? Fuck him and the horse he rode in on. Not a single word of thanks. Ungrateful bastard.'

Composing a brief email to Hallam, he attached the artwork and fired it off.

He stood up and walked over to the electric kettle sitting on the floor near the window. Bending down, he opened the door on the little wooden cabinet sitting adjacent to it. Parting the row of his favourite go-to Amazingly Noodlicious pots, he selected a packet of leek and potato soup from the small assortment at the back.

As he flicked the switch on the kettle and set about opening the soup, he repeated – this time with a hint of venom – 'Fuck *him*.'

In truth Terence Hallam was delighted with Banks's report. Things were progressing far more smoothly than he could possibly have hoped. Not that he'd have let Banks know how he felt, of course. People like him had to be kept firmly in place.

He sucked enthusiastically on a large Cuban cigar, gripped firmly between fat fingers decked out with an array of ostentatious gold rings.

Nevertheless, he thought, he'd chosen well with Carl Banks. He'd run a full background check on the man of course – preserving old friendships in Whitehall had its benefits – and he'd unearthed a couple of nuggets to be stored away for future use; one could never have too much ammunition where dealing with hired hands was concerned. But Banks had been glad of the work – hardly surprising given his recent history – and proved himself a worthy and pliable employee. That's why Hallam had taken the extra step and entrusted the man to organise the construction work on the island. An enterprise such as this relied on the loyalty and devotion of its workers.

But what he liked most about Banks was the fact that, completely unsolicited, he addressed him as Sir. A single deferential word, but it gave him a sense of power that he thrived on.

Hallam smiled to himself. Yes, he'd chosen very well indeed.

The only light in the room emanated from the bank of computer monitors arranged in a semi-circle around him. Hallam ruffled his mop of unkempt hair, so unrealistically silver that it could easily be mistaken for a bad toupee, and leant forward in his high-backed leather chair. He pressed one of the buttons on the complex-looking console before him and the screens lit up. Relaxing back into the chair, he unpopped a button on his immaculate pinstripe jacket, always that little too tight around his obscenely corpulent form.

For as long as he could remember he'd wanted to make a difference and his plans for doing so were now coming close to fruition. It excited him and he was relishing every second of it.

He watched as one by one the screens filled with a sea of expectant faces, all partially hidden in shadow.

'My friends,' he said aloud. His thick, blubbery lips glistened with spittle. 'I'm pleased to inform you that the promotional work is ready to roll and it'll be activated on schedule on the 1st of next month.'

The room filled with the murmur of appreciative voices. Hallam leant forward, delighting at the sight of the heads nodding in unison.

He took a puff on the cigar. 'Whilst work at the resort continues – and I can confidently predict it will be completed within the next three weeks – I shall personally undertake the vetting process and then once the advertising is launched it will be all systems go.'

Hallam reached forward and pushed another button. His email in-box opened up on one of the screens. There at the top was the message from Banks. He selected it and clicked on the attachment. A garish logo with the words **Hallam Holidays** filled each of the screens in front of him.

He smiled contentedly and returned the screens to conference mode. 'Yes, my friends, Hallam Holidays is now ready to begin selecting those who fit its criteria. This is innovation unlike anything the world has ever known. And I want you to know that all the good we're about to do has only been made possible by each of you and your generous investments.'

The murmuring of voices again echoed in unison around the room.

'Rest assured, my friends, those investments will reap you immense satisfaction. Never doubt it for a moment: We're undertaking something monumentally virtuous here and together we're going to make history.'

CHAPTER 2

'This is not a bloody library, Mister Jamie. How many times am I having to tell you this?'

Kabir Baddi frowned at the man perusing one of the adult publications among the small selection on the far wall of the shop.

'Yeah, yeah, I know.' Jamie Trot took a last wistful look at the picture of a blonde thrusting her generous breasts at him – 'A bloke could die happy between them puppies,' he mumbled – and returned the magazine to the top shelf. He walked over to the counter where Kabir was still frowning at him. 'Sorry, Kabir, my son,' he said. 'Won't happen again.'

'You are saying this every time you come in here,' Kabir said with mock exasperation. He grinned, displaying a mouth full of perfect white teeth. 'Nice pictures, I see, yes?'

'Huh?'

Kabir nodded downwards and Jamie followed his eyeline to the trace of a swelling on the front of his shorts. He sheepishly looked back up at the shopkeeper. 'Oh, er... yeah. The old fella hasn't seen much action recently.' He laughed. 'Doesn't take much to get him twitchin'.'

Kabir grinned again. 'Understood. So what can I do for you today, my friend? The usual?'

Jamie eyed up the selection of lagers lining the shelf behind Kabir. 'Yeah, two four-packs of Stella. And 20 B&H.' He felt in his pocket, pulled out a few notes and quickly examined them. 'Actually, no, make it 40 B&H. Cheers.'

As Kabir turned to reach for the alcohol, Jamie surreptitiously slipped a handful of chocolate bars into his jacket pocket. He paid for the goods and walked to the door. As he got there Kabir called out, 'You are sure you're not wanting the magazine?'

Jamie didn't even look back. 'Maybe next time, old son.'

Kabir smiled and shook his head as he watched the door swing shut.

Outside Jamie stopped, ripped open one of the cartons of cigarettes and lit up. A few yards away on the street corner two women in their late teens were stood talking and sharing the scrappy remnant of a cigarette. One of them had her back to him, but Jamie immediately recognised the other. They were both attired in tops that barely reached their upper midriffs and skirts so insubstantial that the lower curvature of their buttocks peeped out.

Jamie approached them. 'Mornin' Jade.'

The woman looked up. 'Alright, Jamie?'

Her friend glanced round at him, but said nothing.

'Here.' Jamie smiled and held out the carton of Benson & Hedges cigarettes. 'Have one each on me.'

Jade smiled and accepted the offering. 'Aww, cheers babe. I owe you one.'

Jamie looked down at her ample bosom. 'Or two,' he chuckled.

'Oi, eyes up you cheeky bugger!' Jade's laugh was throaty.

Jamie waggled his eyebrows mischievously. I hope that boyfriend of yours knows how lucky he is.'

'He fuckin' well oughtta.' She laughed again.

'So who's yer lovely mate?' Jamie nodded towards the second woman as he offered her the cigarettes. She declined with a shake of her head.

'Oh, this is Nicole. We went to school together.'

'Pleased to meet ya, Nicky.'

'Likewise,' Nicole replied without the slightest hint of sincerity. 'But it's Nicole, not Nicky.'

There was an awkward silence.

'Yeah, well,' Jamie said cheerfully, 'I can't stand here chit-chattin' all mornin'. People t'see, fings to do.' He cast his eyes towards Jade's chest again and grinned. 'We can discuss what ya owe me laters.'

With that he strode off, with that all too familiar cocky swagger that can only be an affectation and actually makes men look the complete opposite of cool.

Jade scowled as she watched him cross the road. 'Fuckin' creep,' she said.

'Totes,' Nicole retorted.

Jamie Trot lived with his partner, Vicky Hazelwood, and their two daughters in a concrete monstrosity languishing on an East London housing estate with the misleadingly pleasant name Churchill Hamlets. It was anything but pleasant, a relic just biding its time until developers bulldozed it to the ground. Like so many similar estates across the country it had sprung up during the high demand for housing in the 1960s. There was no disputing that in a sane world it would have been condemned and fallen victim to a wrecking ball decades ago. Its hundreds of poky flats were still fully occupied and the outside walls – as well as those of the rabbit warren of corridors within – were daubed with the work of a thousand graffiti artists, painted over and reapplied countless times. As someone might once have said, if Southwark was a dog, all you had to do was lift its tail and that little hole right there... well, that was Churchill Hamlets. Even on a bright sunny morning the place gave off an aura that felt like a little piece of hell on earth.

The elevator was still out of order – it had been for weeks – but Jamie's flat was only on the third floor. He bounded up the communal stairs, taking the steps two at a time. As he rounded the corner where the staircase turned back on itself, two teenage lads – both wearing hoodies pulled up over their heads, one black and one grey – appeared on their way down.

'Awright Jamie, bruv?' the one in front said.

Jamie acknowledged them with a nod.

The boy continued. 'Ma old man say if I was to see ya, come in Tuesday and he'll have ya bush.'

'Cheers, Moz, tell him I'll be round.'

The two boys moved aside to let Jamie pass.

'Say hi to Bobbi-Leigh for me, cuz,' the other lad called as Jamie disappeared up the stairs.

The boy called Moz sniggered.

Looking slightly affronted, his friend turned to him. 'Wot?!'

'Bobbi-Leigh?!' Moz sneered.

'She's *fuckin'* peng, bruv!'

Moz grinned and playfully slapped his friend upside his head. 'Yeah, but firstly she's just a kid. Jamie would rip yer junk off, bruv. And fourthly she's well outta your league, she'd never put out for a melt like you!'

Jamie's voice echoed down the stairwell. 'I can hear every word, ya dirty little fuckers!'

The two boys stared at each other for a moment, then they both burst out laughing and took off down the stairs at a pace, kicking a discarded beer can, which rattled off ahead of them.

As soon as Jamie walked into the flat his partner, Vicky looked up from her phone and glared at him. 'That took ya long enough.'

Jamie closed the door and walked across to the kitchenette. 'Yeah, got gabbin' to Kabir. Fuck me, Vik, he don't half waffle.' He set down the alcohol on the table. 'I bumped into Little Moz on the way up.'

'Yeah?' Vicky said. 'I spotted that cheeky little shit spray-painting a cock and balls on Reg's front door last week.'

Jamie laughed. 'Ah, it was him was it? I saw that. Half a job though, he didn't add the jizz.'

Vicky rolled her eyes. 'Well Reg come stormin' out and caught him in the act. He was fuckin' livid too.' She laughed. 'Still, serves him right. Reg Avery's a grumpy old bastard and he's always shoutin' and hollerin' at the kids round here.'

'Me, I'd have gone back later and finished it,' Jamie chuckled.

Vicky scowled at him. 'Course ya would.'

'Well a cock and balls ain't a proper cock and balls unless there's a bit of jizz squirtin' out the end.'

Vicky rolled her eyes again. 'Child!'

Jamie pulled one of the cans of Stella Artois out of its plastic ring holder. 'Anyway, Little Moz said Big Moz will have our weed for us Tuesday.'

'Sweet. I'm down to dust now.' Vicky hadn't bothered to get dressed yet. She slipped her phone into the pocket of her fluffy dressing gown, scooped up an empty coffee mug from the floor, climbed off the sofa and padded over to Jamie. She dropped the empty mug on the draining board and tightened the cord around her gown. 'Don't s'pose those'll last ya long,' she said, eyeing the cans of lager disapprovingly. 'Did ya get my fags?'

'Yep.' Jamie handed the two cartons to her.

'Oi, ya shady cunt!' she exclaimed, examining the open one. 'Half of 'em are missing!'

'Don't exaggerate, babe, I only had two on the way back. I was gaspin'.' He felt in his jacket pocket, pulled out the bars of chocolate and held them out to her. 'I bought ya some sweeties too though.'

'Bought 'em or chawed 'em?'

Jamie's face fell. 'Well that's fuckin' choice, ain't it? I treats ya to some sweeties and all ya can do is accuse me of thievin'.'

'Well it wouldn't exactly be the first time, would it?' Vicky took them from him and examined the wrappers. 'I can't eat this shit anyway, it's got nuts in.'

Jamie grinned. 'Ya never used to complain about puttin' nuts in yer mouth.'

Vicky hurled the chocolate at him. 'Fuck you.' Jamie deftly dodged the projectiles and they skittered across the floor. 'I tell ya, Kabir's gonna catch ya one of these days. That'll wipe the stupid fuckin' grin off yer face.'

Jamie looked at her indignantly. 'What makes ya fink I nicked 'em? Jeezarse, Vik, can't ya just accept I did somefink nice for ya?'

Vicky stared at him in silence, trying to gauge the sincerity on his face. 'Okay,' she said, satisfied. 'Sorry.'

'Is that it? Call that an apology?'

Vicky loosened her dressing gown and stepped towards him. She slipped her arms around his waist and drew him close. 'I'm really sorry I accused ya of nickin' the sweets, babe.' She planted a kiss on his lips. 'That better?'

'Yeah, well, I should fink so too.'

They kissed again. Jamie set down the can of lager and slipped his hands into Vicky's gown, across her hips and round to grip her naked buttocks. For a 30-year-old woman, he thought, she had the most perfectly formed, amazingly smooth bum. He looked deep into her eyes and grinned. 'You know what?'

'What?'

'I did nick 'em.'

Vicky's eyes flashed and she pushed him away from her. 'I fuckin' knew it, ya scummy cunt!' She closed the front of her gown and tied the cord.

Jamie chuckled. 'I had ya going for a moment there though.'

'You can fuck right o…' Vicky stopped and screwed up her face. She was looking past him.

Jamie frowned. 'What?'

'Bronson's eatin' the chocolate.'

Jamie glanced round just in time to see their Rottweiler enthusiastically devouring the remains of the confectionary, forcing the shredded pieces of silver wrapper out of the side of his mouth with his tongue. 'At least someone's grateful,' Jamie said.

Vicky shook her head in disbelief. 'Chocolate's poisonous for dogs, ya prick. Everyone knows that.'

'Is it?' Jamie looked bemused. He shrugged. 'Well it's too late now.'

The sound of raised voices suddenly erupted from the next room: 'For fuck's sake, Bill, you've been usin' my lippy again. Why don't ya buy yer own?' – 'Christ, stop bitchin', I'll get ya some more. I had a date with Tyler last night and I'd run out. It's not like ya never take my stuff!' – 'Bollocks. I'm tellin' Dad.' – 'Hah! Like he's gonna give a shit.'

Jamie looked at Vicky. 'Fuck's sake, they shouldn't be usin' language like that. Bob's only 13.'

Vicky shot him a look. 'She's 15 – or will be next month.'

'Nah, nah, nah. That's Bill.'

'Bill's 16.'

Jamie looked confused. 'You sure?'

The expression on Vicky's face was a mixture of disdain and pity. '*Seriously*?!'

Jamie frowned. 'Whatever. They shouldn't be fuckin' swearin' like that.'

No sooner had the words left his mouth than Vicky's two teenage daughters – Bobbi-Leigh, closely followed by Billie-Jo – appeared from their bedroom.

'Dad, Bill's been usin' my make-up again without askin',' Bobbi-Leigh screamed. 'She's such a cock!'

This was a dispute Jamie really couldn't be bothered to get involved in. 'Language!' he said. He turned his back on them, picked up the seven cans of lager and took them to the fridge.

Billie-Jo grinned at her sister. 'Told ya.'

Bobbi-Leigh looked at her mother. 'Mum!' she began.

Vicky held up a hand. 'I don't wanna hear it. Just sort it out among yerselves.'

The girl stamped her foot. 'God, it's so fuckin' unfair. You always side with Bill,' she protested.

'Enough!'

'But *Mum…*' Bobbi-Leigh trailed off as she saw the expression on Vicky's face. She might have protested further but the hard done by look on her own face suddenly changed to one of disgust. 'Ewwww…' she shrieked, putting a hand to her mouth to prevent herself from gagging.

Jamie looked up from the fridge. 'Jesus Christ, what now?'

'Bronson's pukin' his guts up all over the carpet.'

Vicky glanced over at the Rottweiler, which was indeed doing exactly what her daughter had said. She picked up a dishcloth from the draining board. 'It's alright, yer Dad's gonna clean that up,' she said calmly. She glowered at Jamie and threw the cloth at him. 'Ain't ya, babe?'

Grimacing – 'That's well rank,' Billie-Jo muttered, looking just as queasy as her sister – the two girls hastily disappeared back into their room.

Jamie pulled out a bottle of Kleenit from the cupboard beneath the sink. He walked over to the mess on the floor and lashed out a foot at Bronson, who yelped and scampered into the corner where he sat down looking very sorry for himself. Stella, a chunky brown and white Staffordshire Bull Terrier that had been curled up snoozing in a cardboard box beside the television, stirred and looked up sleepily as Jamie got down on his knees and began to scoop up the mess into the cloth.

Vicky pulled out a bottle of vodka from the kitchen cupboard. She filled a glass to the halfway point and returned to the sofa. Stretching out, she lit a cigarette and retrieved her mobile phone from the pocket of her dressing gown.

Jamie finished cleaning up the mess deposited on the carpet by Bronson and went over to the kitchen sink. He dropped the bottle of cleaner into the pedal bin. 'This Kleenit stuff is utter shit. That puke's gonna stain,' he grumbled.

Vicky didn't look up. She was totally engrossed in her phone, scrolling through her Facebook page. 'Like one more stain is gonna make a difference on *this* fuckin' carpet,' she said absent-mindedly.

Just about managing not to throw up himself, Jamie ran cold water over the cloth, ringing out the thick brown sludge into the sink. It collected around the plughole, refusing to go down. Jamie pulled a spoon from the drawer and implemented some force. Finally it broke down and swirled away. Glancing over his shoulder to check that Vicky wasn't looking, Jamie dropped the not entirely clean spoon back into the drawer.

'Here babe, come over here and take a squint at this!' Vicky exclaimed. She was staring wide-eyed at her phone screen. Beneath an image of an idyllic sandy beach were the words:

HALLAM HOLIDAYS
is delighted to offer you the opportunity to win an all expenses paid holiday of a lifetime at our exclusive island resort on the Ionian Sea! Click here for more details.

Jamie didn't look round. 'What?'

'There's a thingy here to win a free holiday on an island in the Ionian Sea,' Vicky said with evident excitement in her voice.

Jamie threw the cloth in the bin and turned to face her. 'Where the fuck's that?'

'Not a clue, I've never heard of it. Hang on.' She clicked the link and scrolled quickly down the screen. 'Oooo, nice, it says it's near Greece.'

Jamie picked up his can of lager and came over to the sofa. 'Shift yer plates then.' Vicky swiveled herself into the sitting position and he flopped down beside her. 'All these fings are a con, babe.' He opened the ring-pull on the can and drank several big gulps. He belched loudly. 'There's always a catch that ends up costing ya.'

'I dunno,' Vicky said, studying the screen. 'It looks pretty pukka to me. And get this. It's exclusive entry for the underprivileged.'

Jamie grinned salaciously and slipped a hand under Vicky's gown. He squeezed her leg. 'Feelin' underprivileged, babe? I can help out with that.'

Vicky gave him a filthy look. 'Not a fuckin' chance. You stink of dog puke.'

Jamie's grin faded and he withdrew his hand.

Vicky returned her attention to the phone. 'Pin back yer lugholes. This comp is a piece of piss. All ya gotta do to be in with a chance is tell them all about yerself and be able to prove yer on a low income.' She glanced disdainfully at her boyfriend as he guzzled greedily from his can. 'Or no bleedin' income at all.'

Jamie belched again. 'So they just wanna hear people's sob stories?'

'Well fuck me, we've got more than enough of those! And the prize is three nights at a brand new luxury holiday resort on a private island. We've got to give it a go.'

Jamie wasn't convinced. 'It's a complete waste of time, babe. The chances of gettin' picked are a shit-ton less than nuffink,' he scoffed. Draining the can, he let out another objectionably vociferous belch.

Vicky punched his arm. 'Pig! Look, it says they're gonna choose four winning families. Why shouldn't we be one of them? I'm enterin' us.' Her eyes filled with a faraway look. 'Just imagine if we won. It'd be the first break we've had for years.'

Now it was Jamie's turn to roll his eyes. 'Don't hold yer breath. There ain't no way we're gonna win. Just remember where you heard it. Anyway, what was wrong with that weekend away we had last year?'

Vicky grimaced. 'That was *two* years ago. And don't get me started on *that* weekend from hell.'

Jamie looked a little perplexed. 'Well I enjoyed it.'

'You were so pissed I'm surprised you can even remember it!' Vicky picked up her glass of vodka and downed it in one. 'Here, girls,' she shouted. 'How'd ya like the sound of a holiday in the sun?'

Billie-Jo and Bobbi-Leigh appeared in the bedroom doorway. 'Really?' the older one said excitedly. Her face dropped. 'Mum, Stella's shitting on the carpet.'

Vicky turned her head and saw the Staffie squatting beside her cardboard box. 'Oh, fuckin' great! She's still got the squits too. You useless prick,' she snapped at Jamie. 'Didn't you put her out this mornin'?'

Jamie looked suitably contrite. 'Sorry, babe, I didn't fink.'

CHAPTER 3

Two hundred miles north, on the balcony of a top floor flat not dissimilar to the one in which Jamie Trot was bending down to wipe up excrement, Grant Kinley was savouring the spring morning air, a mug of steaming hot tea – tiniest splash of milk, two sugars – and his first roll-up of the day. They were little pleasures to be sure, but pleasures that an ex-con had learned never to take for granted.

Grant had served more than a quarter of his 30 years on the planet behind bars. The last time had been a three-year custodial stretch for wounding with intent. Mind you, the bastard had deserved it, coming right up in his face and screaming the N word at him. But when he'd got out he'd sworn to Jenny that he'd never brawl on the street again. Two years had passed since then and he'd been good to his word.

He took a sip of tea and gazed out across the parade of high-rises on the grimy Manchester council estate that had been his home since he was a child. He smiled to himself. Yes indeed, he'd learned to curb his rage and now he only ever let his fists fly behind closed doors.

He squashed out the end of his cigarette on the balcony railing and flicked the remains over the edge. Then he stepped back inside and switched on the TV. He idly browsed through the channels and stopped on an episode of *Classic Cars Extreme: Thrashed and*

Trashed!. Pumping up the sound, he sat down to finish his tea, staring at the screen without really watching.

As usual, Jenny wasn't out of bed yet. And as for the boys... well, Grant didn't know where they were, they'd disappeared as soon as he'd got up. Probably knocking about with that kid from two blocks down, he mused. What was his name again? Doji? Dopi? Dopey more like. Almost as bad as his own two.

He looked up at the photo on the mantelpiece. A pair of prepossessing pale brown faces topped by thick black curls beamed down at him. Why did they never smile at him that way? That was school photos for you, he guessed. They weren't bad kids as such, but certainly way too introvert for his liking. That was their mother's fault, of course; she mollycoddled them.

The bedroom door opened and Jenny appeared. Her long auburn locks were in a state of disarray and she looked pale and bleary-eyed. Dressed only in her underwear, she was pulling on a loose-fitting sweater.

'Where are the boys?' she asked sleepily.

'Out.' Grant drained the last of his tea and held out the mug towards her.

Jenny came over and took it from him, went into the kitchen and added it to the crockery piled up in the sink. Stifling a yawn, she called out, 'Are they with Dopi?'

'What?'

She walked back to the kitchen door. 'I said are they with Dopi?'

'No idea. Probably.' Grant muted the sound on the television and stared at her with undisguised disgust. 'If you crawled out of your pit a bit earlier you'd know where they are.'

'Sorry, I overslept.' Jenny hated herself the moment the words left her lips. She had nothing to say sorry to *him* for, yet it had become habitual, the apologies just kept slipping out.

'Oh yeah, and I suppose it was nothing to do with having a skinful last night – again.'

Jenny didn't answer. She turned and went back into the kitchen.

Through the open doorway Grant watched his wife, her back to him, standing at the sink. What had he seen in her? There must have been something, but it was so long ago now he could barely remember. Looking at her now there certainly wasn't much resemblance to the fresh-faced girl with perky tits and legs that went on forever he'd met all those years ago. How many was it now? At least 15. Her once pretty features had become hard and sallow. It was difficult to believe she was only a few years older than him. Mind you, he thought, the drink would have had more than a little input on that. She was still a good screw... well, on those occasions when she was sober at least. And preferably from behind so he didn't have to look at that face. But if she wasn't sober it was like fucking a corpse.

Yes, he thought, sex was the sum total of her worth to him nowadays.

Jenny reappeared in the doorway, her hands wet and covered in washing up suds. 'I meant to say, we had a letter from Jack's teacher yesterday.'

'Yeah?' Grant turned his attention back to the television.

'Yeah. She's really pleased with his progress this term. She says he's really come out of his shell a lot.'

'That's cool.' A sleek, metallic blue Jaguar E-Type appeared on the TV screen. Grant unmuted the sound and the roar of its engine filled the room.

Jenny had to raise her voice to have any chance of being heard. 'I wish Jordan was doing as well,' she continued. 'He hasn't handled the move to secondary very well. He hasn't said so, but I think he's being picked on.'

Grant didn't take his eyes off the screen. 'He needs to man up. They both do.'

Jenny gave her husband a look filled with contempt. He was, as usual, more interested in the television than he was in the well being of the boys. 'They've become very reliant on each other the last couple of years. They don't seem to do so well when they're separated.'

Grant didn't answer. She had lost his attention to a couple of idiots racing sports cars through a desert canyon.

Conversation between them these days was infrequent and even on those occasions when they did speak it was usually fractious.

Jenny gave him a last look and returned to the sink. Her head was thumping like a bass drum; she would have to take something before it split. She sighed. Grant had been right about *that* she conceded. At least three too many G&Ts again last night.

She dried her hands on a towel and ferreted about for a packet of painkillers in the drawer. Filling a glass with water, she swallowed two capsules. Then she resumed the washing up.

When Grant had promised her that he was done with life behind bars she'd been doubtful. Thrilled to hear him say it, of course, but still very doubtful. Now, ever increasingly it seemed, there were days that she wished he had broken that promise. Although life was hard enough with or without him around, it was definitely less tumultuous when he was away. He'd been out of work for almost a year now and having him sitting around the house all day had put even more strain on their relationship. How many arguments had there been? How many black eyes?

And as for always having a dig at her about her drinking, didn't he realise that it was him who'd driven her to it years ago and even now continued to fuel her dependence? The bottom line was she didn't really care what Grant thought of her anymore, but she wished he wouldn't be so hard on Jordan and Jack. Or lash out at them so often. The least little thing and he'd fly off the handle. It was bad enough when he hit her, but she couldn't stand it when he struck her boys.

Jenny had given up everything for Grant Kinley. Five years ago – it felt like a lifetime now – she had been so close to her mother, as close as a mother and daughter could be. And Jordan and Jack had loved their grandma to bits. But the last time Grant went inside she'd given Jenny an ultimatum: 'Divorce that wastrel, Jenny, or I'm afraid I won't have anything more to do with any of you. Your life is making *me* ill.'

Well, Jenny had come to her decision – which she now recognised as being one of the worst she had ever made – and she hadn't seen her mother since. Actually, that wasn't entirely true. They'd seen each other a couple of times in the street. The first time Jenny had smiled at her mum and it had broken her heart when the woman averted her eyes and walked into a shop she'd evidently had no reason to enter. The second time they'd locked eyes for a few seconds and both turned away.

Yes, Jenny had made her bed and now she had to lie in it. At least she had the two boys and they were a constant source of solace to her. But, God forbid, if Grant ever suspected for a moment that little Jack wasn't his, he'd kill her – and Jack too. She was convinced of it. And it would all be that Noel Brandon's fault.

A plate slipped out of her hand and shattered on the floor. The sound of the television in the next room ceased abruptly. Jenny glanced fearfully back through the open doorway. The TV was off and Grant was looking at his mobile phone. Fortunately, it seemed, he hadn't heard.

Jenny bent down to pick up the broken shards.

Yes, Noel Brandon, the owner of Brandon's Brush-Up where she had been employed as a mop-pusher for just a month. One of the many jobs she'd landed, ballsed-up and lost over the years. She'd got that particular one just before Grant had been banged up for another year, guilty – again! – of assault. And she had almost lost it in the first week when Noel caught her drinking. God, she thought, how she'd pleaded with him not to sack her, explained how badly she needed the job because she had a three-year-old kid to provide for, and how sorry she was to have let him down.

That was when he'd pushed her up against the wall and forcefully kissed her.

She'd shoved him away, of course, but he'd stood in front of her and very matter-of-factly explained that drinking on the job meant instant dismissal. She'd begun to cry. But he'd pulled out a handkerchief and with an undisguised hint of deviant pleasure gently wiped away her tears, adding that provided she was prepared to prove to him that she was worth keeping on, he would let her stay.

At least Noel had been young and fit, and she'd always had a thing for black guys anyway – that's what had first attracted her to Grant.

But good-looking or not, the incident was the catalyst for what would be the most degrading and humiliating few weeks of her life. Frequent blow-jobs in the storeroom (at least he was clean, but she'd still thrown up afterwards... on more than one occasion) and urgent, passionless thrusting (to mercifully swift climax) on the floor of his office.

Less than three weeks later, thanks to a split condom, she was pregnant. And when Jenny had told him, Noel sacked her anyway.

She had never quite regained her self-respect. But the one good thing to come out of that nightmare was her lovely little Jack. Abortion hadn't even been a consideration – she had lived up to her devout Catholicism in that respect at least. And she'd thanked her lucky stars, however reluctant she was feeling at the time, that she and Grant had had sex just before he was incarcerated. The maths had worked out perfectly and saved her bacon.

'Hey, come and look at this on Twitter!'

Jenny snapped out of her thoughts and dropped the broken crockery in the bin.

Grant was beckoning to her enthusiastically. He pointed to his phone. 'This looks fucking mint!'

Jenny walked over to him and leant in. 'Hallam Holidays,' she said, looking at the phone screen. 'You should be looking for work, not browsing holidays we can't afford.'

'Read it,' he said. He held out the phone for her to take. 'This one's free. Besides, I can look for work any time.'

She frowned. 'And yet you don't.'

Grant moved so fast that Jenny almost let out a cry of surprise. He dropped the phone and sprung out of the chair, one of his fists tightly balled. 'Or maybe *you* could try a bit harder to find something that brings in a bit more coin. Hanging around that launderette gabbing all day doesn't begin to cover the bills.'

Rooted to the spot, Jenny flinched, waiting for the impact and the all too familiar searing pain. Thankfully it didn't come.

Grant dropped his fist. 'Now why don't you just fuck off and make me another brew.'

CHAPTER 4

Kirsty Mason's eyes fluttered open. She turned her head and the radio alarm clock on the bedside table came slowly into focus: 8:53.

She had slept soundly – that didn't happen so often these days – and had a vivid dream in which she and Daisy were sitting in the little garden at Castanea, both of them laughing hysterically about something; she had no idea what.

Suddenly Kirsty felt hot. She always slept naked, yet she never failed to overheat, even under the thinnest quilt. Kicking her legs free, she rolled over and looked at Nick, who was laid on his side with his back to her. She could hear soft, steady breathing.

'You awake?'

Nick grunted something unintelligible.

'Was that a yes or a no?'

He grunted again.

'Sorry, I didn't catch that,' she said impishly.

'A no.'

Kirsty smiled. She draped an arm across him and snuggled in close. Pressing her lips to his ear she planted a soft kiss on the lobe. 'What are you thinking about?'

'Nothing,' he mumbled. 'I'm asleep.'

'It's almost nine. We should get up. I need to email the council about the trouble out back again last night. And Charlie will be looking for his breakfast.'

Nick started to turn over and Kirsty shifted back to her side of the bed to give him room.

'He's old enough to get his own breakfast. It's Saturday morning and I'm having a lay in.' Nick settled on his back and turned his head to look at his wife. 'How come you manage to look so beautiful after ten hours in bed? It's just not normal.'

Kirsty moved forward and gave him a peck on the lips. 'There's those that have it and those that don't,' she said, reaching up and brushing her hand through his thick greying hair. She moved in close again and nuzzled her face into his neck, her fingers making little clockwise circles in the soft hair on his chest. 'So what *were* you thinking about? I could almost hear the cogs turning.'

'All sorts.'

'Yesterday?'

'Well, yesterday too, obviously,' he sighed.

Kirsty's fingers stopped moving for a second and then resumed their ministrations in the opposite direction. 'Don't fret about it, love. Something will come along. You know it will.'

'Yeah, I know. But I was *so* sure with this one. I really thought I had it nailed.' Nick rubbed a hand back and forth across his chin. 'What a bloody disaster. I tell you, that bunch of jokers really need to sort out the job description. Wasting people's time. And as for the two goons doing the interview, they made the Chuckle Brothers look savvy.'

Kirsty laughed and prodded him playfully. 'To me, To you.'

He forced a half-smile. 'Over an hour I sat in there – a bloody hour! – and I came out not one iota wiser about what they really wanted. One thing was pretty clear though: they sure as hell didn't want me.'

'You were way too good for that place anyway. And you really wouldn't have been happy working nights.'

'I guess.' He sighed again. 'But honestly love, it just feels like one crappy bit of luck after another. This time last year I was making great money, we had the cottage... we had...' He paused. 'Well, now look where we are. Shitsville.'

'I'm not going to pretend Castanea wasn't our dream home. Who wouldn't want to live in a little cottage near the sea? And Portskewett was a lovely place to be.' She smiled at him reassuringly. 'But it's hardly important. As long as we have each other it doesn't matter *where* we are, we'll be there *together*. Think about it. If we can get through everything that's been thrown at us this past year, we can survive *anything*.'

Nick kissed her forehead. 'I know. But I still feel like I've let you down. And Charlie. And...'

Kirsty cut him short. She could see where this was going. 'You haven't, love. You *really* haven't.' She moved back and propped herself up on one elbow. 'Slough isn't so bad...'

'It's not Portskewett.'

'Nothing else could be.'

He grimaced. 'Honestly though, they couldn't have found us a worse place to live if they'd tried.'

'It doesn't matter. We still have a roof over our heads. And the good times will return soon, I know they will. *You* know they will.'

Nick inhaled deeply, fighting back tears. 'I miss her, love. I miss her *so* much.'

Kirsty felt herself beginning to well up. 'So do I. We all do.'

'Twelve-years-old.' Nick almost choked on the words. 'Twelve for Christ's sake!'

Kirsty looked at him. 'I know. Please, love, can we not do this?' she implored.

He wiped his eyes with the back of his hand. 'I tell you, that guy's lucky they banged him up for life. If I'd have got my hands on him I swear I'd have torn him apart.'

'And then *you'd* have been locked up!'

'It would have been worth it.'

'Not to me and Charlie it wouldn't.' Kirsty sighed. 'Why are we even having this conversation again, love? Karma will take care of that scumbag. We have to cling to that.'

'And what about Charlie?'

'What about him?'

'Losing his sister like… like *that*.'

Kirsty put a finger to his lips. 'Please, love, stop beating yourself up. Charlie's coping. He's coping really well, you know he is. He's doing great at school and he hasn't wet the bed for ages. Every day I see a little bit more of the old him coming back to us.'

'Yeah.'

Her face filled with concern. 'It's you I'm more worried about.'

Nick rolled on to his side to face her. No matter how bad things got, self-pity had never really been his style. He smiled. 'There's no need to worry about me, I'll be okay. It's just like you say, something will come along.'

'It will.' Kirsty leant forward and their lips touched, gently at first, then with escalating passion. They broke off for a moment and gazed intently into one another's eyes. 'Thank you,' she said.

'For what?'

'Being you. Being mine.'

'I love you,' he said. 'So much.'

Kirsty brushed her lips across his cheek and up to his ear. 'Then prove it,' she whispered.

An hour later, showered, shaved and dressed, Nick was busy preparing a breakfast of bacon and eggs.

He had barely been able to hold back the tears as they'd made love and Kirsty had clung to him more passionately than she had in a long time.

Daisy's death had been beyond horrific and their lives had changed dramatically; whose wouldn't in the wake of losing a child so young? Their daughter had been gone for almost a year now, yet it still felt as raw as ever. He knew Kirsty felt the same, but she was far better at hiding her emotions than him and her ability to seem nonchalant about it bugged him more than he'd ever let on. In a way he kind of envied her for it.

Still, he had to admit to himself that although he'd carry the scars of Daisy's death for the rest of his life, the black cloud of depression that had engulfed him for so long had actually dissipated a little since the move. Losing his daughter, his job and his home had battered his pride to such an extent that he had been in fear of losing literally everything.

GX Electronics had been good to him though. They'd cut him far more slack than he possibly deserved, certainly more than he'd have cut himself if he'd been in their position. He had tried so hard, but his focus was gone. And considering Nick had only been with GX for a couple of years, Mike Stanton – God bless him! – had been good enough to ensure he had departed with a few pennies in his pocket. The problem was, that was over six months ago and try as he might he hadn't been able to find another job yet.

The bloody Chuckle Brothers, Nick thought. He couldn't help smiling.

Kirsty came downstairs. She was barefoot and wearing denim cut-offs and a T-shirt adorned with a picture of a cat and the slogan **100% Cattitude**. Her long dark hair, still damp from the shower, lay in tangles around her shoulders. 'Have you seen my slippers?'

'Nope.'

'Mmmmm, that smells yummy.' She kissed Nick quickly on the cheek. Taking three plates out of the cupboard, she set them down on the kitchen table. She laid the cutlery and was just filling three glasses with orange juice when her son, yawning loudly, came plodding down the stairs.

'Morning sleepyhead.' Kirsty brushed his hair aside and kissed him on the forehead.

Nick glanced over his shoulder. 'You're up late, buddy. Just as well me and your Mum decided to have a lay-in too.' He winked at Kirsty. She didn't react but Nick would have sworn he could see her blush. It made him feel warm inside.

Charlie rubbed his eyes sleepily. 'I didn't sleep very well. I smelled the bacon.'

Nick frowned. 'Ah, well, you see, here's the thing, buddy. We figured you probably wouldn't want any, being as it's so late. I've only cooked enough for us.'

The boy cast his father that familiar look that said *yeah, right Dad.*

Nick chuckled. 'Sit down then. Dad's bacon and eggs extraordinaire coming right up.'

Charlie took a seat at the table and Kirsty sat down beside him. 'Why didn't you sleep well, buddy?'

'Bad dreams. I just kept waking up. But I put the light on and read my book for a bit – that always makes me sleepy – and eventually I went off again.'

As four slices of toast popped up in the toaster, Nick came over with the sizzling pan and distributed the food around the three plates. 'What are you reading, buddy?'

'*Lord of the Flies.*'

'Blimey!' Nick exclaimed. 'I'm not surprised that put you to sleep. William Golding – an instant cure for insomnia!'

Kirsty flapped her hand at him. 'He's reading it for school.'

'Even more evidence that it's a yawn fest. Eh, buddy?' Nick winked at Charlie and the boy smirked.

'It is a bit of a mission, Mum.'

'When I was at school...' – Nick placed the empty pan back on top of the stove – '...we had to read *The Great Gatsby*. It was so boring, I hated it with a passion. But for some reason I can't remember now, four or five years later I decided to give it another whirl. And you know what?'

'You appreciated it much more?' Kirsty said.

'Nope.' Nick sat down at the table. 'I still hated it with a passion. I didn't even make it half way through second time round.'

Charlie laughed. He picked up a piece of crispy bacon and popped it into his mouth.

Kirsty smacked his hand. 'Oi, use your knife and fork. And don't encourage your father.'

Nick and Charlie exchanged a smile.

'In my class,' Kirsty began, 'we had to read *To Kill a Mockingbird*. I really liked it.' She started on her breakfast. 'It was a wonderful story.'

'You're one of the lucky ones then,' Nick said. 'When I was at school there weren't many books on the curriculum that didn't bore kids to tears. In fact, a couple of the boys in our class took a copy of *The Great Gatsby* and...' He trailed off as he saw the expression on Kirsty's face. 'Yeah, well, it's all part of your education, buddy. Stick with it.'

Charlie swallowed a mouthful of food. 'I'm actually quite enjoying it.'

Kirsty smiled sweetly at Nick. 'You see? We're not all philistines.'

'Hang on.' Nick looked a bit bemused. 'I thought you said it put you to sleep!'

Charlie took a piece of toast from the rack in the middle of the table and dipped it in his fried egg. 'Not the story.' He crunched on the toast. 'It's just reading in bed that makes me sleepy. Ten minutes and I can hardly keep my eyes open.'

Nick smiled at his son. Kirsty was right, the boy really was starting to seem a lot more like his old self. The uprooting from Portskewett and moving to Slough had been a bit traumatic. In the space of a few months Charlie had lost his sister and his circle of friends. But he was a bright kid and to both Kirsty and Nick's surprise he'd fitted into his new school well. It helped that Kirsty had secured a secretarial position there; most boys of Charlie's age would have been mortified to have their mum working at their school – the potential for merciless ribbing was infinite – but it had given Charlie a boost of confidence. Sure, he'd been quieter than he used to be. He'd had the wind knocked out of his sails, and for a long time he would come home from school, disappear into his room and barely be seen again until he was heading out the door the next morning. But now he was definitely showing signs of bouncing back.

Kirsty finished a piece of toast. 'Me and your Dad were talking last night and we were thinking it might be nice if we had a little holiday away somewhere.'

Charlie took a sip of juice. 'That'd be cool. Where?'

'We haven't decided. I'm going to have a look online this morning and see what's available late August or early September.'

'Somewhere by the sea and really hot?' Charlie said excitedly.

'We can do the sea, but the temperatures will be down to the great British summer weather, buddy,' Nick said. 'I'm afraid the budget won't stretch to anything exotic.'

They finished up their meal in silence.

Nick got up and put the kettle on. 'The weather forecast for today is looking pretty grim. What do you say we take in a movie this afternoon. I can't remember the last time we all went to the pictures together.'

Charlie's face lit up. 'Can we?'

Nick smiled. 'Sure. I think there's a new James Bond on at the Odeon, at least there was. We can check to see if it's still playing. Sound good?'

'Everyone at school's seen it – well, not everyone, obviously – but it's supposed to be really brilliant.'

'Well, make your Mum a cuppa and help me with the washing up and it's a done deal.'

'But…' Charlie's smile faded.

'Come on, you've got to earn your ticket.'

'It's not that,' Charlie said, biting his bottom lip. 'It's just… I mean, I know things are a bit… What I mean is, if we're going on holiday, can we afford it?'

Kirsty thought her heart was going to melt.

Nick grinned. 'Sure we can. It's Mum's treat.'

Kirsty helped to clear the table and then left them to it. She took her mug of tea, went through to the living room and sat down on the sofa, curling her legs up underneath her.

She could hear Nick and Charlie laughing together in the kitchen and she had to fight off the overwhelming urge to burst into tears.

Things *were* tough at the moment, but she had meant what she said: they still had each other.

She reached for her laptop off the side table and clicked on the Google Chrome icon symbol, the gateway to the Internet. She spent fifteen minutes browsing various staycation travel sites but there was nothing within their budget for the months she wanted.

Deciding she would look again later, she logged on to her Facebook page. She scrolled past a video of a man with a huge snake draped across his shoulders and a picture of someone's dinner… Why the hell did people do that? 'No-one cares what you have for dinner every night, Gwyneth!' she muttered.

She was about to log off when the words **FANCY A FREE HOLIDAY?** jumped out of the screen at her. She clicked on the **more…** option underneath and the link expanded to reveal the Hallam Holidays emblem.

CHAPTER 5

The rain lashed relentlessly against the windows of the Number 33 bus from Clay Hill to Hartcliffe on the outskirts of Bristol.

It was 1.30 am, it was the last bus of the night and Lisa Page was the only passenger on board. Dog-tired, she had just completed her 10-hour shift at the filling station, the bus had been early and if she hadn't made a mad dash to the stop she would have missed it.

For some reason the 25-minute journey felt as if it was taking forever tonight. Lisa peered out into the darkness and shivered. Given that it was mid-summer, it had been chilly for days and tonight, accompanied by the incessant rain, there was a real snap in the air.

I really should have brought my coat, she thought.

Breathing hard on the glass, she drew a little smiley face in the condensation. Then she returned her attention to her mobile phone and the advertisement on Facebook she had been reading. A free holiday seemed almost too good to be true; you don't get anything for free in this life, she mused. And if something *sounds* too good to be true, that's because it usually is. There had to be a catch somewhere. Yet Lisa had studied the small print carefully and it really did sound like it was the real deal. Three nights on a Greek island at the height of summer and all travel and resort expenses covered? It had to be worth a punt.

She wouldn't say anything to Warren though, Lisa thought. He would only poo-poo it, just like he did with everything she made the mistake of showing the slightest bit of enthusiasm for. 'Don't be so bloody stupid, woman' – or variations thereon – featured high on his list of put-downs.

Of course, Lisa *wasn't* stupid. She knew only too well that her chances of winning were practically zero – she'd never won anything in her life – but it was nice to dream, wasn't it? What was that saying? It's the hope that kills you? She sighed. And just think if she were to win... if she were *actually* to win! That would show the miserable sod, wouldn't it?

She would take another a look at it tomorrow and double check the small print, she decided. Nothing ventured, nothing gained.

Slipping the phone into her shoulder bag, she looked back at the window, her eyes picking out and following a particularly large raindrop as it meandered its way down the glass.

By the time the bus reached Lisa's stop, the worst of the rain appeared to have blown over.

She covered the 10-minute walk home in double quick time; it wasn't wise to dawdle on the Godley Estate in broad daylight, let alone at 2 o'clock in the morning!

Halfway there the skies opened again and the rain pelted down on her. Lisa increased her pace, the sound of her rapid footsteps on the pavement echoing down the deserted street. There was shouting coming from somewhere up ahead and off to her right she could hear what sounded like a drunken dispute about to turn violent. Eyes forward, keep moving: that was Lisa Page's mantra.

As she came within sight of the house, the sound of breaking glass emanated from across the street and a woman screamed. Lisa didn't even look, she broke into a sprint that belied her generous size and didn't stop until, gasping for breath, she reached her front door. She had never been slim – even as a child she had been the odd one out in a classroom full of beanpoles – but at 36-years-old, a fraction over five feet tall and weighing just shy of 16-stone, she was as out of shape now as she'd ever been. Something else Warren was always remarking upon. As if *he* could play judge!

Lisa felt in her bag for her door key. It wouldn't fit into the lock and for one horrible moment she thought she was going to have to bang on the door to wake Warren again. Cursing under her breath, she waggled it about a bit and she felt the relief as it slipped in.

Dripping wet, Lisa stepped quickly inside.

No sooner had she closed the front door behind her than the door through to the living room burst open and a girl with her blonde hair plaited into two long pigtails, appeared.

'Hollie?'

Without looking at Lisa, the girl brushed past her and scuttled up the stairs. 'G'night, Mum.'

Lisa called after her. 'What are you doing up so late, love? You should've been in bed hours ago!'

Had there been tears in her daughter's eyes? It had been hard to tell without the hall light on.

Lisa felt her stomach tighten. 'And why have you still got your school uniform on?'

Without saying another word, the girl reached the top of the stairs and disappeared out of sight.

'Wait a moment, I…'

The sound of Hollie's bedroom door slamming abruptly curtailed any further questions.

Lisa dropped her bag, slipped out of her shoes and pushing her wet hair back out of her face she went into the living room.

Her husband was sitting in his armchair staring at an old movie on the television, the sound so low that it was barely audible.

As Lisa entered, Warren looked up. 'You're early tonight,' he said, yawning. 'It's five past two, you're not usually in until almost half past.'

'It's tipping down and I didn't have my coat with me. So I hurried.'

Warren peered at her mockingly through the scratched coke-bottle lenses of his spectacles. 'Don't make me laugh, you couldn't hurry anywhere if your life depended on it.'

'Why are you always so rude to me?'

Clearly he deigned the question rhetorical. 'Whatever. Your timing's perfect. I was just thinking of putting the kettle on.'

'Why was Hollie still up?'

After a moment's pause he said, 'She had a bad day at school, so I said she could stay up and watch a bit of telly. Keep her old man company.' The penetrating, dark pools of his eyes studied Lisa intently. 'You got a problem with that?'

Was his tone beginning to get defensive?

'It's a school night, it's way too late for her to…' She could hear herself blathering and she could feel Warren's eyes burning into her, just waiting for her to say it. Okay, she thought, I will say it. 'I don't know. *Should* I have a problem with that?' Lisa could feel her heart pounding.

'You tell me.' The tone was mocking now. 'Should you?'

She looked at her husband. He was only 10 years older than her, but anyone who didn't know could have been forgiven for thinking it was more like 20. The salt and pepper bristles on his face – too long to be called stubble, but too short to be a proper beard – was the youngest-looking thing about him, and what remaining hair he had was matted in thin grey strands across a scalp that was currently shining with sweat. Dressed in a string vest (streaked with what looked like curry) that failed to cover an obscene belly, and a pair of jeans that belonged in the bin, his unsightly bulk was wedged – yes, *wedged* – into the armchair. At that moment he looked to Lisa not a day less than 60.

Warren saw his wife staring at his crotch. He looked down. The zip was undone. He tried to pull it up, but it jammed. For a few seconds he fumbled with it and then gave up. He looked up at her sheepishly. 'Tea then?'

'Why was Hollie still wearing her uniform?' Just asking the question made Lisa feel sick.

'I dunno. I don't dictate to the kids what they should and shouldn't wear.' He took off his spectacles, wiped them on the bottom of his vest and set them down on the arm of the chair.

Lisa swallowed hard. 'And her hair – it's plaited.'

'I like it that way. It suits her.'

'That's not the point. She *hates* it like that.' A horrible thought suddenly flashed through her mind. 'I assume Caine's in bed?'

'You assume wrong then. He went out.'

'When?' Lisa said angrily.

'Three or four hours ago.'

'Where?'

Warren shrugged. 'How should I know?' He chuckled. 'What is this, the Spanish Inquisition?'

Lisa stared at him in disbelief. 'Four hours ago was 10 o'clock. Didn't it occur to you to ask him? I mean, what the hell did he think he was doing going out at 10 o'clock at night?!'

'I told you, I don't bloody know.' The tone in Warren's voice had definitely changed. 'He's 17, he's old enough to look after himself.'

Lisa could feel the bile rising in her throat. 'So you and Hollie have been here on your own all evening? Just the two of you?'

Warren was now glowering at her. 'Well if Caine went out, *obviously* it was just the two of us.' Lisa started to speak and he cut her off. 'I know what you're implying and I don't think I like it!'

He suddenly stood up and took a step towards her, towering over her by a good eight-inches. 'If you've got something to say, woman, fucking well get on and spit it out!' he snarled.

Lisa moved back. 'I'm sorry, I didn't mean to imply anything.' There was a tremor in her voice – almost imperceptible, but it was definitely there. 'I just like to know what the kids are up to, that's all. Hollie's only 14, it's a school night and…' She saw the threatening expression on her husband's face and trailed off. 'I was just asking.'

'Well, *don't*,' Warren said curtly. Then, just as quickly as it had appeared, the menace drained from his face and the equanimity returned. 'Now,' he said cheerfully. 'What about that tea?'

Lisa suddenly realised she had backed up almost to the door. 'I'll make it. Just let me get out of these wet clothes.'

Warren returned to his armchair and Lisa went back out into the hall. As she pulled the door shut behind her the volume on the television went up.

She hastened upstairs, pulling her sodden T-shirt over her head as she went. When she got to the bedroom she unfastened the clip on her skirt, let it drop to the floor, stepped out and kicked it to one side. Removing her underwear, she quickly pulled on a robe, grabbed a towel from the basket at the foot of the bed, and briskly rubbing at her damp hair she went back out onto the landing. She paused at the top of the stairs, listening. She could still hear the sound of the TV in the living room.

Moving swiftly along to her daughter's room, Lisa tapped quietly on the door with the tips of her fingernails.

'Hollie, love, are you awake?' she said quietly. There was no answer. She waited for a few seconds and was about to tap again when a loud bang sounded in the hallway downstairs.

She went to the top of the stairs and peered over the banister. A young lad was standing in the hallway removing a battered bomber jacket.

'Caine!' She started down the stairs.

The boy looked up, an expression of surprise on his face as if he hadn't expected to see anyone. 'Oh, hey Mum,' he slurred.

He'd been drinking – and quite a lot looking at the state of him, Lisa thought. She reached the bottom of the stairs. 'Where have you been?' she whispered angrily.

'Out with Gaz and his brother, we went down The Triangle.'

'You know you're expected to stay in on the days when I'm working a late shift. It's only twice a week, for God's sake.'

'Gaz texted and asked me.' On his third attempt Caine managed to get the locker loop on his jacket over the hook. 'It's his birthday.'

'I'm not interested in reasons,' Lisa hissed. 'You shouldn't have gone out, period. Jesus Christ, Caine, I don't ask for much.'

The boy lazily flapped a hand at her. 'Aww, don't go on at me, Mum. I've got a headache.'

'You'll have a darn sight more than a headache to worry about if you let me down again. Hollie was still up when I got in. I think…'

The sitting room door opened. Warren's immense bulk filled the frame. 'Are we having tea or not?' he said testily. His eyes fell on Caine. 'Oh, you're home then! Your Ma's been worried about you.'

Lisa tried to hide her anger. 'It's okay, he was just explaining. He went out with Baz…'

'*Gaz*!'

'Er, Gaz, yes, sorry. It's his birthday. No harm done.'

Warren squinted at her through the pebble lenses. Lisa felt her heart rate increasing again.

'You see,' Warren said. 'I told you it was nothing to worry about.' He looked at Caine. 'Although I don't know why you hang around with that gashead! Since you're here you can go put the kettle on and make your Ma and me a tea.'

Caine groaned. 'Aww, Dad, I've got a headache and...' He stopped short as he saw the expression on Warren's face. 'Okay, okay,' he said with that childish, hard done by whininess that always made Lisa bristle.

As the boy sauntered towards the kitchen, scuffing his feet as he went, something fell out of his back pocket and bounced on the carpet. Lisa looked down and her eyes widened. It was a switchblade.

'Caine!' she exclaimed angrily.

The boy stopped and turned around to face his mother. '*What*?!'

She pointed to the floor. 'What have I told you about carrying that damned thing around? It's illegal, you'll get yourself arrested!'

Warren chuckled. 'Leave the lad alone, woman, he's not doing any harm.'

Caine bent down to pick up the knife. 'Yeah, Mum, leave me alone. It's only for protection. You can hardly blame me round here.'

Lisa was almost speechless. 'What part of illegal don't you understand?'

Caine shrugged. 'It's perfectly safe.' He flicked the blade in and out a couple of times.

Warren chuckled. 'Nobody is going to mess with my kid.'

Caine cockily tossed the switchblade into the air. It circled a couple of times, but as he reached to catch it, he missed and it dropped to the floor. He bent down, retrieved it and slipped it into his back pocket. Looking sheepish, he turned and went through to the kitchen.

Lisa glared at Warren. 'Just once it would be nice if you backed me up.'

Warren turned back to the living room. 'Oh, don't bloody start again, woman,' he sighed.

'I don't want any tea,' Lisa said. 'I'm going to bed.'

CHAPTER 6

Terence Hallam was feeling jubilant. A month had passed since the contest had gone live and the final pieces of the project on which he had toiled so hard were about to fall perfectly into place.

He sat back and surveyed the three loose-leaf folders laid out in a row on the desk before him. One was slightly out of alignment with the others; he reached out and straightened it. Three down, one to go. He had a thoughtful expression on his face and he took a long draw on the Cuban cigar, lodged between his index and middle fingers.

'What did you do with the Mason file?' he said.

Just beyond his peripheral vision, in the shadows to his right, Caroline Smart had been standing for almost three hours, silently watching her employer deliberating over numerous documents. On the floor in front of her, just beside Hallam's desk, was a pile of folders stacked almost to knee level.

'It's right here.' She bent, down, removed a folder from the top of the stack and handed it to him.

He looked at the name printed on the top right of the folder. 'What does this say?' He held it out for her to see.

Caroline peered at it. 'Robertson,' she said slightly nervously.

'Robertson,' he repeated. 'May I ask why you have given me the Robertson file instead of the Mason file?'

'Oh, I'm so sorry Mr Hallam, it must be on one of the other piles.'

Hallam spun round in his chair and watched Caroline cross the dark room to where several piles of folders were heaped up against the wall.

'I thought I made it clear that the Masons were potential candidates and I wanted them to be placed among the priority profiles.'

'Yes, you did, sir. I...' She sounded flustered and Hallam felt a little tingle of pleasure at her apparent embarrassment.

He spoke with an intentional hint of impatience that compounded her discomfort. 'Then why is it on one of *those* piles – the ones I very clearly said failed to meet the criteria – instead of *this* one.' He pointed a fat finger at the stack beside the desk and looked at her, as if expecting an acceptable answer.

'I'm sorry, sir. There are so many.'

'I see,' he said quietly.

She quickly started picking through the first pile of folders. The bank of computer screens was inactive, and there was no natural light. Beyond the glow from Hallam's desk lamp there was no illumination in the room at all.

Caroline was very clearly struggling to read the names in the poor light. Hallam watched her with mild amusement. He loved to make his employees feel awkward. Watching them mew and mumble and fumble in front of him never failed to give his sense of absolute power a gratifying fix. And what an easy target Mrs Smart was, how timid and subservient. He could upset her with a single carefully chosen word, or by adopting just the right tone, and he did so whenever the moment was favourable.

It's possible she might once have been an attractive woman, Hallam thought as he watched her move on to the adjacent pile of folders. But it was hard to tell. A heavy application of make-up had created an adverse effect, handicapping her with a curious grotesquery.

'I have it!' Caroline stood up and stepped quickly over, handing a folder to Hallam. He glanced at the name on the cover – **MASON** – and opened it up to assess the paperwork inside.

Caroline stood patiently to one side and waited. A minute passed. Then two. Then five.

'Perfect,' Hallam said, closing the folder and placing it neatly alongside the other three on his desk. 'That's the four.'

He spun the chair to the left to face the computer screens and punched a couple of buttons.

'I've been waiting for this moment for so long, Mrs Smart. You have no idea how thrilling it is to be doing something so beneficial to our society.'

Caroline acknowledged him with a polite smile, but said nothing.

Hallam waited patiently as one of the screens came to life, then another and another until each of them displayed the silhouetted heads of his investors, their faces – as always – obscured for the purpose of anonymity.

'My dear friends,' Hallam began. 'As I reported to you last week, all the most essential work on the island has been completed and our resort, though not *quite* finished to full specification, is now ready to receive the first guests.'

A cacophony of approval emanated from the computer screens.

Hallam smiled. 'I'm pleased to further inform you that I have, this very evening, completed the vetting process and have selected four families from across Great Britain who will be our very first guests on the island. Our strategy is ready to launch and we will soon begin to remedy the injustice that plagues us all so greatly.'

A man sitting in shadows on one of the screens spoke; his voice was fed through a modulator. 'This is indeed good news, Mr Hallam. May I ask when we will see our first arrivals?'

'The families I have chosen will be informed immediately. As promised, their holiday will begin when we fly them to Greece on September 1st. I hope that will be satisfactory to you all?'

Another collective mumble of approval echoed around the room.

'Very well,' Hallam said. 'As I've told you before, I am confident that your investment will be worth every penny. All that is expected of you now is to sit back… and enjoy. Goodnight, my dear friends.'

Hallam pushed a button on the console and the screens all turned black.

'You'll dispatch the letters to our lucky winners tomorrow, Mrs Smart,' he said.

'Very well, sir.' She smiled. 'Will that be all for tonight?'

Hallam's face darkened. 'Not quite. There's just one more little matter to take care of and then I think it'll be time for bed.'

Caroline looked slightly agitated. 'Will you be requiring me to stay the night?'

Hallam shook his head. 'No, not tonight. It's late, I'm tired and I have an early start tomorrow.'

The look of relief on the woman's face was overt. Fortunately for her Hallam didn't notice. He picked up a telephone receiver built adjacent to the console and punched in a number.

Lying naked on his disheveled bed, Carl Banks was fighting a losing battle. He was trying desperately to finish the last chapter of his paperback book, but his eyelids had been drooping for the past ten minutes and he'd read the same paragraph over three times. Finally giving in, he dropped the book beside him, closed his eyes and rested his head back on the stained pillow. That was when the phone rang.

He reached out and felt around on the bedside table. He found the phone and peering at the screen through sleepy eyes he tapped the accept option. 'Yes?'

'Banks? Hallam.'

Immediately alert, Banks pushed aside the open box perched on the side of the bed. It slipped off, emptying its contents – a half-eaten meat feast pizza – onto the floor, and swinging his legs over the side he sat bolt upright. 'Mr Hallam, sir. I wasn't expecting you to return my call so soon. Being as you're such a busy man, I mean.'

'Yes, I *am* very busy. What did you want?' Hallam said matter-of-factly.

'I wanted to speak to you about the boat accident. I'm sure you're aware of it, being as it happened so close to your island, I mean.'

'I am.'

Banks paused. Already this wasn't going quite the way he'd played it through in his head. 'There was more on the news this evening. An unexplained explosion on board.'

'And?'

'The four men I employed on your behalf, Mr Hallam. They were good men. I knew them all, but Shaquille was a close friend. All dead.'

'I've seen the news. The last I heard they were presumed missing, not dead.'

Was the man being purposely obtuse?

'I can't believe you think that, sir,' Banks said. 'On the news they spoke to a witness who'd been watching the boat from the beach. He said that one minute it was chugging happily along, the next there was an almighty crack and it was consumed in a ball of fire. If you'd seen the footage of the burnt out wreckage... well, I don't think there's any doubt they're all dead.'

'Get to the point. I haven't got all night.'

Banks was suddenly consumed by a coughing fit. He quickly composed himself.

'I'm waiting,' Hallam said calmly, although there was a discernible trace of irritability creeping in.

'Yes, of course. Well, the thing is, sir, I've done a hell of a lot of work for you...'

'A business arrangement for which you have been more than adequately remunerated,' Hallam interjected.

'Absolutely.' Banks could feel himself beginning to sweat. 'You've been incredibly generous and please don't think for a moment that I'm unappreciative. But I'm a bit strapped at the moment and I was thinking that now you don't have to pay Shaquille and his men, if you get my drift, sir, I was kinda hoping you might see your way clear to extending your generosity a little further.'

The line went quiet.

Banks licked his lips expectantly.

After a moment Hallam spoke. 'I think not. Don't forget that dishonourable discharge from Her Majesty's services rendered you permanently unemployable. I gave you work when nobody else would, work for which you've been exceptionally well paid. I suggest you be grateful for small mercies, take the money and crawl back under whichever stone you came from. Have I made myself clear?'

Banks had another coughing fit. He reached for a tissue and dabbed at his mouth. 'I'm sorry you feel that way, sir.' Ignoring the splodge of blood on the tissue, he screwed it up and tossed it at the waste bin. It missed. 'But I'm sure you understand I had to ask. And of course I was thinking more about you than myself.'

Hallam's patience evaporated completely. 'This is your last chance to get to the point, Banks,' he snapped.

'Okay, here's the thing: I don't think what happened to Shaquille and his men was an accident. As I see it, it was obvious from the work they did for you on the island that your requests were... well, shall we say unorthodox? How long before they let slip to someone about it? It doesn't take too great a stretch of the imagination to think someone in your position would want to tie up loose ends like that. And that being the case, I got to figuring that also makes *me* a loose end.'

He paused. The line was silent again.

Banks took a breath and continued. 'But I want you to know, you've nothing to worry about with me, Mr Hallam. My discretion is guaranteed.'

'I'm pleased to hear it.'

'And provided we can come to an amicable arrangement it'll remain that way. Shall we say an additional £20,000?' Banks grinned. 'For that you get the head, the tail, the whole damn thing.'

'What the hell are you talking about?' Hallam's impatience was escalating.

Banks grinned. 'It's a movie quote.'

'I don't watch movies,' Hallam said flatly.

'It's a really famous one… from *Jaws*.'

No response.

Banks cleared his throat. 'What I'm saying, Mr Hallam, is that £20,000 buys you my absolute guarantee of silence and the promise that you'll never see or hear from me again.'

'Now you listen to me, Banks.' The ire was unbridled now. 'It sounds very much as if you're trying to blackmail me. And I assure you, you really don't want to be doing that.'

'Blackmail?' Banks sounded genuinely surprised. 'Oh, not at all, sir. Not blackmail.'

Again the line when silent. Banks could almost hear the cogs turning in Hallam's head.

A lot of planning and investment had gone into creating his unique venture and Hallam had to be certain there would be no loose lips sinking his much loved and culturally vital ship.

When he spoke the calmness had returned. 'Very well,' he said. 'I'll concede that the work you've carried out for me has been first class. Although I will not be held to ransom, I'm sure a little something extra can be arranged on this occasion.'

Banks smiled. 'That would be *very* much appreciated, Mr Hallam.'

'Very well then. Rest assured that within 24 hours you'll receive what I deem your guaranteed silence justly deserves.'

Without waiting for Banks to reply, Hallam punched a button and ended the call.

'A problem, sir?' Caroline asked.

'Nothing that can't be eliminated. I shall call pest control in the morning.'

Caroline frowned. 'I'll say goodnight then, sir.' She turned to leave, but Hallam reached out and took hold of her arm.

She turned back and looked down at him. In the half-light she could see the spittle glistening on his lips. His eyes were alive and filled with anticipation.

'Not just yet,' he said.

*

Kevin Smart was feeling unwell. As unwell as he had done for a long time. He'd taken all his medications, but for some reason they just weren't cutting it today.

His arm spasming slightly, he leaned carefully forward and picked up one of the two 700ml stainless steel water bottles from the table. He had already drained one – the lid on it didn't sit true and he'd spilt some on himself – and was well on the way to emptying the second. He pressed the straw to his lips, sucked hard and swallowed, feeling the welcome relief as it irrigated his dry throat.

He replaced the bottle on the table and with difficulty managed to move a little to one side in the chair; the uncomfortable sensation beneath him immediately reminded him of the fact he'd soiled himself a couple of hours ago. He hadn't been able to go for days, and now this...

Yep, he solemnly thought to himself, being sick is an absolute bitch.

The sound of the front door opening immediately perked him up.

'Is that you, darling?' he called out, his voice slurred and borderline intelligible.

Caroline appeared in the doorway. She looked very tired and Kevin couldn't help but notice that her lipstick was smeared on one side.

'Who else would it be?' she said wearily.

She looked down at the floor. He'd managed to knock the plate of food she'd left for him onto the rug. She sighed loudly and sauntered out into the kitchen to get a cloth.

Caroline Jones had married Kevin Smart almost 19 years ago. 19 years ago on the 27th of next month to be precise. It sounded clichéd, but it really had been the happiest day of her life. Kevin Smart: former school football captain, A-grade student and breathtakingly handsome to boot. He'd been every girl's dream catch. And Caroline had been the lucky girl who caught him, the envy of all her friends – or so she liked to think.

She didn't feel so lucky now. Fifteen wonderful years they'd had together. And then, holidaying in Scotland, he'd taken that fall on the steps outside the hotel. He'd played it down at first, but a few days later he revealed to her that his legs had been feeling weak for some time. At that point the warning signs that something might be seriously wrong just didn't register. And why would they? After all, his job as a lecturer at the college kept him on his feet all day – and everyone gets achey legs, don't they? It was only when he began to drop things, and the nights when he would wake up with the most excruciating muscle cramps became increasingly frequent ... only then the alarm bells started ringing. Caroline's best friend at school, her grandfather had died from motor neurone disease and she remembered how Amanda had described it to her. Caroline knew she was probably just being paranoid, but she bullied Kevin into consulting a doctor. It turned out it wasn't paranoia after all and their worst fears were confirmed. Early onset motor neurone disease. Incurable, but manageable. Life expectancy: impossible to predict.

Kevin had worked on for as long as he'd been able, but that hadn't been very long at all. So now here he was, three years later, confined to the house, virtually an invalid, reliant on Caroline to shave him, dress him, feed him and –

'I'm so sorry. I've messed myself,' Kevin slurred.

– and, yes, clean up after him too.

'What, *again*?' Caroline said angrily. Any compassion she had ever felt for her husband had long since gone. She took off her glasses and rubbed her tired eyes. 'For God's sake, Kevin! Couldn't you have done that while Gillian was in? As if I haven't had a dreadful enough day as it is!'

She marched over and pulled him roughly forward. She examined the cushion beneath him and the smell assailed her nostrils. 'Jesus Christ, it's leaked all over the place.' She pushed him harshly back into the chair. 'I think I'm going to be sick!'

'I'm sorry,' he said, the tears stinging his eyes.

'Yeah,' she sighed. 'Sure you are.'

She crossed to the door. 'I'll run you a bath.'

Out in the hall she kicked off her shoes and went on through to the downstairs bathroom in the extension they'd had to have built to accommodate their unfortunate new lives.

She sat herself down on the toilet seat and the tears flowed.

How had her life come to this? Not for the first time she regretted that she and Kevin had never had children. They'd tried, of course, but it had turned out that she was barren and that was the end of that.

Since she had been a little girl, Caroline had imagined having a daughter. At one stage it had almost been an obsession. After the discovery that she couldn't conceive, they had discussed adoption, but for one reason and another it had never happened.

Then Kevin had got sick and all talk of children was over and done with. As for sex… well, that was pretty much off the cards now too. On good days – and there weren't so many of those any more – Kevin would try to make love to her, but it was pathetic. She'd even said that to his face once... and immediately regretted it. But the very thought of him even touching her these days filled her with repulsion.

Caroline had considered leaving him on more than one occasion. But the fact was he owned the house. And after 19 years she was damned if she was going to walk away and have nothing to show for it. So reluctantly she'd stayed.

She had needed to find work too. Better paid work at least. It had never been Caroline's intention to become a career woman, she'd been more than happy working in Pat's Patisserie. But needs must and she'd not only had to become Kevin's part-time carer – Gillian came in every morning to deal with some of the essentials – but the breadwinner too.

So this is my life, she thought. Ball-and-chained to a man who's all but incapable of wiping his own backside. And personal assistant to an absolute monster who, if I want to keep the job, expects me to give him fellatio, or hand relief – or sometimes let him screw me. And I am supposed to look bloody grateful while I'm doing it.

She stood up and looked at herself in the mirror. Her lipstick was smudged, her mascara was running down her face in little rivulets and – oh, God... for a moment she thought she was going to throw up – there was a trace of dried ejaculate on her chin.

She quickly ran some hot water into the sink, picked up the bar of rose-scented soap and scrubbed her face clean. Then she set the bath running and went back through to the living room.

Kevin looked up at her. His eyes were moist and full of apology.

Once upon a time Caroline's heart would have melted at that. She would have taken him in her arms, kissed him and told him not to worry; these things happened.

Once upon a time... But not any more.

She pulled over the wheelchair that was parked up against the wall and roughly yanked him forward in the chair. 'Come on then,' she said bitterly. 'Let's clear up this mess.'

CHAPTER 7

With a newspaper tucked underneath his arm, Jamie came in through the door of the flat beaming.

'Hey, Vik, have you seen Reg's front door? Look what someone's added to Little Moz's handiwork!'

Vicky looked up from the sofa, a disinterested expression on her face as Jamie held out his mobile phone to show her the picture he'd taken. Added to the crudely drawn outline of male genitalia – slightly faded where Reg had attempted to scrub it off – were a couple of little spurts.

'I told ya,' Jamie cackled. 'Ya gotta have jizz!'

'You really are a fuckin' child,' Vicky said. 'What's that?' she added, pointing at the cluster of envelopes in Jamie's other hand.

'Oh, it's the post.' He handed it to Vicky. 'I passed postie when I was comin' up the stairs. He said we was the only delivery on this floor today and asked me to take it. I would've let him come up and put it through the door, but he looked knackered – he must be at least 75 – and as he asked nicely I took mercy on the poor fucker.'

'You're a real Samaritan, babe,' Vicky said sarcastically, leafing through the fistful of envelopes. 'Bill... bill... another cuntin' bill...' As she worked her way through she casually tossed each one aside.

Jamie dropped his newspaper on the table beside the sofa and disappeared into the bedroom. 'Bin 'em,' he called out. 'If they's expectin' to get paid anytime soon they've got another fink comin'.'

'Fuck me!' Vicky exclaimed. She was staring at one of the envelopes; it was emblazoned with the Hallam Holidays logo. Her fingers shaking, she tore it open and eagerly scanned the contents. Her eyes lit up.

'Babe,' she shouted. 'Come look at this.'

A cry came from the bedroom: 'For fuck's sake!' Dressed only in his underpants and one slipper – the other he was holding out at arm's length – Jamie appeared in the doorway. 'One of your bastard mutts has shit in my slipper. *Again*!'

'Never mind that now, come over here and take a look at this.' She held up the letter.

Jamie rolled his eyes at her lack of concern for his dilemma. 'Hang on.' He went over to the kitchen sink and dropped the soiled slipper nonchalantly into the washing up bowl.

With a look of abject disgust on his face, Jamie walked over to the sofa, kicking the two cardboard boxes in which the Rottweiler and the Staffie had been dozing soundly. They both woke and looked apprehensively at Jamie as he stood looking contemptuously down at them. 'Your fuckin' days are numbered,' he said, addressing the pair of them.

'Never mind them,' Vicky said. 'You know that contest I entered?'

Not taking his eyes off the two dogs, Jamie sat down beside her. 'You enter thousands of contests.'

'The free holiday one. You remember.'

Jamie looked at her. 'Read my lips. No. I don't fuckin' remember.'

'Well we've only gone and won!'

At the sound of the word won, Jamie suddenly became interested. 'You're jokin' me.'

'No, for real, babe.' Vicky handed him the letter. 'Look. We've won. Three nights on a Greek island. Woo-hoo!'

She jumped to her feet. Gyrating her hips and waving her arms in the air she started chanting. 'We woooon it. We woooon it!'

Billie-Jo and Bobbi-Leigh appeared from their bedroom.

'What's going on?' Billie-Jo said.

Jamie was staring at the letter in his hand as if he were in a trance. 'We've won a holiday,' he said quietly. He looked up at the girls and suddenly became animated again. He waved the letter in the air. '*And...* wait for it, wait for it... we're going next week. We won. We *fuckin*' won!'

The two girls looked at each other in disbelief.

'I never won nuffin' in the whole of my life,' Vicky said excitedly.

Jamie tossed the letter to one side, stood up and took her in his arms. 'You won my heart, babe.'

Vicky grinned. Her eyes were moist with tears. 'Fuck off, ya soppy cunt.' Then she pulled him close. 'Come here,' she said, kissing him hard on the mouth. 'You might just get lucky tonight.'

Jamie's eyes lit up.

'I love ya, babe,' Vicky said.

'Mum...' Bobbi-Leigh had a worried look on her face.

'Love you too, babe.' Jamie kissed her again.

'Muuum…'

Frowning, Jamie glanced over at her. 'What the fuck, Bob? Can't ya see your Mum and me's havin' a moment here?'

'You said we're going next week,' Bobbi-Leigh persisted.

'So what?'

'Who's gonna look after Bronson and Stella?'

Both girls appeared to be genuinely concerned.

Jamie scowled at the two dogs looking up at him, their tails slowly wagging. 'Fuck 'em. It's only a few days. They can stay here.'

*

Dressed in her robe and slippers, Lisa descended the stairs yawning. She bent and picked up the assortment of post and junk mail leaflets laying on the doormat. She was about to drop them on the hall table to attend to later when the colourful logo in the corner of one of the envelopes caught her eye. She recognised it immediately. Her heart skipped a beat and she let out a little gasp of excitement.

Warren stirred at the sound of his name being called repeatedly. At first it was distant, but it was getting louder and closer.

He opened his eyes as Lisa came hurrying into the bedroom, out of breath and clutching a letter in her hand. 'I've got something to tell you,' she cried breathlessly. 'But you have to promise not to get cross.'

With a bit of effort, Warren propped himself up on the pillow. 'Dear God, woman, I thought the house was on fire.' He shifted to make himself more comfortable and rubbed the sleep from his eyes. 'This had better be important, I was having a lovely dream.' He wiped the traces of drool from the corner of his mouth with the back of his hand.

'It *is* important,' Lisa said. 'But I don't want you to get cross.'

'So you said.' Warren reached for his spectacles on the bedside table and slipped them on. He looked up at his wife inquiringly. 'Well. Go on.'

'I would have told you before, but the chances were so slim I didn't even really think it was worth mentioning, well, truthfully I suppose I didn't want you to talk me out of it.' Lisa was beginning to gabble.

'Out of *what*?'

'You promised not to get cross, it's...'

'Who's getting cross?'

'But it's something good.'

'Then spit it out, woman!' Warren was glaring at her now.

Lisa waved the letter at him. 'I... what I mean is *we* have just won a holiday!'

*

Kirsty and Nick were seated at their kitchen table. They'd read the letter through twice and still couldn't quite believe it.

Kirsty's face was glowing. 'It almost sounds too good to be true.'

Nick placed his hand over hers. 'Yeah, well, you know what they say about things that are too good to be true, love: They usually are.'

'I read through the small print scrupulously when I entered,' Kirsty said. 'If there's a catch it was invisible to me.'

Nick smiled at her. He'd not seen her this enthusiastic about anything for months and it made him feel good inside. 'Maybe I shouldn't be so cynical.'

'You? Cynical?' Kirsty leant over and kissed him softly on the cheek.

'So tell me about this outfit, er…' – Nick glanced down at the letterhead – '…Hallam Holidays.'

'There's not much to tell. I did Google them, but all I could find out is it's a privately owned company, established this year, with the sole intention of funding free holidays for families in need.'

Nick sighed. 'I had my reservations when you told me you'd entered us. I'm not sure I like the idea of us being a charity case.'

'We're not a charity case. But times have been hard and…'

'You didn't let me finish.' Nick's eyes were twinkling. 'I don't *like* being a charity case, but neither am I stupid enough to look a gift horse in the mouth. Is there any more information about the resort?'

'No, no-one's been there before. It's like it says here in the letter, we'll be the first guests. Well, us and three other families.'

Nick smiled at her. 'So what do you reckon then?'

'I reckon I can't wait to tell Charlie we're going on holiday. He's going to be so excited.'

Nick shook his head. 'What I meant was, what about the caravan holiday you booked for the end of October?'

'Oh!' In the excitement Kirsty had clearly forgotten about that. 'If we cancel, we'll lose the deposit,' she said forlornly.

Nick winked at her. 'Then we'll have that too.'

Kirsty smiled, folded the letter and tucked it back into the envelope. 'You know what? I really think our luck might be turning a corner.'

'Yeah?'

She gave Nick another quick kiss. 'Yeah.'

*

Jenny cursed angrily under her breath.

Her arms were full – she'd forgotten to take a carrier bag with her to the shop and she always refused point blank to pay for one – and now she was going to have to put the shopping down to get her door key out of her shoulder bag.

She set down the loaf of bread, the bottle of milk and the litre bottle of gin at her feet.

As she turned the key in the lock a voice called out from along the walkway. 'Good mornin' to ya, Mrs K!'

Jenny looked up and saw the postman approaching.

He grinned at her, flashing a row of tombstone teeth. 'How ya doing?'

Jenny hastily bent down and retrieved her shopping, trying without too much success to tuck the alcohol out of sight behind her back. 'Hiya, Malik. I'm fine, thanks. You?'

'Yeah, all good. Baby's due any day now.'

Jenny's face lit up. 'Aww, that's wonderful news!'

Malik handed her an envelope – 'Just the one for ya today.' – and walked breezily past. 'Have a good one.'

'You too. Pass on my best wishes to Aniyah.'

'Will do,' Malik called back over his shoulder as he disappeared round the corner at the end of the walkway.

When Jenny walked into the flat she was relieved to find that Grant didn't appear to be up yet. She hurried across the living room and out to the kitchen where she put down the loaf of bread, the milk and the envelope on the table.

Glancing furtively behind her and cocking an ear to ensure there was no indication that Grant was moving around, she bent down to the cupboard underneath the sink. She moved aside a bottle of bleach, a can of fly spray and various assorted cleaning products and, getting down on her knees, she pushed the bottle of gin right to the back. Then she returned the other items to where they belonged and took one last look to satisfy herself the alcohol was safely stashed out of sight. Jenny couldn't recall the last time Grant actually lifted a finger to clean the flat anyway.

She closed the cupboard door and had just stood up when Grant appeared in the doorway behind her.

'Oh,' she said. 'You made me jump.'

Naked and scratching lazily at his crotch, Grant padded over to the fridge. 'You been out already?'

'Yes,' Jenny replied, gathering up the milk and loaf of bread from the table. 'Pop this in the fridge for me would you?' She held out the bottle of milk towards him.

Grant glanced at her. 'What did your last slave die of?' He took the bottle from her and slid it on to the top shelf on its side. 'I thought I had some beers in here?'

Jenny tutted. 'It's 9.30 in the morning.'

'Says the fuckin' alcoholic,' Grant snapped back. He slammed the fridge door.

She immediately looked contrite. 'Sorry. I'll pop out again later and get you some more.'

'Yeah, you do that.' He noticed the envelope on the table. 'What's that?'

'Oh, sorry, it's just a bit of junk mail, I meant to put it in the bin.'

As she picked it up Grant sprung forward and snatched it out of her hand.

'Junk mail my arse!' he exclaimed. He pointed at the logo in the corner. 'Hallam Holidays! You know what this must be!'

Jenny looked at him blankly.

'Hallam Holidays. The competition I entered. For fuck's sake, wake up!'

Jenny's eyes widened. 'You don't mean…'

'I dunno. Maybe!' Grant's fingers were scrabbling to open the envelope. Pulling out the letter, his eyes darted rapidly back and forth absorbing the content.

Jenny could feel her heart racing. 'Well come on, don't keep me in suspense!'

Grant raised his head. He beamed at Jenny and the gold front tooth she hated so much flashed in the sunlight streaming through the kitchen window.

CHAPTER 8

In certain places the cool waters of the Ionian Sea are crystal clear and boast some of the most dazzling hues imaginable. At Palaiokastritsa, for example – one of the most beautiful spots in Greece, on the northwestern coast of Corfu – the sea really is that shimmering azure that one sees on picture postcards; the ones splashed with the words *Wish You Were Here!* that tourists glance at on those squeaky rotating racks and scoff, convinced that they must have been digitally augmented.

A lot of them are, of course, but Kirsty Mason was now gazing in awe at the vista stretching out before her and getting first hand proof that seeing is believing. The colour of the water was simply breathtaking.

She was sitting at the back of a traditional Greek caique. Destination: the privately owned isle of Mástiga and the holiday of a lifetime.

Behind Kirsty was a flagpole, atop which a pennant bearing the initials **HH** flapped vigorously in the warm sea breeze.

She closed her eyes, inhaled deeply and turned to Nick. 'I absolutely adore the sea air.'

He smiled at her. 'There's no other smell quite like it, I'll give you that.'

'It always takes me back to my childhood,' she added. 'This is all so surreal, it feels a bit like a dream.'

'I was just thinking exactly the same thing.' Nick looked at Charlie. 'What do you reckon, buddy?'

The boy was peering intently through a pair of binoculars he'd received two Christmases ago, studying the lofty Cypress trees dotted along the coastline of the island ahead of them.

'It's amazing!' the boy replied.

Nick leant in close to Kirsty's earlobe. 'Shame we're the only ones who seem to be appreciating it,' he whispered.

In front of them there were a dozen other people. Waiting to board the caique at the mainland harbour at Piraeus an hour earlier they had all enthusiastically introduced themselves to one another. Now, not one of them was paying the least bit of attention to the glorious scenery.

Seated furthest away from them at the front was a tall black man and his caucasian wife. Their two little boys were scampering up and down the aisle, screaming excitedly about nothing intelligible. One moment Jack and Jordan appeared to have settled in the seats with their parents, the next they were up on their feet again and shouting up a storm.

Grant and Jenny Kinley seemed to be completely oblivious to their unruly children; either that or they just didn't care. They were deep in conversation with a plump lady occupying the aisle seat across from them.

Lisa Page was chattering more than sufficently to compensate for the fact that her husband wasn't joining in. Warren looked a bit green. The sea had been as flat as the proverbial millpond when the caique left Piraeus, but it had quickly become choppy and he had been sick over the side a couple of times. He appeared to have recovered and found his sea legs now though, and was leaning over the back of the seat in front of him, talking to a teenage girl who was staring miserably out at the water. Most of the people aboard were attired in keeping with the temperate clime, although a couple of them Kirsty would have argued were distinctly *under*dressed. Hollie Page, however, stood out by virtue of the fact she had bundled herself up in a pair of jeans and a baggy sweatshirt.

Next to her was a lad with long, lank hair. He was listening in on his mother's conversation with the Kinleys, chipping in with an occasional remark that he clearly thought was witty but which appeared to contribute nothing of any real value. He also kept casting a furtive glance at the two teenage girls, both dressed in skimpy bikinis, who were sitting in front of Charlie. Neither had noticed the attention they were drawing from Caine; both of them had their faces buried in their mobile phones.

When everyone had been waiting to board at the harbour, the younger of the two girls had come over and introduced herself to Charlie as Bobbi-Leigh: 'You can call me Bob.' Not sure what to say, Charlie had muttered an awkward reply out of courtesy. And then when they all boarded, much to his dismay, he'd found himself seated directly behind the girls. None too subtly, Bobbi-Leigh kept craning her head to look at him. Once she'd caught him looking back and smiled at him, highly amused when he'd quickly looked the other way in embarrassment.

Across the aisle from the two girls, immediately in front of Kirsty and Nick, a woman dressed in an obscenely insubstantial bikini that was barely able to restrain her generous breasts was cosying up to the man next to her. He was wearing an equally ill-fitting pair of shorts and an inappropriate T-shirt bearing the legend I'm not a gynaecolgist but I definitely know a c*nt when I see one. Vicky Hazelwood was busily thrusting her tongue down his throat, so enthusiastically in fact that it looked as if she was attempting to chew on Jamie Trot's tonsils. She paused to take a breath.

'Fuck me!' Jamie gasped.

Vicky cackled. 'Careful what you wish for, babe.'

Jamie's eyes widened. 'What brought all this on?'

'I dunno, must be the sunshine. Soon as we're settled in I'm gonna fuck yer brains out!'

'Not if I fuck yours out first, babe!' They clamped mouths again.

Wide-eyed in disbelief at what she was witnessing, Kirsty glanced at Nick aghast. The look that passed between them said far more than words.

Now, as she surveyed the motley ensemble of their fellow contest winners Kirsty felt as bemused as her husband that every one of them was engaged in anything *but* admiring the scenery. 'Their loss,' she whispered to Nick.

'Look!' Kirsty cried excitedly, pointing at the water. 'Are those jellyfish?'

Nick peered over the side. 'Yeah! Look at that. There's masses of them too!'

As they sat gazing in awe at the bloom of tiny pulsating creatures, they were suddenly enveloped in a cloud of smoke. Nick turned his head in disgust to see both Jamie and Vicky had lit up cigarettes. He bristled and was about to say something when a loud voice shouted out from the front of the boat.

'Hey there please!'

Nick looked up and saw the helmsman glaring at Jamie and Vicky. 'No smoking allowed on board. Is very clear!' He gestured to the multiple No Smoking signs lining both the sides of the boat.

Vicky flicked her cigarette over the side into the water.

'Fuckin' Nazi,' Jamie grumbled. He took a last puff, snuffed it out with his fingers and tucked it neatly behind his ear.

'Hey,' Nick said, changing the subject. 'I meant to say. I Googled a bit about the island just before we left yesterday.'

'Yeah?'

'Yeah, it was really interesting. Do you know what Mástiga actually means?'

'Okay, look. There's something I never told you about myself...' There was a note of concern in her voice.

'What?'

'You have to promise not to get mad. I always wanted to tell you, but I couldn't summon up the courage. I'm so sorry, love.'

Nick started to look worried. '*What?*'

'I have a confession to make... I completely flunked out on the ten years of Greek classes I took at school.' She buried her face in her hands. 'I feel so ashamed.'

Nick gave her a sarcastic look. 'Oh, *very* funny. You should try stand-up.'

Laughing, Kirsty looked back up at him. 'Well, honestly, how would I know what Mástiga means? Come on then, educate me. What *does* it mean?'

'Scourge.'

'Lovely.'

'Apparently, two hundred years ago it was a penal colony where they sent men *and* women. There were two vast concrete buildings to house them, separated by high fences. Which didn't stop the sexes mingling, of course, although those that were caught were executed. The place was a hive of villainy, perpetrators of every conceivable crime, everything from petty theft, prostitution and affray to arson, rape and murder.'

Kirsty screwed up her face. 'Yeah, well, like you say, that was two hundred years ago. Australia was full of British convicts as well once.'

'Sure. But listen. The prison governor – Cyrus Paraskev... Paraskevo... I'm probably not pronouncing it properly, but I think it was something like Paraskevopoulos...'

'Not so clever now are you Mr I Know What Mástiga Means!' Kirsty playfully stuck her tongue out at him.

Nick smiled and kissed her nose. 'Yeah, okay. But here's the thing: This Cyrus guy, it turned out he was worse than any of the people they had locked up. A real sadist by all accounts. He tortured the men for no discernible reason beyond his own amusement. And he systematically raped the women, and if he got them pregnant they were simply made to disappear. Anyway, one night back in 1843, a riot broke out in the men's block, spilled over into the women's block and the whole place ended up razed to the ground. But get this too: Paraskevopoulos's body was never found. Most people believed that in all the commotion he fled the island. But rumours persisted that the prisoners had got hold of him, dragged him into the woods and buried him alive. Either way he was never seen or heard of again.'

Kirsty shuddered. 'That's just horrible.'

'Yep. And to this day some people are convinced that his ghost stalks the island, waiting to exact his revenge on innocent tourists.'

Kirsty's face dropped. 'You're *kidding* me!'

Nick grinned. 'Okay, I made that last bit up.'

'You!' Kirsty playfully punched his arm.

'Well, sort of,' Nick continued. 'About 30 years ago some enterprising guy bought a boat with the intention of running a service for locals out of Piraeus to the island. You know, day-trips, that sort of thing. But the venture belly-flopped because the locals genuinely believed that Cyrus's spirit haunted the place.'

Kirsty shuddered. 'I do kind of wish I'd learned all this *after* our holiday.'

Nick chuckled. 'There's no need for nightmares. Nowadays Mástiga is apparently renowned for its natural beauty and it's been a popular stop-off-and-look-see on boat tours of the islands for the last 20 years. Well, up until last year, I guess, when this Hallam fellow purchased it and started developing it.'

Kirsty sighed. 'Imagine being able to afford to buy your own island though!'

'I know,' Nick said. 'But he probably got it cheap. Greece has been in serious finanical shtook for years.

Selling off a few of their islands had to be a no-brainer for the Government. And it is pretty small. If they dropped you smack bang in the middle, it's only something like 15 miles to the coast in any direction.'

Kirsty rolled her eyes. 'Oh, is *that* all?'

Nick laughed.

'Ladies and gentlemen...' The helmsman had turned to face the group. The tops of his tanned, muscular legs disappeared into a pair of tight black shorts and his unbuttoned, white short-sleeve shirt billowed open in the breeze, revealing a golden brown chest covered in a mat of black hair. With the back of his hand he mopped the sheen of sweat from his forehead. Speaking perfect English with a thick Greek accent he said, 'We will shortly be arriving at Mástiga.'

CHAPTER 9

It was approaching 3 o'clock in the afternoon.

The helmsman looked back over his shoulder and waved a cheerful farewell to the holidaymakers, left standing on the jetty surrounded by a heap of suitcases and hand luggage as they watched the caique head off back to the mainland.

'Phwoar!' Vicky exclaimed, waving back at the sun-bronzed Greek man. 'I tell ya, I'd give *him* one any day of the week. What d'ya say, ladies?'

Lisa and Jenny both looked slightly uncomfortable. Kirsty forced a half-smile.

'No?' Vicky said incredulously. 'Oh, well, all the more for me then.'

'Babe...' Jamie sidled up to her. 'You're embarrassing yerself.'

'No, babe.' Vicky cackled. 'I'm embarrassing you.'

Jamie looked at Grant and said – as if there were a need to say anything at all – 'She's only kidding, mate.' He shot a glance over his shoulder to check that Vicky couldn't hear him; he could see her busily ferreting in her shoulder bag for something. 'She's more than well taken care of in that department,' he added quietly.

Picking up a suitcase in each hand, Jamie started off along the jetty.

Everyone else followed his lead, gathering up their belongings and making their way along the slatted walkway. At the far end they stepped out onto the dusty track and set down their cases.

Nick looked off along the deserted stretch of road that ran along the coastline for about a quarter of a mile before curving inland and disappearing off among the Cypress trees.

Jamie turned to face the others. 'What now then?' he said, addressing no-one in particular.

'The itinerary said we'd be met off the boat by a coach,' Grant ventured.

'Exactly.' Jamie scowled and raised his arms as if to illustrate the obvious: there very clearly wasn't *anyone* to meet them. 'So where the fuck is it then?'

'Yeah, it is a bit piss poor,' Grant agreed.

Vicky and Jenny exchanged glances. 'Let's just be a bit fuckin' patient shall we?' Vicky said. 'There's no point gettin' wound up before we even start.'

Jamie was about to tell her where to get off when the air was filled with the cacophony of various mobile phone message tones going off in unison. Moments later a handful of phones had been withdrawn from pockets, all of them iPhones with the exception of one.

Nick looked at the old Nokia in his hand. He'd never been someone who gave much truck to keeping up with the Joneses, but nevertheless he hastily tucked it back into his pocket.

It quickly became apparent that everyone's phone had received the same text message:

> Terence Hallam, Chairman and Director of Hallam Holidays, is delighted to welcome you to the private holiday island of Mástiga. Click on the link below within one hour of receiving this text to be eligible for entry into a draw to win a £1000 cash prize at the end of your stay. Every member of your family with a phone must activate the link. Failure by any one member to

> do so will unfortunately result in your entire family being
> excluded from the draw. Good luck!

'A thousand squid! Mint!' Grant said, flashing his gold-toothed smile.

'An hour?' Jamie chimed in. 'Who are they kiddin'?! I'm havin' me some of that gravy right now!'

'Us too!' Warren cried enthusiastically. It was the most animated he'd been since they'd left the mainland. 'Come on,' he said, turning to Lisa, Caine and Hollie. 'Get clicking, we don't want to miss out!'

Caine and Hollie plonked themselves down on top of the family's twin suitcases and tapped on the link.

There was a mumble of general agreement.

Jack and Jordan, both clearly too young to have phones of their own, were hopping up and down trying to see Jenny's. 'Show us, Mum!' the older one cried excitedly.

'There's nothing to see,' she said wearily. 'It's just a link.'

'What's a link, what's a link?' the smaller one chimed in.

Jenny ignored them. She turned to Kirsty. 'I've clicked on it and there's a picture of a palm tree come up. But I'm not sure what purpose it serves.'

Kirsty was examining her phone too. 'Me neither. It doesn't actually seem to have done anything.'

Vicky shook her head in disbelief. 'What d'ya want, jam on it? If there's a chance of winnin' a grand that's good enough for me.'

Kirsty looked at Nick, who was standing looking out to sea. She walked over, hooked her arm through his and smiled. 'Come on, love,' she said. 'Aren't you going to enter the prize draw?'

'You know very well I can't,' he said.

Kirsty moved round in front of him and slipped her arms around his waist. 'I know, I'm only teasing.'

'Bloody iPhones,' he mumbled. 'People treat them like toys. They can't stay off the things for five minutes. Look at those girls on the boat, they barely looked up once! All that beautiful scenery they missed out on.'

'Oh, come on,' Kirsty said, giving him a little peck on the cheek. 'Don't get grumpy.'

'I'm not.'

Kirsty looked at him doubtfully.

'Really, I'm not,' he said. 'I just don't see what the point of iPhones is. My Nokia can send texts and it can make calls. That's all I need. All this swipe me, click me, like me nonsense, it's just rubbish. I don't need games, or music, or weather reports, or gimmicks that make me look like a cartoon character, or…'

'Camera?'

'I have a perfectly good camera. Why would I want to take pictures on a phone?'

'Internet access?'

Nick sighed. 'Yeah, alright,' he acquiesced reluctantly, 'I suppose that would come in useful from time to time.'

She kissed him again. 'Maybe if we win the £1000 we'll look into getting you upgraded.'

'I can think of better things to spend the money on.' He smiled at her. 'But yeah, maybe.'

'Do you think if we won I might be able to have a phone?' Charlie had stepped up quietly behind them.

Nick grinned and ruffled his son's hair. 'We'll see, buddy. Gotta win first though. Unlike all these other folks, we've only got the one entry on your Mum's phone.'

The conversation was suddenly interrupted as Jamie let out a cry. 'Here they fuckin' come at last!'

A low rumbling noise sounded in the distance. Kicking up a cloud of dust, a minibus appeared from between the Cypress trees, heading in their direction.

Billie-Jo was standing with her back to the sea taking a selfie. She tapped at the screen. 'Aww, for fuck's sake! Fuckin' signal's dropped out.'

Vicky waved at her. 'Never mind that, the bus is comin'. Come on girls, get yer lazy arses over here and help with the cases.'

'But I wanted a pic for Tyler,' the girl said petulantly. 'I promised I'd send him one soon as we got here.'

Jamie shot her an angry look. 'Never mind that useless poof Tyler. Yer mother said help, so get the fuck over here and help.'

Bobbi-Leigh grinned at her sister.

'Fuck off, skank!' Billie-Jo scowled, slipping the phone into her bag. 'And he ain't no poof. Trust.'

Everyone moved forward expectantly as the minibus got closer. Warren stepped away from his family and deftly manoeuvered himself so that he was standing right behind Bobbi-Leigh and Billie-Jo. 'Exciting all this, isn't it girls?'

They both looked back to see him leering at them hungrily.

Frowning at him, Billie-Jo said, 'Yeah, I s'pose.' But as they dismissively turned their backs on him she glanced at her sister and silently mouthed, 'What the actual fuck?!'

Warren peered lasciviously downwards towards the two bikini-clad bottoms and behind the thick lenses of his spectacles his eyes widened.

His little moment of reverie was curtailed as Lisa, red faced and puffing, stepped towards to him. 'Can you give me a hand with this suitcase please? I think we packed everything but the kitchen sink!'

Casting one last sly look at the teenage girls, Warren snapped, 'Give it here then,' and grabbed the suitcase from her hand.

Nick, who was standing at the back, whispered to Kirsty, 'I hope they'll prove me wrong, but I don't think we're going to be attending too many intellectual soirees this weekend, do you?'

As Kirsty put a *shoosh* finger to her mouth she looked over and noticed the disdainful expression on Vicky's face. She smiled at her, but Vicky turned away and sidled up to Jamie. Whatever she said to him was lost behind the sound of the engine rumbling as the minibus pulled up in front of them. But Jamie chortled loudly and the smug look he shot at Kirsty made her feel really uncomfortable.

The doors of the minibus hissed open and the sound of a Nana Mouskouri song blared out. The driver reached out, shut off the music and grinned down at them. 'Welcome, welcome, people,' he said. 'I am Dimitri. Please, get aboard.'

'What about our luggage, pal?' Grant gestured towards all the suitcases and bags.

'Plenty of room inside.' He beckoned. 'Please, come. I help.'

Dimitri climbed out and reached for Jamie's suitcase. Jamie snatched it back. 'Oi, I'll do that.' He turned to the others. 'Ya can't trust these day-glo wops!'

Vicky guffawed. 'It's dago, ya fuckin' muppet!'

Grant bristled, but said nothing.

Everyone shuffled forward and started to board, depositing their belongings into the wire cages in front of the seats.

*

Hallam puffed on his cigar and smiled. Things were going exactly as planned.

He and Caroline Smart had arrived on Mástiga the previous morning. He had immediately spent several hours walking the whole 2000 acres of his holiday resort, surveying the work carried out by Carl Banks's associates. There was the odd aspect he might have tweaked — mostly just a case of dotting the i's and crossing the t's — but largely speaking he had been very much impressed.

It had been a shame about Banks, Hallam had mused. Despite his discharge from the army for sexually assaulting two Officer Cadets, he had turned out to be perfect for Hallam's needs. He could have proved useful in future too. It was just a shame the man had to get greedy. Still, that was no longer a problem; Banks was gone.

Now, sitting in an office in a small building on the outer reaches of the resort – one not dissimilar to his UK bolthole in terms of the technology installed – he was finally getting to see the fruits of years' worth of planning and was basking in the thrill.

'Avarice, Mrs Smart, the guaranteed facilitator of compliance.'

'Indeed, Mr Hallam.' Caroline adjusted her glasses. She was, as usual, standing dutifully at his side.

'If there's one thing I've learned in life it's that all you need to do is dangle the right carrot and the proletariat will bite your hand off. Our surveillance beacon registered tracer signals from 11 iPhones. That's 11 between the 15 of them.'

'I assume the younger children don't have one then,' Caroline said.

'Precisely. Although it wouldn't have surprised me if they had. These days they seem to have them before they can even talk.' He gestured at the bank of TV screens before him, on all of which was displayed the same CCTV image of the families boarding the minibus. 'Look at them, my dear. 24-hours ago they were sitting around in their council estate hovels, now they are about to get what they're long overdue.'

Caroline nodded approvingly.

'Right then.' Hallam stood up. 'I must get changed. We have guests to welcome.'

CHAPTER 10

The trip from the jetty to the resort was slow but educational. Listening in on the conversations between his fellow travelers, Nick was able to ascertain that within each family unit the mother was the sole source of income. He felt a fleeting twinge of shame and put his arm round Kirsty, hugging her tightly.

She smiled up at him. 'You alright?'

'Yeah.'

There was with one exception, however. The slightly obnoxious woman who had introduced herself as Vicky – 'Ya can call me Vik if yer like' – seemed to be very proud of the fact that she and her other half hadn't worked a day in their lives and lived quite happily 'off the fuckin' social of course!', as she so eloquently put it.

A little under 15-minutes after leaving the coast to head inland, the minibus passed alongside a high steel mesh fence that ran parallel to the road for about half a mile or so.

'Looks like a bloody prison fence,' Grant muttered under his breath.

Nick flashed a knowing look at Kirsty.

Then, a little further along, they drew up in front of a pair of gates, over which was a cast iron arch bearing the now familiar **HH** crest coated – hastily and not particularly well, Nick thought as he peered up at it – in glittering gold paint.

Mounted on either side of the gates was a security camera. Grant looked at them warily.

Dimitri picked up a keyfob from the dashboard and pressed it. The tall gates whirred into life and gracefully opened.

The minibus crawled forward and once it had passed through Dimitri paused, pressed the fob again and the gates slid shut behind them.

'Doesn't it strike you as odd the place is fenced off?' Nick said quietly to Kirsty.

Jamie overheard him. 'Keeps the fuckin' riff-raff out, mate!' He cackled.

'It's meant to be a private island,' Nick countered. '*What* riff-raff?' He leaned in close to Kirsty and whispered, 'They obviously haven't factored in our present company.'

The minibus continued for several hundred yards up a narrow track, then swung to the left onto a large open forecourt in front of a small building. The façade was decked out with brightly coloured bunting and a short flight of steps led up to a doorway above which was the ubiquitous **HH** emblem.

The minibus pulled to a halt outside, the doors hissed open and amidst a discord of excited chatter the families climbed out, eagerly collecting their cases as they did so.

'Happy holidaying to you, lovely peoples,' Dimitri shouted, then waving frantically he accelerated away at speed.

As the minibus disappeared round the bend, the double-doors of the building flew open and Hallam, wearing a garish open-neck shirt, strode purposefully down the steps, with Caroline following closely in his wake. He stopped at the bottom, withdrew the large cigar from between his lips and smiled broadly. 'Well now, isn't this absolutely marvelous?' He spread his arms wide. 'Welcome to the island of Mástiga, ladies and gentlemen. Welcome, welcome!' He took a step forward. 'My name is Terence Hallam and I am your host and humble servant.'

The families, standing in their own little clusters, all nodded and smiled politely.

Hallam continued 'As you know, you have been specially selected as the maiden guests at this,' – he raised his arms triumphantly – 'my brand new holiday retreat. My guinea pigs if you like, eh what?'

He chuckled boisterously, turning to Caroline as if expecting her approval. She smiled respectfully.

'Now,' he said, 'we here at Hallam Holidays appreciate that some people don't always get what they deserve in life. With the benefit of private funding our aim is to bring underprivileged families like your good selves here, completely free of charge, and give them the experience to end all experiences.' The smile faded a little. 'However, I do have an apology to make.'

'Here it comes,' Nick whispered to Kirsty.

Hallam took a puff on his cigar. 'I have to tell you that unfortunately the resort isn't quite finished yet. The clubhouse with its pool area won't be ready until next year. We considered delaying the launch, but I'm sure as our lucky contest winners you'll appreciate it was important to us that we get things moving along and bring in our first deserving guests before summer's end when the rains come in.'

Nick leaned in close. 'You do remember that hotel in *Carry on Abroad*, don't you?'

Kirsty elbowed him in the ribs. 'Shhh!'

'Nevertheless,' Hallam went on. 'There's a natural lake at the far end of the resort, it's idyllic, it's completely safe and you're perfectly at liberty to make use of it. If you enjoy exploring, there's plenty of woodland to indulge yourselves with. You'll make your own entertainment, and you're free to go wherever – and *do* whatever – you choose. Or if you simply want to relax…'

'Hang on, if there's no clubhouse, what about all the free booze… er, I mean drinks we was promised?' Jamie was looking at Hallam with an expression on his face like that of a deprived child.

'Fear not, Mr…'

'Trot.'

'Trot. Yes, of course. Well, don't you worry about that, Mr Trot. All your chalets have been stocked with a cornucopia of beverages, both alcoholic,' – he winked playfully at Jenny – 'and non-alcoholic.'

Jenny blanched and squirmed internally. Is it possible he might know?

Jamie exchanged glances with Vicky. 'Sweet!'

Hallam continued. 'And of course there are plenty of other surprises awaiting you around the resort and you'll discover those over the next few days. We're a little short staffed at present, I'm afraid, but myself and my assistant here, Mrs Smart, will be on hand should you require any assistance.' He took another puff on the cigar. 'Now, before I let you pootle off and start enjoying yourselves, are there any questions?'

Nick raised a hand. 'I hope this doesn't come across as ungrateful...'

Hallam peered at him with interest.

Nick felt the dark eyes burning into him. He swallowed. 'This seems like a lovely resort. I'm just curious as to why you chose to build it so far inland. Wouldn't it have made more sense for it to be closer to the sea?'

'Not ungrateful at all, Mr Mason,' Hallam said.

The fact Hallam appeared to know everyone's names wasn't lost on anyone.

'In fact it's a very good question,' Hallam continued. 'It's simple really. A large part of the land we've used for construction was already cleared for its former purpose many years ago.' He chuckled. 'It saved a considerable amount of the money invested in this enterprise that would have been required for excavation had we chosen a location by the coast and started from scratch.'

Nick nodded appreciatively. 'Thanks.'

Grant spoke up. 'Why all the fences?'

Anyone who'd been watching might have noticed Grant Kinley had been looking increasingly twitchy since they'd passed through the gates. As it happened, no-one other than Jenny had. But then again, she knew the reason behind Grant's twitchiness.

Hallam smiled. 'Again, a very good question. Thank you, Mr Kinley. It's nothing sinister though, merely a precautionary measure to keep out the indigenous wildlife.'

'It's a bit like something out of *Jurassic Park*!' Warren chuckled.

'I hope you're not breedin' fuckin' great big dinosaurs here,' Jamie said, cackling loudly.

'I agree the fences may appear a tad imposing,' Hallam said. 'But I assure you they're only here for your safety.'

Grant looked unimpressed. 'Must be some serious wildlife,' he muttered. 'That fence is 20ft. high if it's an inch.'

Hallam didn't respond to Grant's remark; either he didn't hear or he chose not to offer any further explanation.

'Right then,' he said. 'If there are no further questions I'd just like you to each take one of these.'

He gestured to Caroline, who smiled sweetly. Removing her glasses, she tucked them into her pocket and stepped forward to begin distributing wristbands in two different colours, each bearing the **HH** logo.

Hallam grinned. 'Blue for the boys and pink for the girls, eh what? You must be sure to keep these on at all times for access to an array of surprise bonus treats!'

Caroline finished handing out the wristbands and returned to her place at Hallam's side. He stood and watched with mild amusement as the holidaymakers all eagerly slipped on the coloured bands. Dangle the right carrot…, he thought to himself.

'Splendid!' he exclaimed just as Jenny was fastening the last band around little Jack's wrist. 'Now, I'm afraid there is one small catch to all of this and I wouldn't be doing my duty if I didn't come clean, so to speak.'

'I fuckin' knew it,' Jamie grumbled under his breath.

Hallam looked at the sea of faces, all suddenly tinged with doubt. 'As you're well aware, ladies and gentlemen, your holiday is being fully paid for. But now that you're here...' He paused for dramatic effect. '...The catch is – and it's a Hallam Holidays rule, so there must be absolutely no exceptions – the catch is...' He paused again.

Christ, this is painful, Nick thought to himself.

The big man smiled. 'We expect, nay *demand*, that you have the most wonderful time!'

He roared with laughter and again turned to Caroline to ensure she was laughing along. She was.

'Right then!' Hallam clapped his hands together. 'Enough of my waffle. You've had a long journey and I'm sure you're tired and want to get settled in. Mrs Smart will escort you to your accommodation nestled in our beautiful woodland.' He waved a hand towards the line of trees encircling the forecourt. 'And remember, if there's anything at all you need – not that I suspect there will be once you've seen everything that's been laid on for you in the chalets – you know where to find us.' He pointed at the building behind him. 'All that remains for me to say then is go forth and enjoy yourselves.'

CHAPTER 11

From somewhere off through the trees an eruption of loud voices, music and laughter rudely pierced the late evening silence.

'We could always go and join the party, you know,' Kirsty said. She looked at Nick and was delighted to see she had provoked exactly the reaction she was hoping for.

He scowled at her. '*Really*?!'

She laughed. 'Of course not!'

As soon as they'd unpacked their luggage, Kirsty had prepared a light salad from the generous choice of goods in the fridge. Now they were sitting in comfortable chairs on the veranda of their chalet, sipping the ice-cold Moscow mule cocktails that Nick had rustled up; vodka, ginger beer and a wedge of lime over crushed ice.

Until the music started, the two of them had been completely relaxed, gazing up at the breathtakingly beautiful night sky, alive with the flicker of a million distant stars.

Charlie was sitting on the steps in front of them gazing upwards through his binoculars. Nick looked down at him. 'You really need a telescope for that, buddy,' he said. 'Those aren't really powerful enough.'

'I know,' Charlie replied, continuing to look skywards through the treasured field glasses. 'Did you know that the nearest star to Earth – other than the sun, of course, which is 93 million miles away – is called Proxima Centauri, 4.2 light years away?'

Impressed, Nick looked at his son. 'That's pretty cool. I *didn't* know that. How far is a light year then?'

'9.7 trillion kilometres.'

Nick laughed. 'What does that translate to in miles then, smarty-pants?'

Charlie didn't hesitate. '6 trillion. Or thereabouts.'

Nick did a quick calculation in his head. 'So this Proxima Centauri is about 25 trillion miles away.'

'25.2,' Charlie said matter-of-factly.

Nick raised his eyebrows and looked at Kirsty. 'We've got ourselves a pretty smart kid here.'

She smiled. 'We have. NASA will be calling on him before he even leaves school.'

Still glued to the binoculars, Charlie felt a little glow of pride. He continued, 'The two brightest stars though are Alpha Centauri A and B, and they're 4.3 light years away.'

Nick leaned forward in his chair and ruffled his son's hair. 'That's enough education for your old Mum and Dad tonight, buddy. Time for bed, it's been a long day.'

Charlie looked a little disappointed, but he didn't argue. He got up and kissed each of them on the cheek. 'Goodnight.' He paused in the doorway. 'Do you think Squeaky is okay?'

Before they'd left home there had been some upset about who would look after Charlie's beloved pet hamster. But Kirsty had popped next door and had a quick word with their neighbour, Mrs Colebrook, a widow, slightly reclusive yet pleasant enough if you got talking to her. And so it was arranged that Squeaky could have a little vacation of his own.

Kirsty looked up at her son. 'Of course he is. He's safe in Mrs Colebrook's hands. She told me her own children kept hamsters when they were small.'

'Do you think he misses me?'

'Of course he does.'

Charlie seemed to be satisfied with that and he retreated into the chalet.

'Do you think he's having a good time?' Kirsty said.

'Squeaky?'

Kirsty laughed. 'No, idiot. Charlie!'

'Yeah. I think so.' Nick sighed contentedly. 'After all, it's a bit of alright this, isn't it?' he added.

'It is. You glad we came?'

'Yeah.' Nick held up his mobile phone. 'That girl was right though,' he said. 'No signal.'

'That's because you've got a phone that's about 20 years past its shelf-life.'

Nick frowned. 'Okay, okay, I get it. I need a new phone. Have you got any signal on yours though?'

Kirsty pulled her phone from the pocket of her shorts and shook her head. 'No, nothing.'

'There you go. That kid was right.'

'But does it really matter? A few days out of touch with the world isn't going to kill anyone.' She reached out and plucked the Nokia out of Nick's hand.

'Speaking of killing,' Nick said, 'I hope you realise we could be sitting on the very spot where that Cyrus whatshisname raped and slaughtered all those convicts.'

Kirsty rolled her eyes. 'Don't start with all that nonsense again!'

Nick laughed. 'It's not nonsense! Hallam said they'd built this place on land that had already been cleared. It makes sense this is where the prison was situated.'

'Seriously though,' she said. 'Happy?'

He nodded. 'Very. I admit I had my doubts, but it's actually okay.'

'Just okay?'

Nick smiled. 'Well, maybe a smidge more than okay.'

Kirsty finished her drink and waggled the empty glass at him. 'Another?'

'I'll make you one if you want. I don't think I will.'

'Nah, don't worry then.' She set down the glass, got up and went over and perched herself on Nick's lap. 'I love you.'

He kissed her. 'Love you back.'

A stream of foul language drifted over through the trees, followed by raucous laughter.

Nick shook his head. 'I was about to say I can't believe how relaxing this is,' he said. 'I've been so stressed for so long.'

The volume of the music increased.

'Someone's having fun,' Kirsty said.

Nick frowned. 'Depends on your definition of fun, I suppose.'

Kirsty stifled a little yawn and gazed into his eyes. 'Come on now, Mr Grump. I think it was obvious from the outset that we aren't likely to be spending much time with any of that lot. Let them get on and do their thing, we'll do ours.'

'I guess you're right.'

She winked at him. 'What do you say we have an early night?'

Nick's frown disappeared. 'You took the words right out of my mouth.'

Stretching, Kirsty said, 'My shoulders are aching and as luck would have it I remembered to pack the patchouli oil. I was thinking if you were to give me a massage… well, you never know, it might get me in the mood.' She adopted a coy, doe-eyed look; Nick loved it when she looked at him like that.

'Right,' he said and stood up, abruptly tipping Kirsty off his lap. 'That's enough stargazing for tonight then. Race you to the bathroom.'

Nick took off leaving Kirsty behind. She made no attempt to race him. She just smiled contentedly.

*

The digital clock above the bank of TV monitors changed from 02:05 to 02:06.

'As long as they keep those wristbands on we'll be able to track their every movement.'

Hallam flicked a switch on the console in front of him and the largest of the screens lit up, displaying a plan of the entire resort and 15 tiny flashing red dots closely clustered in one spot.

'I suspect your suggestion of additional treats will be all the incentive they need to keep them on,' Caroline said.

'Exactly.'

'What you said about the clubhouse and the pool though, sir. I must say, I hadn't realised there was still that much work to do.'

'There isn't going to be any clubhouse or pool.' He spun round in his chair to face her. 'This enterprise has cost a small fortune.' His tone smacked of impatience. 'The fact is this resort isn't quite as extensive as I'd originally envisioned. There *was* going to be a clubhouse and pool, but there isn't. I wasn't going to waste money on unnecessary luxuries, our guests aren't going to be here long enough anyway. But it's of no consequence. As it stands what we have here is perfectly adequate for their needs. And ours.'

He swung the chair back to face the screens.

'I was wondering, sir. Would it be alright if I made that phone call home now? I promised Kevin I'd keep in touch, but I haven't since we left the mainland two days ago.'

Hallam was about to refuse, but at the last moment he decided to throw her a bone. Things were going well, he was feeling benevolent. 'Very well,' he said. 'Use the phone next door. We're pretty much finished for the night now anyway. I suggest your make your call and then hit the pillows. I've one last thing to do and I'll be turning in myself.'

'Thank you, sir. Goodnight.'

He waited for her to leave the room and then pushed two buttons on the console. All the screens came alive, each displaying a different view of the rooms within his guests' chalets. All bar one of them was in darkness. The one that was lit showed a crystal clear, high angle image of Vicky Hazelwood standing naked in front of the sink in a bathroom.

Hallam's eyes widened. He licked his lips and observed her with apparent excitement.

Vicky removed the last of her make-up. Looking at herself in the mirror, she squinted and stuck out her tongue at herself. Then she opened the cabinet above the basin and started picking through the contents. There were all the usual fripperies one might expect to see – small bars of brightly-wrapped soap with various fragrances, a bottle of mouthwash, packets of dental floss and...

Her hand paused, hovering over a small, plain white box.

Hallam shuffled forward expectantly in his chair.

Vicky removed the box from the cabinet and studied it. There was a little label attached to it.

Hallam watched her read it. 'With the personal compliments of Terence Hallam,' he whispered.

Heart rate increasing, he continued to watch as she opened the box, withdrew a little bottle of scent, squirted a tiny bit in the air and sniffed.

'Ooo, nice,' she said aloud. 'I'm takin' that home with me.'

Hallam couldn't hear what she said. The surveillance system wasn't equipped with sound. Another cost-cutting measure he'd been unhappy about, had argued against, but eventually conceded was necessary.

Right now he wished they'd spent the extra money.

'Here, babe,' Vicky shouted. 'There's some right posh smellies in here!'

Making a mental note that the next time he spoke with the investors he would underline his displeasure at the absence of sound on an otherwise exemplary CCTV system, Hallam continued watching as Vicky placed the bottle back in the cabinet. She gave herself one last look in the mirror and flicked back her hair. She ran a hand underneath each of her breasts, raised it to her nose and sniffed. Satisfied she'd pass muster, she crossed to the door and flicked off the light. The screen in Hallam's office went dark.

Hallam sat back in his chair. He felt the disappointment wash over him. He'd hoped she might have made use of his little gift.

*

Sleep was evading Kirsty. The sound of Nick's snoring as he lay beside her wasn't helping either.

For more than an hour they'd made love tenderly – she had reached climax with the most amazing orgasm, the first she had experienced for many months – but immediately afterwards Nick had rolled over and gone to sleep. She hadn't minded. But then she had lain awake for hours, a thousand thoughts swimming in unresolved circles around her head and the sound of the neighbours' party chuntering away in the background. She was tired but she just couldn't sleep.

She looked at the clock: 02:37.

Sliding carefully out of bed so as not to disturb Nick, she quietly pulled on a long T-shirt that came down to her waist and crept across the room.

She went out to the small kitchen and ran a glass of water. Then, stepping sleepily out onto the veranda she inhaled deeply; the cool air nipped at her nostrils.

The noise from up the way had finally dwindled half an hour ago and the silence was exquisite. But all of a sudden a girl's voice sounded in the distance. 'Just leave me alone!'

Kirsty was instantly alert. She stood stock-still and looked off into the trees, now shrouded in inky blackness and unnervingly threatening. She strained her ears, listening intently.

After a moment's silence another voice sounded; a man's voice, slightly slurred, possibly intoxicated. 'Come on, sugarcake. Just one little goodnight kiss for Daddy.'

Kirsty felt her stomach turn. She stood for a few minutes listening. The air had fallen silent. She shook her head sorrowfully, turned and went back inside.

As the door closed behind her, she failed to hear the sound of faint sobbing drifting through the trees.

CHAPTER 12

Shafts of morning sunlight sparkled through the trees causing Nick to squint. He was dressed in his pyjama bottoms, relaxing on the veranda sipping coffee.

It was early, but already the air was beginning to warm up and the rhythmic drone of cicadas was almost deafening. Not that it bothered Nick. He found the low frequency sound to be strangely hypnotic, pleasantly tranquil even.

Suddenly, as if out of nowhere, Grant Kinley with his two boys in tow appeared on the path at the bottom of the veranda steps. As he walked past, Nick could hear him muttering under his breath.

He called out. 'Morning.'

Startled out of his thoughts, Grant turned his head sharply. 'Oh, morning, er...'

'Nick.'

'Yeah. Listen, you haven't had a chance to scout this place out yet have you?'

'No, not yet.'

Grant didn't look at all happy. 'Well I have and there isn't a damned soul around.'

Nick shrugged. 'It's early. And Mr Hallam did say there isn't much in the way of staff at the moment.'

'What, fuckin' *no-one*?!' Grant spat out the words. 'I thought fatso said if there was anything we needed we only had to ask.'

'Problem?'

'Yeah. Jenny – my wife – she's not, er... very well.'

'Nothing serious I hope,' Nick said. 'Anything I can do to help?'

Grant looked at him with interest for a second, sizing him up. 'Nah, it doesn't matter. Forget it.'

Nick stood up. 'Are you sure?'

'You deaf, pal?' Grant snarled. 'I said no, didn't I?' He looked Nick in the eye. 'Now fuck off!'

There was a time when Nick would have reacted to someone who spoke to him like that, but he wasn't about to start anything here. He took a pace back and held up his hands. 'Okay, no need to get all riled up.'

Giving Nick a last look of disdain, Grant grabbed Jack and Jordan roughly by their hands and marched off, dragging them tripping and stumbling over the uneven path behind him.

Nick shook his head. Why the hell did he have to end up with this lot as campmates? It could only happen to him, he thought.

Kirsty stepped out onto the veranda and slipped her arms around him from behind. Nick could still detect the sweet earthy scent of the patchouli oil that he'd tenderly rubbed into her neck and shoulders the previous evening.

'Who was that you were talking to?' she asked, yawning.

'The black guy. Kinley I think his name is. One of the charming people we're sharing this paradise with for the next few days. He said his wife's not well. He had his kids with him.'

'The two little boys?'

'Yeah, but they didn't say a dicky bird. I tell you, love, I realise we don't know diddlysquat about any of these people's backgrounds, any more than they do about ours for that matter. But you've gotta wonder how some of this mob got lucky enough to win.'

Kirsty reached up and took Nick's coffee out of his hand. She had a sip. 'Relax. We only just got out of bed and you're getting up tight already. We can just keep away from them.'

'Oh, we're going to. Trust me on that.' Nick turned around to face her. 'You enjoying that?'

She took another sip of the coffee. 'Mmmm. It's good.'

'There's plenty in the cafetiere if you wanted one, you know.'

She smiled at him sweetly. 'No, this one's fine.'

She set down the mug on the table and Nick took her in his arms. 'Morning, gorgeous lady.' He was about to kiss her, but reeled back. He sniffed. 'What's that awful smell?'

Kirsty screwed up her face. 'Vile, isn't it? I found it in the bathroom cabinet. It's perfume, a personal gift from our host. It's obviously not Chanel No 5.'

'Well, *personally* I can assure you it's pretty bad.' He wafted a hand in front of his nose.

'I know,' Kirsty said. 'Thank God I only sprayed a tiny bit on the back of my hand.' She frowned. 'I had a weird feeling when I was sitting on the loo.'

'I have those sometimes,' Nick chuckled.

Kirsty punched him on the shoulder. 'I'm serious!'

'What sort of feeling?' Nick said.

'This is going to sound a bit ridiculous, but it felt… well, like I was being watched.'

Nick laughed. 'That'll be the ghost of old Cyrus.' He realised Kirsty wasn't laughing and put on a serious face. 'Really?'

'Yeah. It really creeped me out. And another thing, I was up in the night, I couldn't sleep. I came out onto the veranda for some air and I heard voices. I think there's something bad going on with that family – the one with the sad-looking teenage girl, I mean. The Pages.'

'There's something not right with the whole damned lot of them!' Nick said tetchily. He saw the look on Kirsty's face. 'It's alright, I'm calm, I'm calm.' He looked at her quizzically. 'Go on…'

'I don't know, I'm not sure. But I think her dad might be abusing her.'

Half an hour later, showered and dressed in cut-offs and a T-shirt, Kirsty started preparing breakfast.

Nick appeared from the bedroom wearing jeans and doing up the buttons on an open-neck shirt with the sleeves rolled up to the elbows. 'Morning, buddy,' he said.

Charlie was stretched out on the sofa reading a Stephen King novel with a picture on the cover of a terrified-looking girl, her face splashed with blood. He looked up. 'Hi, Dad.'

Nick walked over and gave Kirsty a peck on the cheek. 'How long till we eat?'

'About ten minutes.'

Nick nodded. 'Perfect. Listen, I'm just gonna take a little stroll over to reception. See if I can find anyone.'

'Okay.' Kirsty stopped what she was doing. 'Can I ask why?'

'Yeah, well, I know what I said about avoiding these people. And I know it's none of our business.' Nick slipped his feet into a pair of loafers. 'But I've been thinking about it and I'm a bit bothered about that Kinley guy's wife. He strikes me as an A-grade arsehole.'

Charlie looked up from his book. 'Dad!'

Nick smiled and slapped himself on the wrist. 'Sorry.' He walked to the door. 'I shan't be long.'

Kirsty blew him a kiss. 'You're a good man, Nick Mason.'

*

As Nick was leaving the chalet and setting off along the path to the reception building, a couple of hundred yards in the opposite direction Grant was seething with rage.

'You just can't control yourself, can you?'

He was standing over Jenny, still wearing her disheveled clothes from the night before and slumped on the sofa in their chalet.

From their chairs at the table, Jordan and Jack watched in fearful silence as their father grabbed their mother by her shoulders and shook her violently. '*Can* you?!' he almost screamed.

Her head lolling, she looked up at him groggily. 'Leave it, Grant, will you? I can't argue, I haven't got the strength. I'm sick.'

'Sick?' Grant exploded, pushing her back down. '*Sick?!* Well, there's a fucking surprise. A whole bottle of booze and shit knows how many pills. I ain't surprised you're sick, you useless bitch!'

'It was just a few,' Jenny protested. 'For my head.'

'For my head,' Grant said, mimicking her whiny tone. 'You couldn't even manage to stay sober for four days, could you? Four fucking days!'

'It was a party. Everyone was drinking. *You* were drinking.'

'But not two bottles of gin to myself!' He scowled down at her. 'You're pathetic, do you know that? How many pills did you take, *Ginny*, huh? C'mon, how many?'

'Don't call me Ginny,' Jenny slurred. 'You know I hate it when you do that.'

'Aww, am I hurting the pitiful little drunk's feelings?'

Jenny managed to prop herself up on her elbows. 'Why are you always so horrible to me? It's not like it's my fault.'

'Not your fault? *Whose* fault is it then? The boys? *Mine*?'

Jenny sat up and got unsteadily to her feet. She seemed to rally herself a little. 'Maybe if you were a bit nicer to me, maybe I wouldn't have to drink to try and black out my miserable fucking life.'

She poked at his chest with her index finger and he angrily batted her hand away. 'Don't poke your fucking bony finger at me!'

But she hadn't finished. 'And maybe... maybe if you hadn't spent half your life in prison...' She paused, then said it anyway: 'Well, maybe I wouldn't have had to suck cock to hold down a job!'

Grant's eyes blazed. He lashed out and slapped her hard across her face.

The two boys gasped, their eyes filled with fear.

The skin on her cheek burning pink, Jenny stared at him defiantly. 'Oh, that's right, the answer to everything. The big tough guy beating on the defenceless woman.'

Grant took a step towards her.

'Dad, no!' Jordan had jumped to his feet.

'Sit down and shut your mouth, or else!'

The boy hesitated for an instant, then did as he was told, cradling his terrified brother in his arms.

With his fist clenched, Grant struck Jenny again. But she moved her head a fraction to the right – barely more than an inch, but it undoubtedly saved her a broken nose – and he caught her a hard blow across her cheek with the edge of his signet ring.

Dazed, she took a step backwards, but somehow managed to stay on her feet. She held a hand to her face, whimpering softly. Her fingers felt wet. She looked at them and saw the blood. 'Fucking bastard!' she exclaimed, stumbling towards him.

Certain she was about to pitch forward onto the floor, Grant stepped deftly aside, but to his slight surprise she remained upright and tottered clumsily past him to the door.

'I'm going out,' she sobbed.

Grant was about to grab hold of her and pull her back when he changed his mind. Let the bitch go, he thought. In prison he'd quickly learned that striking a

113

woman was something you didn't boast about. Nevertheless she always managed to wind him up to the point he had to teach her a lesson.

He watched her disappear through the door, bashing her arm on the jamb as she went. 'Yeah, that's right, get the fuck outta here,' he shouted after her. 'And don't bother coming back till you've sobered up, you fucking alky slut!'

He grimaced at the smear of blood – that *bitch's* blood! – on his fingers.

Their eyes brimming with tears, Jordan and Jack watched their father in silence as he strode past them and into the bathroom to wash their mother's blood off his hands.

CHAPTER 13

Nick had made no secret of his scepticism about this whole free holiday lark. But both Kirsty and Charlie had been so excited; who was he to deprive them of a sunshine holiday he himself was in no position to give them? So he'd pretty much kept most of his misgivings under his hat.

But now, standing on the steps outside the reception building where they had been so warmly welcomed yesterday, it was clear something wasn't quite right. He walked up to the doors and rattled them. They were locked. Cupping his hands over his eyes, he pressed up against the semi-opaque glass and strained to see inside. The vestibule was in darkness, but he could just make out the outline of a reception desk and a potted Yukka plant.

He tapped gently on the glass and called out. 'Hello?'

Frowning, he walked back down the steps and stopped to momentarily survey the forecourt. Aside from the distant sound of the omnipresent cicadas chirruping away, there was an eerie silence. Grant had been right, this really was a bit odd.

Nick set off back towards the chalet.

Jamie, dressed only in an unsightly pair of underpants, was sitting on the veranda of his chalet when he heard the sound of feet on the path and Nick walked past. 'Morning,' he called out. He might have taken an immediate dislike to Jamie, but as a man raised with good manners he set aside his feelings to greet the man in a civil fashion.

Jamie took a sip of his coffee. 'Mornin',' he replied oafishly.

Vicky appeared from inside and the pair of them watched with undisguised contempt as Nick disappeared off down the path.

'Cunt,' Vicky said.

'Ya know, fings would be perfect here if it weren't for that toffee-nosed fucker,' Jamie said.

Vicky nodded. 'Yeah, I know. Did you see him and his bitch wife sizin' everyone up on the boat yesterday? Judgin' us all? You could see on their faces what they was thinkin'. Snooty fuckers.'

'Forget him, babe. The others are alright.'

'Yeah. That Warren seems a bit weird, but at least he ain't walkin' around like his shit don't stink.'

Jamie thrust his hand into his underpants and had a good scratch. 'I was just finkin',' he said. 'Maybe we could go find that lake this mornin', take a few drinkies along with us. Maybe ask the others if they wanna come, make a bit of a party of it. Well, not *that* lot obviously!' Jamie gestured in the direction Nick had gone. 'What d'ya think?'

'Yeah, I fancy a swim. It's a right piss off that the pool ain't finished!'

Vicky turned and went back inside, passing Bobbi-Leigh, who was coming out. The girl was clutching a glass of orange juice. 'Hey, Dad, what d'ya reckon?' she said, thrusting it up under Jamie's nose.

Jamie winced and turned his head away. 'Fuck's sake, what's that? It smells like piss!'

'Citrus-O, it says on the label. It's s'posed to be orange juice I fink. Mingin', ain't it?'

She crossed over to the edge of the veranda and emptied the contents of the glass into the bushes. Turning away, she failed to notice the juice, fizzing unnaturally and dripping off the leaves, which were shrivelling up.

'Can I have a coke instead?' she asked breezily.

Jamie stared at her. 'It's 8 o'clock in the mornin'!' he said. Then he chortled. 'Course ya can.'

As Bobbi-Leigh went back inside he called after her, 'And grab me a lager while you're at it.'

Further up the pathway, a noise through the trees to his left stopped Nick short in his tracks. It sounded like a child sobbing.

He stepped off the path and carefully made his way through the foliage. There, with her back up against a tree, Hollie was sitting crying quietly. She was dressed in shorts, the sweatshirt Nick had seen her wearing the previous day and a pale blue baseball cap with the letter H embroidered in green above the peak.

Nick immediately recalled what Kirsty had said to him on the veranda.

He gave a little cough to announce his presence and she looked up. Her eyes were red and her face was streaked with tears.

'Hi there, kiddo, you alright?' Nick took a step closer. 'I don't mean to intrude, but I heard you crying.'

She didn't answer. Instead she turned her head away and wiped her tears on the back of the sweatshirt sleeve.

'I'm Nick. And you're... Mollie was it?'

The girl continued to look away from him, but after a moment she quietly replied, 'It's Hollie.'

'Sorry,' Nick said. 'I know I only heard it yesterday, but I'm completely useless at remembering names. I'll forget my own one day. The joys of getting old.'

Hollie said nothing.

'Hollie,' Nick continued. 'That's a pretty name. With a Y?'

'I E.'

Nick squatted down on his haunches a few feet away from her. 'Hey listen. I know it's got nothing to do with me and you probably want to be on your own, so you can tell me to buzz off and mind my own business if you like. But a young girl like you shouldn't be out here on your own. You're on holiday, you should be having fun with your folks.'

Hollie turned her head to face him. 'It's my Da...' she began and pulled herself up short. She looked at him. 'Forget it, it's nothing. Just having a bad morning. I'm fine.'

Nick nodded and stood up. 'Okay. Like I say, it's got nothing to do with me. But if you want to talk about it you can, you know.' He smiled. 'I had a daughter about your age. You actually look a lot like her. But I remember myself when I was young – and trust me, that was a *long* time ago! – I wasn't very forthcoming, but sometimes it's good to get stuff off your chest. Maybe even easier if you're talking to someone you don't know. A problem shared and all that.'

'No, it's cool.'

'Oh, I don't mean me,' Nick added hastily. 'I'm just a silly bloke. But my wife, she's a really good listener. If you felt like talking.'

Hollie shook her head. 'No, really, it's cool.'

'Okay, but we're here if you change your mind.' Nick turned and started to walk away.

'You said you *had* a daughter…'

Nick turned and looked back at her. Astute lass, he thought. He smiled. 'Yeah. As I say, you know where to find us.'

'Thanks, mister,' Hollie said.

'It's Nick. You can call me Nick.'

Hollie sniffed and wiped her nose on her sleeve. She smiled up at him, showing braces fitted across her top teeth. 'Thanks, Nick.'

*

Jenny's head was swimming. After hurrying from the chalet 20-minutes earlier she had crossed the path and plunged headlong into the woods. The ground was uneven and whichever way she turned the terrain looked exactly the same: trees, trees and more trees. With no noticeable landmarks she had quickly become disoriented and she was now well and truly lost in the dense woodland.

The further in she went, the thicker the foliage had become. The branches tore unforgivingly at her clothes, and only after gashing open her calf on a protruding limb did she finally come to a stop. Dropping to her knees, she threw back her head and screamed. 'Bastaaaard!'

She flopped over on her side, rolled onto her back and stared bleary-eyed up through the gently undulating treetops at the cloudless blue sky.

'What the hell am I doing here?' she muttered.

Slowly her eyelids closed.

*

When Nick got back to the chalet he found Kirsty and Charlie both heartily tucking into generous bowls of muesli.

'Hey, you started without me!' he said as he grabbed a piece of toast and sat down.

Kirsty paused, the last spoonful of muesli hovering at her mouth. 'I told you: ten minutes. We gave you an extra five as it is.' She consumed the cereal and dropped the spoon into her empty bowl.

'Yeah, sorry,' Nick said, crunching on his toast. 'I got a bit waylaid.'

Kirsty rose and picked up her empty bowl. Charlie handed his to her.

'Cereal?' she said.

'No, I'll stick with the toast, thanks,' Nick replied.

Kirsty crossed to the sink and put down the bowls. 'What would you like to drink, Charlie?'

'What have we got?'

Kirsty bent and opened the fridge. 'Just about everything by the looks of it. Choco-milk, plain milk, cola – way too early for that – or…' She turned her head and smiled at him. 'Someone's favourite.'

Charlie's face lit up. 'Juice?'

'Coming right up.' Kirsty hooked out a bottle of orange juice. 'Citrus-O,' she said, looking at the label. 'Not heard of that one. Must be Greek.'

'It's all Greek to me, Mum!'

Nick laughed. 'Good one, buddy.' He held up the palm of his hand and Charlie high-fived him.

Kirsty brought over the bottle, set it down on the table and took her seat.

Charlie eagerly grabbed hold of the bottle and unscrewed the cap. 'Juice, Dad?'

Nick shook his head. 'Not for me.'

Charlie looked at Kirsty. 'Mum?'

'No thanks, love.'

Charlie shrugged. 'All mine then!' He poured himself a large tumbler-full of the bright liquid.

'God knows what's in it,' Nick said. 'You need sunglasses just to look at it.'

Charlie giggled.

Reaching for another piece of toast, Nick slathered a large spoonful of marmalade on it. 'That Grant guy was right,' he said, looking at Kirsty. 'There's not a soul about. No-one. Not even Hallam or that woman who was with him. The reception place is all locked up.'

'It's still early. Maybe things take a while to wake up round here.' She selected a slice of toast for herself and offered the rack to Charlie. He took a piece.

'Maybe,' Nick said. 'But I'm not sure. Something doesn't feel right.'

Charlie was sniffing at his glass of juice and he didn't seem too impressed. He put it down.

'And I'll tell you something else,' Nick said. He took a bite out of his toast, wiped the smear of marmalade from the corner of his mouth and sucked it off his finger. 'I bumped into that girl Hollie. She was pretty upset. What you said earlier…'

Kirsty stopped buttering her toast and her mouth fell open. 'No! Oh God, abuse?'

'Well, it may not be physical abuse, but there's definitely something wrong between her and her dad. It might just be an awkward teenage thing.'

'I know what I heard,' Kirsty said quietly.

Nick nodded. 'I don't doubt it. I'm just not sure. I had a word with her but she wasn't very talkative.' He suddenly became aware that Charlie was listening with interest. 'Anyway,' he said. 'Conversation for another time.'

He tapped his fingers on the table. 'Listen up. I thought we might go exploring after breakfast,' he said cheerfully. 'Maybe find the lake Mr Hallam mentioned and have a swim.'

Charlie swallowed a mouthful of toast and picked up his glass of juice.

'That sounds like a plan,' Kirsty said. 'What do you say, Charlie?'

The boy paused, the tumbler pressed to his lips. 'Sounds good.'

'And maybe Mum can do us a packed lunch,' Nick said. 'How does that sound, buddy?'

Again Charlie was about to take a drink. He paused and set down the glass for a moment. 'Can we have chicken sandwiches?'

'I expect so. There's all sorts in the fridge, I think I spotted some chicken in there.'

'And crisps?'

'I don't know. Nick looked at Kirsty. 'Can we, Mum?'

She smiled. 'I think we can arrange that too.'

'Yes!' Charlie cried triumphantly. He picked up the tumbler and took a large swig of juice. As he swallowed he began to cough.

Kirsty leaned over and patted him on the back. 'Take it easy.' But the boy continued to cough. She frowned. 'Charlie, love, you okay?'

The boy tried to speak, but now his face was turning scarlet and he was hacking violently. He lurched back in his chair.

'Nick, he's choking!'

Nick jumped to his feet, but Charlie waved a hand and gasped. 'It's okay, I'm okay,' he cried hoarsely. He took another sip of juice and cleared his throat. 'It just went down the wrong way.'

Her face filled with relief, Kirsty flopped back down onto her chair. 'Just take it easy in future.'

'Yeah, you had us worried there for a moment, buddy,' Nick said, returning to his seat.

'Sorry, Dad. Sorry, Mum.'

'This picnic then,' Kirsty said. 'I'll pack up plenty of goodies. It'll be lovely, just the three of us.'

'Well I'm certainly not planning on inviting the neighbours,' Nick said. 'But listen. Before we head out

I thought I might go up to Kinley's chalet and check everything is okay with his wife.'

Kirsty looked at him questioningly. 'Why would you do that?'

'I don't know. He seemed pretty keyed up. What can I tell you? Good, bad or indifferent, I suppose I just don't like seeing people in trouble.'

Kirsty smiled at him. 'Like I said, you're a good man, Nick Mason.'

CHAPTER 14

Jenny's eyes snapped open. There was something crawling on her face. She let out a squeal and brushed off a little green bug.

Laid flat on her back among the leaves and staring up at the sky, she frowned as she tried to remember where she was. Then the events that had brought her battered and bleeding to this spot came flooding back and the tears welled in her eyes. To her horror it occurred to her that whatever had been on her face might have been feeding on her blood; the blood from the cut where that bastard Grant had hit her. Involuntarily she shuddered.

She sat up and looked around her. How long had she been here? She had no idea. More importantly, where the hell *was* "here"?

A shiny black centipede, perhaps four-inches long, crawled from the leaves and across her hand. She felt its tiny legs tickling and looked down. Letting out a shriek, she shook her hand violently. The insect clung on for a few seconds – 'Get off, get off!' – then fell, but not before its jaws had punctured the skin. Jumping to her feet, Jenny tried to stamp on it, but it moved fast and snaked away into the leaves out of sight.

She examined her hand. 'Mother-fffffff...!' she exclaimed angrily. There on the side just above her thumb were the twin angry red pinpricks where the vile insect had administered a shot of its venom. The wound burned, it was weeping clear fluid and it was already starting to swell. She needed to get back to the chalet and put some antiseptic on it.

As she stepped forward she became aware of the throbbing in her leg. She looked down and saw the gash on her calf where the branch had speared her. It was bleeding quite badly.

Looking around to make sure she wasn't being watched – it was second nature, pure instinct; she knew perfectly well there was no-one around – Jenny pulled off her T-shirt and attempted to tear it. It refused to surrender and she felt her wrist click. 'Oww!' Why did they always make this look so easy in films?

She chewed at the hem to try to make a hole that would give her some purchase, but to no avail.

Poking around on the the ground among the debris she found a semi-sharp piece of wood. After several attempts, she managed to make a hole in the bottom of the shirt into which she could insert her fingers, and with some difficulty she managed to tear off a strip of the fabric.

Kicking aside a patch of leaves to make sure there was nothing lurking undernearth, she sat back down. Binding the piece of cloth tightly around her calf – the searing pain made her wince – she stood up again.

She squirmed back into what remained of her T-shirt, pulling it down as far as she could over her hips so the missing piece didn't notice too badly, and looked around to try to get her bearings.

'Some holiday this has turned out to be!' she grumbled.

She looked to her left, then to her right, came to a decision and limped off through the bracken. Had she turned her head to the left she might have noticed the movement in one of the trees as a CCTV camera, partially hidden among the branches, turned slowly and silently to track her path. But she didn't.

A little further on she heard the faint sound of running water.

Picking up the pace, she emerged from the undergrowth and stumbled, almost taking a fall. In front of her the ground dropped away precipitously into a narrow gully.

Jenny immediately realised she must have made the wrong choice. Looking at her surroundings, it dawned on her that she had to be even further away from the chalet now.

The eye of another CCTV camera mounted high in the tree watched impassively as she turned back and moved to her left... just one small step. Hidden from sight beneath the carpet of leaves, the touch-sensitive steel plate was activated.

What happened next did so without warning and with such suddenness that Jenny didn't stand a chance.

Tossing debris and dust into the air as it shot up from the undergrowth, a length of high-tensile wire lashed out at her. She instinctively raised her hands to protect herself, but it was a fraction of a second too late. The wire slashed her diagonally across her face. She screamed in pain and stumbled backwards. The ground gave way beneath her feet and she felt herself start to fall. Her arm flew out and she tried to grab hold of a hanging branch. Her hand scrabbled feverishly at it for a few precious seconds, desperately trying to find purchase, but it slipped through her fingers. With a guttural howl she plunged into the gully, bouncing off the rocky sides as she plummeted down to the shallow stream at the bottom. She hit the water hard, impacting her head on a rock, and her skull split open.

With her spine shattered, she lay splayed out across the rocks like a discarded rag doll, glassy eyes staring up the face of the gully, yet seeing nothing.

Up on the precipice there was a rapid swooshing sound and the wire, still dripping with Jenny Kinley's blood, whipped into the air and swiftly retracted back into the undergrowth out of sight.

*

His face flushed with excitement, Hallam took off his tie and loosened the collar of his shirt. The back of it was sodden with sweat and clinging to him. He reached round and with a handkerchief he mopped up the beads dribbling down his neck .

He'd been tracking his guests' movements since sunrise. He'd thrilled at the sight of wet bodies emerging from showers – both the men and the women. Although he very much considered himself a ladies' man, as he'd got older he had started to find the naked male form aesthetically pleasurable to look at and in some cases very arousing. It didn't go unnoticed that two of the men, Messrs Trot and Page, didn't shower. Jamie had flicked soap and water under his armpits, but Warren hadn't washed at all. When the youngsters were occupying the bathroom, Hallam had switched off the cameras. Unlike the odious, twisted specimen who couldn't even be bothered to take a shower, he had absolutely no interest in children.

Hallam had watched the families dress, he'd observed them eating breakfast in their chalets and on their verandas. He'd seen Hollie Page shout something at her parents, storm away from the breakfast table and walk off into the woods alone. He'd watched Grant Kinley and the two boys walk down to reception and back. He'd seen the brief and apparently splenetic conversation between Grant and Nick Mason; that one had particularly delighted him. He'd witnessed Nick's futile visit to reception, the brief interaction with Jamie Trot and his encounter with Hollie in the woods. He'd seen the argument between Grant and Jenny and watched with excitement as she'd angrily left the chalet and blundered off among the trees. He had known at that moment that she would most likely be the first. Thanks to the tracker wristbands and the CCTV cameras dotted across the whole 200 acres of the resort, he'd kept track of her as she had managed to get lost, and he'd watched with heightening anticipation when she eventually came to the gully. And then...

Hallam grinned. 'Did you enjoy that, my friends?'

A mumble of approval echoed around the room and someone applauded.

'A mere aperitif,' Hallam continued. 'It was only a matter of time before this useless, drunken excuse for a woman met her maker. Fate and justice, intrinsically linked, playing out for your delectation on our little stage. Just wait until realisation sets in and they turn on each other like the rabid weasels that they are. *That's* when the dominoes will fall and *that's* when your investment will really come to fruition.'

He reached forward. 'Stay tuned, good people. The fun is only just beginning.' He flicked a switch and the murmur of appreciative voices ended abruptly.

Glancing at another screen, he stared at the moving red dots on the map intently. He focussed on one in particular; it was static. He stared at it hard for several minutes, then satsified that it was going to remain static he turned away.

He picked up a cigar from the ashtray where it was gently smouldering and took a puff.

'My entire life I've stood by and watched scum like our esteemed guests here on the island – I mean, what are they? Can we even *call* them human? These *animals* bring down our great country with their feckless indolence, their greed, their blind pig ignorance. It's all about me, me, me. I'll do whatever *I* want to do whenever *I* want to do it, and anyone who doesn't like it can be damned.'

Someone made a slightly muffled sound of acknowledgement.

Hallam set down his cigar. 'And then what? You're saddled with a lily-livered Government that has Mother Nature's gift handed to them on a plate, a virus with the efficacy to wipe out the proletarian infestation. And what do they do? Allow natural selection to perform a cleansing sweep? No, no, no, far too obvious.' He was sweating profusely and panting, and the spittle flew from his plump lips. 'They strive to protect a health service that they've spent years crippling so they can save the filth. *This* filth and their grubby offspring.

Millions of them, like termites, destroying everything that's good. A major opportunity missed. Well, I'm telling you, reparation isn't coming – it's here. Here and happening right now. And you're privileged to share in the glory, my dear.'

Beneath the desk Caroline paused in her ministrations. She was on her knees between Hallam's legs, her blouse unbuttoned and her plump breasts spilling out of a brassiere at least two sizes too small. She took a breath. Her lipstick smeared and her spectacles slightly crooked, she looked up towards him. 'Thank you, Mr Hallam,' she said and returned to the business at hand.

'History in the making, my dear.' He suddenly twitched and let out a gasp of pleasure. With an expression of immense satisfaction on his face, he eased back into the chair. 'History in the making,' he sighed.

CHAPTER 15

As Nick made his way up the path towards the Kinleys chalet he could hear indistinct, but clearly angry shouting emanating from inside.

He walked up the steps and crossed the veranda to the front door where he stopped. He listened to the voices coming through the window: 'Why did you shout at Mummy?' – 'Because Mummy's a silly fucking bitch not fit enough to look after herself, let alone you two! If you think…'

Nick rapped on the door and the voice fell silent. A few seconds later the door was flung open wide and Grant stood looking out angrily at him.

'*What*?!'

He'd known what he had intended to say, but Nick suddenly felt very awkward. 'Hi. Again. I was just checking…'

'Yeah? I think I already told you once to fuck off. What was you "just checking"?!'

Nick realised that coming up here had been a fool's errand. But he was here now, so… 'Look, I think we might have got off on the wrong foot.' He reached out to shake Grant's hand. 'Nick Mason.'

Grant didn't offer his hand in return, he just stood in the doorway glowering at Nick. '*And*?'

Nick looked at him expectantly for a moment and then withdrew his hand. 'Well, I thought I'd have a little look around. I went down to the reception block and you're right. The place is deserted.'

'So you thought you'd have a little look around, did you?' There was an unmistakable note of sarcasm.

'Yeah, I did.'

'So me saying the place was deserted wasn't good enough for you. You thought I was lying.'

Nick shook his head. 'Of course not. Look, this is ridiculous.'

Inside, Jordan and Jack were sitting on the sofa; both of them were upset and looked frightened. On Jordan's face was a bright red slap mark which he was tearfully nursing. Jack was clutching a small, threadbare teddy close to his chest. They were both watching their father at the door having an argument with the man they'd seen earlier that morning.

Jordan nudged his brother and motioned for him to follow. Without taking their eyes off Grant, they got up, moved quickly across the room and went out through the open back door.

Meanwhile Nick was struggling to keep his temper. 'The point is, I agree with you that something isn't right here, I just don't know what. But it might be better if we got together with the others to discuss it. I figured if your wife is...'

Grant was losing his patience now. He was a heartbeat away from punching this man's lights out. 'If my wife is *what*? Listen, pal, and listen good.' The vitriol spewed out. 'My wife is an alcoholic slut unfit to look after her kids. It's down to me to keep them on a leash while she's off her head half the time. What we *don't* need is interfering fuckers like you...' – he jabbed his finger angrily at Nick – '...poking their noses into our business, right? What we *do* need is to be left the fuck alone. Now how about you do like I already told you and piss off?'

Before Nick could respond, Grant slammed the door in his face.

Grant turned round and his eyes fell upon the empty sofa where, moments earlier, his two boys had been sitting. He let out an exasperated growl.

'Unbelievable!' Nick exclaimed as he walked down the steps. 'Fucking unbelievable. Well, you can't help people who won't help themselves,' he muttered resignedly. Shaking his head, he set off back along the path in the direction of his chalet.

The path snaked down among the trees and the sound of talking drifted over from his right.

'Go on, sugarcake,' the voice was saying huskily. 'Touch him. He's not gonna bite.'

Nick stopped. What now? This so-called holiday was turning into a living nightmare.

He stepped off the path and peered covertly through the bushes.

In a small clearing, Hollie was standing – back up against a tree – with Warren's full weight pressed up against her. The man might have had his back to him, but Nick could that see Hollie was helpless, wedged between her father and the tree. There was no doubt in Nick's mind that what he was seeing was patently inappropriate.

Nick hesitated, unsure what to do. He could see the fear in Hollie's eyes.

Warren was speaking to her softly. 'There was no need to make a scene at breakfast. I thought we'd discussed it and decided it was best for us – for *everybody* – if your Ma doesn't know. It's always been our little secret. Surely there's no reason it can't stay that way.'

'Just leave me alone.' Hollie wriggled in an attempt to break free, but Warren pressed up even closer.

'Come on, Daddy's sorry. I didn't mean to hurt you last night. How about a little kiss, just so I know you've forgiven me, eh?' He nodded downwards. 'Then I've got a little something for you,' he whispered lasciviously.

Puckering up, he leaned in towards her.

Hollie turned her head away. 'Get *off* me!'

Nick couldn't stand by any longer. He felt physically sick. 'Hey!' he shouted angrily, stepping out from the bushes into the clearing.

Startled, Warren spun round, hastily zipping up the fly on his shorts... but not before Nick had glimpsed his state of arousal.

Seizing the opportunity to run, Hollie ducked away to the right. Warren grabbed for her arm, but she wormed free and her pink wristband came off in his hand. She sped across the clearing and disappeared off among the trees.

'Hollie, get back here *now!*' Warren shouted furiously. But she was gone.

Run, girl, just run, Nick thought.

Stuffing the wristband in his pocket, Warren turned angrily to face Nick. 'Can I help you, mate?'

It took every ounce of Nick's strength not to march straight up to the man and punch him square in the face. 'Yes,' he said, with as much composure as he could muster. 'There's something not right on this island and I was thinking everyone should probably get together and discuss what we're going to do.'

Warren stared at him fiercely through the pebble lenses. 'Not right? What do you mean, "not right"?'

'I'm not sure. It's…'

'Well if you're not bloody sure, what's the all the fuss about?'

This sort of attitude was becoming seriously tiresome. Nick sighed. 'No fuss. I just…'

'Then fuck off, mate.'

Nick looked off into the trees. There was no sign of Hollie. 'That's the second time in a few minutes someone's said that to me,' he said calmly.

'Then why don't you just get on and do it? I'm busy.'

Nick was really struggling to keep his temper. 'Busy, huh?' he snapped.

Warren looked momentarily uncertain, but he didn't back down. 'Yeah, busy. So go on, mate. Do one.'

Nick took a pace towards him. 'I just saw exactly what busy means, you twisted piece of shit!' He spat out the words. 'And if I see you lay a finger, or if I even *hear* you've laid a finger on Hollie, I'll…'

'Don't you say her name! Don't you *dare*!' Warren took a step back. 'Who the hell do you think you are telling me what to do? I don't have to answer to you, I don't have to asnwer to *anyone*. It's not cool to threaten people like that, mate.'

Nick's reply was measured and calm, but his words left Warren in no doubt whatsoever. 'It's not a threat – *mate*. It's a promise.'

Warren turned on his heels. 'Don't think for one moment you'll get away with this,' he growled, and he set off in the direction Hollie had fled.

'Jesus Christ!' Nick hissed through gritted teeth.

Whatever promise this holiday might have shown when they had first arrived was going to hell in a handbasket.

*

After Jordan and Jack had escaped the chalet, they had headed straight off into the woods. They'd chased each other through the trees, and finding a couple of suitable sticks they had played sword fights for a few minutes, which had cheered Jack up a lot.

Then they had swung on the overhanging branches of a vast olive tree, making screeching noises like monkeys.

Now they were sitting on the ground, breathless and laughing hysterically.

Eventually they stopped. Jack said, 'Do you think Mummy and Daddy will be okay?'

Jordan shuffled his bottom over so that he was sat next to his brother. He put an arm round him. 'Of course they will,' he said comfortingly.

'I hate it when they shout at each other.' Jack hugged the teddy bear tightly. 'It scares Mooch.'

'It'll be fine,' Jordan said. 'It always is.' But he really wasn't so sure this time.

Jack perked up. 'Let's play hide and seek!'

'Okay,' Jordan said. 'I'll hide.'

'No, I want to hide,' his younger brother said petulantly. He waved the teddy in the air. 'You've got to find *us*.'

'Go on then,' Jordan said. He put his hand over his eyes and started to count. 'One... two...'

Jack grinned, got up and scampered off as fast as his little legs would carry him. Spotting a fallen tree, he dashed over to it, climbed carefully over to the other side and ducked down low. He set the teddy bear down on the leaves and put a finger to his lips. 'We have to be quiet, Mooch,' he whispered.

'...eighteen... nineteen... twenty!' Jordan jumped up and spun around. 'Coming ready or not!'

Jordan made his way through the trees, stopping and listening at regular intervals.

Suddenly he heard a twig snap. Jack evidently hadn't understood the game; he was supposed to be hiding, not walking about.

Jordan darted behind a tree, and waited to jump out and give Jack a surprise. As the sound of footfall got close, he leapt out with a cry. 'Gotcha!'

Warren jumped. 'Bloody hell, lad, you nearly gave me a heart attack!' He put a hand to his chest.

Jordan's face dropped. 'Sorry. I thought you were my brother. We're playing a game.'

To their left Jack's head popped up from behind the fallen tree.

'Look, there he is,' Warren said. 'You're the Kinley boys, aren't you. Jack and...'

'Jordan.'

'Of course. I don't suppose either of you two scamps have seen my little girl round here, have you?'

The two boys shook their heads. Picking up his bear, Jack clambered back over the tree and came to join his brother.

Warren frowned. 'I've lost her, you see.' He looked around. 'Where are *your* parents? You're not out here all alone are you?'

'We…' Jack began, but Jordan nudged him.

'Our Dad's just over there.' He waved at hand at the trees.

Warren looked in the direction Jordan had indicated. 'I can't see anyone,' he said. He took a step towards them.

'Well he's there,' Jordan said firmly.

Jack stepped back a little and shielded himself behind his older brother.

Warren eyed them suspiciously for a moment. Then he smiled. 'Okay, well if you or your Dad happen to see my Hollie, tell her I'm looking for her, would you?'

They both nodded.

With that Warren turned and hurried away.

'I don't want to play any more,' Jack said sullenly as they watched Warren recede into the woods.

'Why not?' Jordan said. 'Come on!' He snatched the teddy bear off Jack and took off at speed.

'Give me Mooch!' the little one cried, taking chase.

They ran through the trees shouting and laughing. Just as Jack had almost caught up with Jordan, the older boy suddenly hurled the teddy into the air. It bounced off a tree and spiraled off out of sight on the far side of a ridge.

'Moooooch!' Jack shouted and raced off up the ridge, disappearing over the crest and down the other side.

Jordan sauntered after his brother.

'Come quick!' The voice sounded panicky.

Jordan quickened his pace. He hurried to the top of the ridge and stopped, looking down at Jack who was standing at the edge of a clearing in front of a huge sandpit in which there as a slide, a swing and a trampoline.

'Look,' Jack said, pointing.

On the opposite side of the sandpit was a small pebble-dashed hut, the front of which was bedecked with brightly coloured streamers. Over the doors there was a huge placard bearing the words *Ice Cream Parlour*.

'Wow!' Jordan ran down the slope and joined his brother. He grabbed hold of his arm. 'Come on!' he said excitedly.

'Hang on,' Jack cried. 'Mooch!'

The bear was laying in the middle of the sandpit.

'Quick then,' Jordan said, and they both stepped out onto the sand. It shifted beneath their feet and they promptly sank up to their ankles.

'Wait!' Jordan said, grabbing hold of his brother's arm.

'But I've got to get Mooch.'

Jordan pulled his feet out of the liquefied sand and stepped back away from the pit, dragging little Jack after him.

'I know. But we'll have to find something to hook him with.'

The little one frowned. 'Why?'

Jordan looked his younger brother in the eyes. 'You remember that Tarzan film we saw on telly? The one where the baddie got stuck in the sand and it slowly dragged him under?'

'Yeah, that was brill!'

'Well this sand is like *that* sand. It's dangerous. We mustn't walk on it or we could die.'

The younger boy nodded his understanding.

'Come on,' Jordan said. 'Let's go and find something that we can use to rescue Mooch.'

Several hundred yards away Grant was stampeding through the woods.

'Boys!' he shouted angrily. 'Come on, stop messing around.'

His foot caught on a root and his ankle jarred awkwardly. 'Fuck!'

He hobbled to a stop. 'Boys!' he yelled again. 'Come on, don't be silly now, I didn't mean to get cross with you.'

The only response he got was a flapping of wings as a little Olive-tree Warbler took flight from the branches overhead, closely pursued by its mate.

He took a step and a sharp pain shot through his ankle. 'You wait till I get my hands on you, you little fuckers,' he said under his breath. 'Your mother too.'

Limping badly now, he moved on.

A little further on he came to the ridge. Stepping up, he saw Jordan and Jack on the far side of the pit doing something with a length of tree branch.

'Boys! There you are.'

Jordan and Jack stopped what they were doing and looked up at their father fearfully.

'What are you doing?' Grant said as he limped down the slope. Then he saw the teddy bear laying in the middle of the sand pit. 'What's old teddy doing there, Jack?'

Neither of the boys said anything. They took a quick step back.

'Come on, now.' Grant walked towards the sandpit.

'Daddy, don't…' Jack began, but Jordan elbowed him to be quiet.

Grant marched straight out into the pit. 'I'm sorry I…'

Immediately the sand gave way beneath him. Before he could even comprehend what was happening, he was waist-deep in the morass.

'What the fuck…?'

The boys stood watching in silence as their father thrashed about in an attempt to find a footing. Jack looked alarmed, but there was an unquestionable glimmer of excitement in Jordan's eyes.

Grant chuckled, clearly not having quite grasped the gravity of the situation; quite literally the gravity – or lack thereof.

'Boys! Don't just stand there, come and give your Dad a hand here.'

Jack and Jordan remained rooted to the spot.

Grant was getting angry now. The silt was sloshing around his chest. 'Jordan, please. Get over here and help me,' he cried.

The boy ignored his plea.

As Grant desperately looked at them for help, he had a sudden moment of clarity. Had he not seen or heard somewhere that floundering around in a situation like this causes a person to sink faster? It felt as if his entire body was being drawn down by the suction and his every instinct was to fight against it. Nevertheless, with an immense mental effort he managed to still himself.

He gently shifted a little, hoping to find some sort of anchorage, but his sense of feeling had gone and he couldn't be sure his feet were even moving. The result wasn't what he had hoped for; instead of stabilising, he sank a little further. He stopped still again and considered his options. Distribution of weight would help, he thought. If only he could flatten himself out. But that wasn't going to happen, he was already in too deeply.

The boys were still watching him. Okay, he thought, *they* are my only option. He'd already tried the softly-softly approach. Time to engage the fear factor. That always got them moving.

'Get the fuck over here and help me,' he screamed. '*Help* me, damn you!'

Still the boys didn't move. Jack had turned away, but Jordan was still watching Grant with a mixture of fear and excitement on his face.

'Wait till I get my hands on you, you little fuckers!'

Maybe he could manually try to free his legs a little. It was a risk and might worsen the situation, but at this point Grant couldn't think of anything else to do. He slowly reached a hand down into the sludge to feel for his legs. But as he did so, he lurched sideways at an angle. His head – from the neck up – his right shoulder and his arm were now the only parts of him that weren't submerged.

Realising that his options had run out – if there had even really been any to begin with – and reluctantly accepting his fate, he let out a big sigh and resignedly closed his eyes.

Then his foot touched something solid beneath him.

An indescribable thrill coursed through him as hope came rushing back. His eyes sprung open.

There, a couple of yards away from his face, was a scorpion. It was moving swiftly towards him across the surface of the quicksand like a skater on ice. It stopped a few inches from his face, as if unsure of what it had encountered. Cautiously it moved forward an inch and Grant saw the shiny surface on the jet-black carapace covering its head.

A bead of sweat rolled down Grant's forehead and he swallowed hard as one of the pincers reached out inquisitively towards him.

For all he was worth Grant tried to remain still, but as the tip of the pincer touched his nose, survival instinct kicked in and he flinched away.

Tail raised defensively and with its venom-tipped stinger twitching, the scorpion moved back a little. Not nearly far enough for Grant's liking though. Without thinking, he lashed out with his right hand to bat it away.

But the creature was too fast for him. With an incredible display of reactionary speed, it scuttled to one side and the stinger arced upwards, finding its target in the side of Grant's hand.

He cried out and jerked his hand away.

The liquid soil shifted beneath him and Grant promptly sank up to his chin... then his mouth... then his nose. He threw back his head and took a final desperate breath.

The last thing Grant Kinley saw as the unforgiving sludge engulfed him was his eldest son staring at him wide-eyed – the clear trace of a malevolent smile on his lips – raising a hand and giving him a little wave.

And then he was gone.

He might have managed to hold his breath for 30-seconds... maybe 35. But when Grant's lungs had started to burn and his chest felt as if it was about to explode, he would have had no choice but to exhale... followed by the inevitable mortifying inhalation that signed his death warrant. The vile, choking muck would have been drawn in through his nasal cavities, followed by the futile reflex action to expel it again. But of course he'd have been completely bereft of the air required to do so. The unforgiving liquid death would have oozed down into his throat and ultimately deluged his lungs.

As Jack looked up, his eyes darting back and forth searching for his father, loud chimes filled the air. Both boys turned to see the ice cream parlour ablaze with flashing lights.

'Let's have ice cream,' Jordan said.

Jack was staring out across the pit to the spot he'd last seen his father. 'What about Daddy?' Then he saw his beloved teddy bear. 'And Mooch!'

Jordan took his brother gently by the arm. 'We can't get him. It's too dangerous. Let's just go and get an ice cream.'

They walked towards the parlour. As they ascended the steps and walked on to the wooden decking, the floor opened up beneath them.

Screaming, they plunged downwards into the darkness and the doors on the trapdoor slammed shut with an almighty clang.

The musical chimes ceased instantly and all the lights on the small, pebble-dashed hut winked out.

CHAPTER 16

When he'd got back to the chalet, Nick had been absolutely fuming. But the sight of Kirsty and Charlie sitting on the veranda eagerly awaiting his return – a rucksack containing the picnic lunch at their side – had quickly doused his fiery disposition.

Nick had thrown the rucksack over his shoulder and now, as they walked through the serene woodland, he was feeling completely relaxed again.

'I know it's hardly a life-changing decision, but we couldn't make up our minds whether to bring sandwiches or wraps,' Kirsty said with a smile. 'So we made both.'

'I reckon the biggest life-changing decision any of these losers ever has to make is which colour wheelie-bin to put out each week,' Nick said with a grin.

Kirsty laughed.

'If they can even be arsed to put out their rubbish at all,' he added, his brow furrowing.

'Come on now.' Kirsty wagged a finger at him. 'No Mr Grouch today, thank you very much. You can leave him behind.'

Nick stopped walking and raised his hands. 'Fair enough. But honestly, love, you haven't had first hand experience of these idiots.'

They started to trek off again.

'Like I said last night, let them do their thing…' Kirsty said.

'Sure.' Nick frowned. 'I still think it's strange there was no-one around up at reception this morning though. On the way back let's swing by and check it out again.'

'There's no need to let worrying about it ruin our day. I'm sure Mr Hallam or one of his staff will be there. We don't really need them anyway, we can make our own fun. Right Charlie?' she called back over her shoulder.

'Right!' Charlie replied excitedly from several yards back.

Nick adjusted the rucksack on his back. 'What have you got in here? It weighs a ton.'

'Just a few nibbles.'

Kirsty looked round for Charlie, who was standing in the bracken about 10-yards back, peering upwards through his binoculars.

He had been dawdling behind since they had left the chalet and every time he'd spotted a bird he'd stopped to observe it and then made a careful note in the little book he was carrying in the back pocket of his shorts. So far he'd seen and managed to identify the Olive-tree Warblers – which seemed to reside here in their hundreds – and also spotted a Black-headed Bunting, a pair of Chukars and, much to his delight, a beautiful pinkish-brown Hoopoe with a long black downcurved bill. He'd shouted out to his parents to come and see, but by the time they had tracked back to him the bird had opened its striking black and white wings and flown swiftly away.

'Come on, love. Keep up,' Kirsty called.

Charlie continued to look through the binoculars at something up in one of the trees. 'Hey, Dad, come and take a look at this.'

Nick strolled back towards him. 'Come on, slowcoach. When we get to the lake there are sure to be plenty more you haven't seen yet.'

'It's not a bird.'

Nick stepped up to him and Charlie handed over the binoculars. 'There.' He pointed up among the branches. 'It's a camera.'

Nick looked up and sure enough, bolted to the trunk maybe 20-feet above them, was a CCTV camera.

'Probably for security,' he said, returning the binoculars to Charlie. 'It's encouraging to see. I imagine it'd be pretty easy to get lost out here. Come on.'

A few minutes later they came across a tree with its immense roots spouting up out of the ground around it like a fossilised fountain.

'Quick snack break?' Nick suggested, slipping the rucksack off his back.

Kirsty nodded. 'I'm parched.'

They found a place to sit on one of the vast, mossy tree roots and Nick opened up the rucksack and ferreted around inside. He pulled out a bottle of Loux lemon juice and handed it to Kirsty. She broke the seal, unscrewed the top and took a large mouthful.

'Ooo, that's nice. It's sweet, but it's a bit sour too. And it smells gorgeous.'

She handed the bottle to Nick and he took a sip, then handed it back to her.

He pulled out a bottle of Citrus-O. 'Juice, Charlie?'

'No, I'm okay thanks.'

'Sandwich?'

'Later.'

The lad was standing a few feet away, scanning the terrain through his binoculars.

Nick pulled out a package of clingfilm-wrapped sandwiches and sniffed it.

'Yes, they're your faves,' Kirsty said, amused.

Pulling off the wrapping, Nick offered one to Kirsty. She shook her head.

'Look,' Charlie whispered loudly. He pointed up to a branch where the bird he'd seen a few minutes earlier was perched looking down at them. Realising it had been seen, it took flight. Charlie dashed off after it.

'Don't stray too far, love,' Kirsty called after him.

Nick looked around at the serene woodland. He patted the tree root. 'Can you imagine,' he said thoughtfully, munching on his chicken-mayo sandwich. 'Back when this place was a penal colony, when the men and women managed to get it together, this would have been the perfect spot for an illicit liaison.'

'Until they got caught and had their heads chopped off, yeah.' Kirsty said.

'Cannodling convicts, eh? Caught in flogrante dolictoo.'

'In *what*?' Kirsty said, laughing.

'You know. Having a bit of the old how's your father.'

'You mean in *flagrante delicto*!'

Nick grinned. 'Yeah, okay, that too.' He leant over and gave her a kiss on the cheek.

Putting down the bottle of lemon juice, she took his face in her hands and kissed him hard on the mouth. 'I love you.'

'Love you back.'

Nick had been watching Charlie out of the corner of his eye. He was chasing his quarry, and the Hoopoe almost seemed to be treating it as some sort of a game, as it flitted from one branch to the next, maintaining a safe distance but never going so far as to lose its eager pursuer.

Satisfied his son was out of earshot, he said, 'Now we've got a moment to ourselves, there's something I wanted to tell you.'

Kirsty saw the serious look on his face. 'Okay, go on,' she said trepidatiously.

'On the way back from my delightful chat with Kinley, I came across Hollie and her father in the woods. Everything you thought was right on the button.'

Kirsty's eyes widened. 'Oh no. What happened?'

Nick looked a bit uncomfortable. 'I don't really know how to say this, but…'

'Mum, Dad!' The urgent cry came from off through the trees.

Dropping the remains of his sandwich and grabbing the rucksack, Nick jumped up. Kirsty was already on her feet and running.

At the edge of the trees they found Charlie standing on the ledge overlooking the gully.

'Come away from there!' Kirsty shouted.

Charlie did as he was told and immediately stepped away from the precipice.

Kirsty wrapped her arms around him. 'I told you not to wander off!' she said. angrily.

'I'm sorry.'

She hugged him tight. 'It's okay. But don't do it again.'

Nick came up behind them. 'You need to stay close, buddy. I know we're in fenced off land and I'm sure it's safe out here, but we still don't know the area properly yet. You need to stay close.'

Charlie stared up at him. His face was white and he was trembling. 'There's someone laying in the water down there,' he said shakily, pointing back towards the edge of the gully.

'*What*?' Kirsty let go of him.

'Are you sure?' Nick said. He stepped up to the ledge and looked down into the gully.

'Be careful,' Kirsty implored him.

'Christ, he's right,' Nick exclaimed. 'There *is* someone down there.'

'Doing what?'

'Nothing.' He turned back to face her. 'It looks like she's had a fall.'

'Is she okay?'

'It doesn't look like it.' Nick got down on his knees and leaned out over the edge as far as he dared, looking to his right and left.

'What are you doing?' Kirsty asked with a note of concern. She looked at Charlie. 'Stay here.'

She stepped up behind Nick and squatted down. He was looking along the length of the precipice for a way down the face of the gully, but as far as he could see there wasn't one.

He leaned a little further over and looked down. 'There are plenty of roots sprouting out of the rock. I just about reckon I could get down there,' he said.

Kirsty stared at him in disbelief. 'You can't be serious! You are *not* going down *there*!'

Nick looked at her. 'I have to. She might still be alive.'

'Then we'll go and find help.'

Nick shook his head. 'And if she *is* still alive, by the time we've found someone and got back here it might be too late.'

Kirsty still couldn't believe what she was hearing. 'And what are you going to do if you do manage to get down there and she *is* still alive? How are you going to get her back up here?' She looked nervously over the edge. 'I don't think it's even possible to get down there.'

'I disagree,' Nick countered. 'And I have to try,' he added adamantly.

'Don't let him, Mum.' Charlie was crying.

'It's okay, buddy. It's not that far. And I wouldn't do it if I wasn't sure I could.'

The CCTV camera above them watched as, still on his knees, Nick turned round and shuffled back towards the edge.

'Take my arm,' he said, reaching out to Kirsty.

'Take your arm?!' she exclaimed. 'I won't be able to hold you.' She was close to tears.

He waggled his hand at her and shuffled down a little further. 'Come on, take it. It's perfectly safe, just hold on until I can…'

'Nick, please don't.' She got down on her knees and grasped his hand. 'I can't hold you, I really can't.' Her palm was sweating, but she held on for all she was worth. 'You're going to fall!'

'No I'm not.' His lower half was already dangling over the ledge.

Suddenly Nick lurched downwards and Kirsty lost her grip. She was dragged forward off her knees, his hand slid out of hers and she fell face first into the dirt. Her head shot up and she watched in horror as Nick cried out and disappeared over the ledge.

Charlie screamed. 'Daaad!'

For a few seconds – to Kirsty it felt like an age – there was complete silence. She felt her throat constrict and she lay on the ground gasping for air, staring in disbelief at the ledge.

Nick stood upright. 'It's okay, buddy. I'm fine.'

From her position laying in the dust, Kirsty could only see him from the shoulders up and for all the world it looked to her as if he was suspended in thin air.

'I told you it was safe,' he said. 'There's an outcrop of rock.' He glanced down. 'And there's a huge bit of root sticking out underneath it.'

'For Christ's sake,' Kirsty sobbed. 'I thought for a second I'd lost you.'

'Never. I've done the hard bit getting over the ledge safely. It should be fairly easy to get to the bottom now.'

Charlie was wiping the tears from his eyes.

Kirsty got back up onto her knees. Her heart was beating 19 to the dozen. 'Okay, but keep talking to me all the way down.'

'I'll tell you what, I'll sing.' Blowing her a quick kiss, Nick ducked down out of sight.

The first root was solid and took his weight easily. '*All of me, loves all of you…*'

Kirsty put a hand to her mouth. It was Daisy's favourite song.

Nick was able to worm his fingers into a cranny in the rock face, which enabled him to cover the first few feet downwards quickly and safely. '*All your curves and all your edges, all your perfect imperfections…*' But after that he quickly realised he'd underestimated the complexity of the descent. 'I wish we'd packed a rope,' he called up; the note of nervousness in his stab at humour was patent.

Kirsty's voice echoed down to him from above. 'Do you think you can make it?'

Nick glanced down. He was already halfway there. He swallowed hard and tried to sound confident. 'Definitely,' he shouted. Under his breath he muttered, 'Maybe.'

'*Give your all to me, I'll give my all to you…*' He was sweating freely now. He looked to his left and spotted the curled end of another piece of root. He reached out and pulled hard on it. It didn't even flex. '*You're my end and my beginning…*' Taking a deep breath, he grabbed hold and lowered himself down another few feet. '*Even when I lose I'm winning…*'

Another convenient fissure in the rock and a cluster of roots made the next part of the descent relatively simple.

'You've stopped singing!'

She sounded so far away. Nick looked up. His face was dripping with sweat. 'I don't do high notes!' he shouted.

Suddenly his foot slipped and for a moment he thought he was going to fall. He clung on to the piece of root and fortunately it held his weight. Breathing hard, he continued downwards and despite the doubts he would never have admitted to, a minute or two later his feet touched the ground.

'Made it!' he shouted up to Kirsty.

Kirsty's reply echoed down to him. 'Thank God!'

Now all I've got to do is get back up again, Nick thought.

'Is she alive?'

'Hang on.'

Nick stepped carefully over the slippery rocks towards where the broken body lay, the running water lapping playfully around it.

A large bird – Nick didn't know what, and it didn't matter – was balanced on the rock beside her head, struggling with something in its beak.

As Nick drew closer he saw that the something was an eyeball. It had been plucked out, but was still attached by the rectus muscles that secure eyeballs in their sockets, refusing to yield to the bird's attempts to steal it away.

'Get lost!' Nick flapped at the bird. Reluctant to give up the prize, it hesitated for a moment, weighing up its options. Nick kicked out and splashed water at it. With an angry squawk the bird hopped away, but only a few yards before settling on a rock on the far side of the stream. There it sat, glaring at him angrily.

Nick squatted down. Despite the hideous gash across the face and the mauled eyeball that was now resting on her cheek, he recognised the body as that of Jenny Kinley. He had no need to check for life signs, it was perfectly clear now that she was dead; her brains were splattered all over the rock beneath her.

Suddenly Nick felt a little dizzy. He stood up and turned away from the horrible sight. He looked up towards the precipice some 40-feet above him. A flicker of suspicion crossed his mind as he recalled his fractious encounter with Grant Kinley that morning. Had Jenny fallen? If so she would certainly have been killed on impact. Or had someone pushed her over?

'It's that Grant Kinley guy's wife, Jenny,' he shouted. The sound of his voice reverberated across the walls of the gully. 'She's dead!'

CHAPTER 17

'This is gonna be so fuckin' great!' Jamie took a swig from the bottle of Pilsner in his hand.

Just over an hour earlier, his liquid breakfast still sloshing around inside his belly, he'd taken a stroll along to the next chalet to have a word with Lisa Page about getting everyone together and walking up to the lake that Hallam had mentioned to them yesterday. Well, not exactly *everyone*; he had no intention whatsoever of inviting Nick Mason and his shitty little family. He'd walked straight past their chalet without so much as turning his head.

Lisa had seemed a bit flustered when Jamie first turned up, but she said she would have a word with her husband when he and her daughter arrived back from their walk, adding that she was sure everyone would be delighted to come along. They had been planning to visit the lake anyway and thought it sounded fun to go as a group.

Jamie had then walked further up the path to invite Grant Kinley too. Banging on the door there had been no reply. He had hung around for a minute or two, but deciding he couldn't care less – 'Fuck 'em!' – he'd returned to his own chalet to find Vicky packing a coolbox with more food than they could possibly eat. There not being enough alcohol in his opinion, while Vicky was changing into her swimwear he'd discarded some of the food and managed to crowbar in a few extra bottles of lager.

So now here they were, the procession of happy holidaymakers making their way through the woods to find the fabled lake. Having walked for 20-minutes though, they started to get very fed up that they hadn't found it yet.

Wearing a blue bikini as equally insubstantial as the one she'd worn when they had arrived the previous day, Vicky was chatting away to Lisa, who'd opted for more discreet attire; a black one-piece bathing suit with a white beach sarong wrapped around the bottom half. She was carrying their lunch in a Tesco's bag for life.

Trailing behind, carrying the cool-box between them and not looking very happy about it, Billie-Jo and Bobbi-Leigh were also wearing unsuitably scant swimwear: matching bright yellow bikinis with thongs that disappeared up between the cheeks of their buttocks. It was a revealing sartorial choice that hadn't gone unappreciated by Caine, who was bringing up the rear and enjoying getting an eyeful. He'd been attempting to make small-talk since they'd set out, but both girls had pretty much been ignoring him. So eventually he'd gone quiet and continued to delight in the unhindered view of Billie-Jo's undulating buttocks.

Jamie was leading the way alongside Warren, both of them bare-chested and wearing swim-shorts.

As they walked Warren had rattled on about nothing else except his daughter and for some reason Jamie couldn't fathom he was still making excuses for her absence. 'She's not a bad kid, but she will go off in these strops of hers. Least little thing and she's off sulking. Still, her loss today.'

'Yeah, teenage girls, eh?' Jamie drained the Pilsner in his hand and tossed the empty bottle off into the undergrowth. He belched and turned round. 'Bill, chuck us another bottle.'

Everyone came to a halt and the girls set down the cool-box on the ground.

Jamie looked at Warren. 'Want one?'

Warren shook his head. 'Maybe later.'

'You sure? Hallam's payin'.'

Scratching at his belly, which was hanging obscenely over the top of his shorts, Warren smiled. 'Oh, go on then. I wouldn't want to offend our generous host.'

'Make that two, Bill.'

Billie-Jo bent over and unclipped the clasp on the cool-box lid, affording Caine an unexpected bonus flash.

Warren saw his son gawping and felt a wave of anger... and perhaps not just a little bit of jealousy. Hadn't the damned boy learned his lesson? It had only been three months since the business on the estate with that 13-year-old girl. In Warren's opinion she had been a naughty little tease and he knew if the chance had presented itself he could easily have succumbed to temptation himself. But nevertheless Caine had been damned lucky not to have ended up in serious trouble. And Warren could certainly do without any unwanted attention from the law.

'Caine!' Warren snapped. 'Get your carcass up here and walk with me.'

As the boy moved sullenly past, Billie-Jo reached out and handed him two bottles. 'Here, give these to my Dad!' she said, bending down again to secure the clasp on the cool-box.

'Dad, this is really heavy,' Bobbi-Leigh whined. 'Can't someone else carry it for a bit.'

'I'll take it on the way back.' Jamie grinned at Warren. 'It'll be a bit fuckin' lighter by then!'

Caine stepped over and handed Jamie the bottles of lager. He took them and passed them straight to Warren. 'Hold these a sec,' he said. 'Gotta drain the snake.'

Vicky rolled her eyes. 'We'll never find this fuckin' lake if you keep gettin' tanked up and stoppin' for a piss every five minutes.' She winked at Billie-Jo and Bobbi-Leigh. 'And besides, it's not a snake, it's a worm.'

The girls looked embarrassed. 'TMI, mother!' Billie-Jo exclaimed in horror.

Jamie ignored the jibe and darted off behind a tree.

Vicky turned apologetically to Lisa. 'I'm sorry about this. I can't take him anywhere. No fuckin' social graces whatsoever.'

Lisa forced a smile and swatted at a fly that had been buzzing around her head for a while and getting increasingly annoying.

Vicky noticed and grinned. 'Ya shoulda washed yer minge this mornin',' she said with a throaty chuckle.

Lisa hadn't been keen from the start, but this woman was turning out to be dreadfully uncouth, she thought. In fact, she was beginning to wish she'd just said no to Jamie's invite and stayed back at the chalet.

Warren was whispering angrily with Caine.

'Didn't you learn anything at all with that Charlotte kid?' he hissed at his son. 'You're lucky her parents didn't give a shit about her or you'd have been spending the last of your teenage years in juvenile detention.'

Caine looked a little bemused. 'Her name was Carly,' he said. 'Anyway, what you talking about?'

'Don't you think for one second I didn't see you. Just you keep your eyes off those two girls, you dirty little bastard,' Warren snarled.

'Talk about the pot calling the kettle black!'

Warren's eyes blazed, but before he could respond Jamie reappeared from behind the tree. 'Fuck me, I needed that.' He adjusted his shorts and broke wind.

'Talkin' out your arse again, babe?' Vicky chortled.

'Love you too, babe' Jamie replied sarcastically as he stepped over and retrieved his bottle of Pilsner from Warren. Holding the cool bottle against his brow, he looked at Caine. 'What's that you was saying about blacks?' he said.

'Nothing,' Caine muttered.

'Better not let Kinley hear ya!' Jamie guffawed and turned to face the others. 'Come on then, what you all hanging about for?'

Billie-Jo and Bobbi-Leigh sighed and picked up the cool-box, and they all set off again.

'It's a shame the Kinleys couldn't come too,' Vicky remarked. She looked to make sure Jamie was out of earshot. 'That Grant ain't half fit. And I reckon those two little boys would love being out in the jungle.'

Lisa put a hand to her mouth. 'You can't say that!'

Vicky didn't even notice Lisa's shocked expression. She was busy adjusting her bikini top. 'I reckon the cheeky buggers took off up there early to get the best spot. I hope they're not already off their heads when we get there, or we'll have a bit of catchin' up to do.' She looked ahead at Jamie who was already halfway through his third bottle of lager. 'Well, some of us will anyway,' she said with a note of disdain.

*

It had taken Nick almost three times as long to ascend the rocky face of the gully as it had to climb down. He'd walked along the stream for a hundred yards or so in both directions looking for an alternative, but it was evident there was no easy way back up.

Sweating for England, he had collapsed at the top of the precipice. His clothes were filthy and he'd managed to tear a gaping hole in the sleeve of his shirt.

Kirsty had held him so tightly he'd started to think she would never let go, and then Charlie had come running over and joined them for a group hug.

Once he'd recovered his breath, he pulled his phone from his pocket. 'We need to call an ambulance.'

He pressed the button to activate it and waited for the screen to illuminate.

'What's the Greek equivalent of 999?'

She looked a little dumbfounded. 'Are you serious? How the heck should I know?!'

'Damn it,' he said after a few seconds. 'Still no signal. Here, quick, give me yours.'

Kirsty pulled her phone from her back pocket and handed it to him. Nick fiddled with it for a few moments, clearly having trouble turning it on.

'Give it here,' Kirsty said, taking it back from him. 'Let me do it.'

Nick watched as the screen lit up. She tapped a green icon at the bottom and frowned. 'I can't seem to get a signal either. If I try to use the call option it just flashes up with that stupid palm tree picture.' She looked up at him. 'Wait a minute, we're on a bloody island in the middle of the woods. How on earth are we going to call for an ambulance?'

Nick looked at her, searching for a response that suggested he'd been well aware of that, but he was drawing a blank. 'Good point' he said curtly. 'Come on.'

They set off swiftly through the woods, trying to trace their steps back. Nick set the pace, but both Kirsty and Charlie were struggling to keep up.

'What do you think happened,' Kirsty asked breathlessly.

'Christ knows,' Nick called back over his shoulder. He stopped and waited for them to catch up. 'But her body was in pretty bad shape. I wouldn't lay money on all her injuries having been caused by the fall.' He scratched his head. 'Or maybe they were. I don't know. But the biggest question is what the hell was she doing all the way out here on her own. If she *was* actually on her own.'

Kirsty stopped in front of him. 'What are you saying?'

'When I went up to their chalet this morning there was no sign of her. I mean, she could have been in the bathroom or something, I don't know. But her husband was in a pretty foul mood.'

'Meaning…?'

'Meaning I'm probably adding two and two and making five,' Nick sighed. 'But one way or the other we need to find him and let him know what's happened. Then we need to find someone in charge.'

As Nick was about to turn away, Kirsty pointed over his shoulder towards the bushes up ahead. 'What's that?'

Nick looked over and squinted. Then he saw what Kirsty was pointing at: a blue baseball cap hanging off a branch. He walked over and plucked it down. Turning it in his hands, he saw the little bit of green embroidery above the peak: the letter H.

'Do you think it's Jenny's?' Kirsty asked.

'No,' Nick said solemnly, holding out the cap so she could see the letter H. 'It's Hollie Page's. She was wearing it the last time I saw her.' His eyes scanning the trees, he called out her name a couple of times, but apart from the faint sound of birdsong coming from high overhead, there was an eerie silence.

'What the hell's happening on this bloody island?' Kirsty said. She looked close to tears again.

'I don't know,' Nick said, tucking the baseball cap into the rucksack. 'But I'm damned well going to find out. Come on.'

Charlie, who had been standing back and hadn't uttered a word since they'd left the gully, spoke up. 'Listen.'

His parents looked at him.

'What is it?' Kirsty said.

'Can't you hear it?'

Nick and Kirsty strained their ears.

After a moment, Nick said, 'What are we supposed to be listening for? I can't hear a thing.' As far as he was concerned, aside from the sound of the birds there was nothing *to* hear.

'I can't hear it now,' Charlie said a little forlornly.

'What was it?' Nick said.

Charlie was about to reply when he stopped. 'There!' he cried. 'Hear it?'

Nick shook his head. "I…" he started, but Kirsty pressed a finger to her lips. She looked at Charlie. 'I hear it!' she said.

Nick was on the verge of losing his cool when suddenly he heard it too: Laughter. It was far off, but nevertheless unmistakable.

'Come on,' he said, and they set off in the direction of the sound.

Jamie was killing himself laughing. Caine had caught his foot in a deep divot and taken a tumble. That had been funny enough in its own right. But when Warren had tried to help him up, Caine had ended up dragging him off his feet too. Warren had pitched forward on top of Caine, who'd let out a shriek as the full weight of his father's bulk had piled down on him. And now they were both rolling around in the dirt. Caine was clutching at his groin with a pained expression on his face – 'My balls!' – and Warren, unable to sit up, was complaining about his back. It really was a comical sight, and both Lisa and Vicky, as well as the two girls, were laughing along.

'Come on, you dozey fuckers,' Jamie said, extending a hand to Warren. 'We'll never get to this fuckin' lake if you don't stop buggerin' about.'

He pulled hard and Warren sat up looking distinctly embarrassed. He saw Lisa laughing at him and the vitriol in his eyes was tangible. He made a mental note that when they got back to the chalet she would pay for compounding his humiliation.

Caine was still sitting on the ground rubbing his crotch – 'He's havin' a fuckin' wank now!' Jamie cackled, almost crying with laughter – but Warren had managed to get to his feet and was standing brushing himself down when a shout came from the trees.

'Hey, you guys…'

All heads turned to look and they saw Nick, Kirsty and Charlie stumbling through the undergrowth towards them.

'Oh, fuckin' great!' Jamie exclaimed, grimacing. 'Who invited them along?'

At the sight of Nick, Warren looked uncomfortable and distinctly nettled.

Nick came running up to them. 'There's been an accident,' he panted.

'Yeah, the accident was us bumping in to you,' Jamie muttered.

Nick let that one go. As Kirsty and Charlie hurried up to join him, he surveyed the sea of faces, all of which except for Jamie's were looking at him, waiting for him to elucidate.

'Where's Grant Kinley?' Nick asked.

Vicky was standing with her arms folded, tapping her foot impatiently and staring scornfully at Kirsty. 'How the fuck should we know?' she snapped.

There was a general mumble that indicated nobody had an answer to that, or even cared for that matter.

Caine got up off the ground. 'I saw him first thing this morning. He went past our chalet, he had his two little rug rats with him. But I haven't seen him since.'

Nick suddenly noticed that Hollie wasn't with them either. 'Where's your sister?' he asked, addressing Caine.

'She didn't feel like coming,' Warren interjected. 'Not that it's got anything to do with you,' he added with a note of indignation.

Nick shot him a disparaging glance, but said nothing.

'You said there's been an accident. What's happened?' Lisa said. The only one of the group with even the slightest trace of concern on her face, she was staring at Nick.

'His wife's…' Nick saw the two girls looking at him apprehensively and he stopped himself. 'Never mind,' he said. 'All that matters is there's been an accident and I need to find Kinley.'

Jamie eyed Nick suspiciously. 'Come on, spill. What sorta accident?'

'She had a fall,' Kirsty blurted out. Nick gave her a look of annoyance.

Lisa put a hand to her mouth. 'Is she alright? Where is she?'

'We just need to find her husband,' Nick said firmly.

Vicky scowled. 'For fuck's sake, we've been walkin' bloody miles to find this bastard lake and you're sayin' we've gotta turn round and go all the way back carting all this shit?' She pointed at the cool-box.

'Just leave it then,' Nick said.

'Ya can fuck right off with that one, sunshine,' Jamie exclaimed. He looked at Billie-Jo and Bobbi-Leigh. 'You make sure that cool-box comes back with us.'

'Aww, for fuck's sake, Dad,' Bobbi-Leigh whined. 'You said you'd carry it back.'

'Just do as you're told,' Vicky said.

Charlie stepped forward. 'I don't mind helping.'

Bobbi-Leigh smiled at him sweetly, but just as he was about to take the handle of the box from her, Caine elbowed his way past. 'Out the way, shrimp. The lovely ladies need a man's help.'

Bobbi-Leigh smirked at Billie-Jo and they handed over the cool-box to Caine. It was far heavier than he'd anticipated and he very nearly dropped it.

Billie-Jo sniggered. 'Look at those muscles, Bob. You sure you can manage, mate?'

Caine grinned at her sheepishly. He was evidently struggling. 'No problem,' he said.

Nick frowned. 'Okay. Now we're all sorted, can we please get moving?'

CHAPTER 18

On face value flies are among the most pointless of nature's insect species. Or so one might think. In fact, their significance in the lives of human beings is considerable, not least of which being that they quite literally eat poo. They are scavengers, surviving by consuming decomposing organic matter so that humans don't have to deal with it. It's a compelling argument that, without them, mankind would be up to its neck in faeces and rotting corpses.

Nevertheless, they are vile and disgusting creatures that had no place in Terence Hallam's world. As far as he was concerned, shit-eaters deserved nothing more than a painful demise.

He stood looking out of the window of his office on Mástiga, watching a fly buzzing about on the inside of the glass. It greatly amused him that here he was in Greece, and flies were members of the order Diptera, a name derived from the Greek language; the words *di* (two) and *pteron* (wing).

His eyes followed the insect as it dotted back and forth in a lazy rotation of stupidity, trying desperately to… to what? The window was ajar by 45-degrees, the fly had found its way in through the gap easily enough, tempted no doubt by some tasty morsel its senses had alerted it to. And yet now it was trapped, moronically banging its head up against the glass, unable to find and exit through the self-same gap right there in front of it – a gap umpteen times its own body size.

Lured in by the promise of a treat, Hallam thought, and now incapable of escape. He found the analogy delicious.

He leaned forward and pushed the window open a little further.

'An opportunity, my little friend,' he said. 'You can't claim you weren't given a fair chance.'

Detecting the movement of the window, the fly paused momentarily, almost as if it were deliberating over what to do about its dilemma. But then it resumed the fruitless bouncing against the glass, oblivious to the fact the countdown to the end of its life had begun, whereupon it would be swatted, or perhaps annihilated in a mist of choking insecticide. Or...

As it stopped again, quick as a flash Hallam's hand shot out. Before the creature could react, he pressed down hard with his fat thumb, luxuriating in the pleasure that washed over him as its insides squelched out and smeared across the glass.

Hallam pulled out a handkerchief and wiped his thumb. He looked at the crushed splodge of the fly's corpse on the glass. One less miserable little shit-eater for the world to have to tolerate, he thought.

The door opened and Caroline came in. She waited politely for him to acknowledge her presence before speaking.

'Yes?'

'They're all assembled outside reception, sir.'

Hallam's brow furrowed. 'A little sooner than I'd anticipated, I must say,' he remarked. 'But of small consequence.'

He thought for a moment and then clapped his hands together enthusiastically. 'Right then, let's make an announcement, shall we?'

*

After the trek back through the woods, with barely a word spoken between them, almost an hour later everyone with the exception of Nick was gathered on the forecourt in front of the reception block.

Both Jamie and Warren had put up a bit of a fight at first, claiming that whatever had happened to Jenny Kinley was nothing to do with them. Jamie had even started to get aggressive. But when, having felt himself pushed into a corner, Nick had suggested he believed that the fall might not have been an accident, the two women had brought pressure to bear. Vicky in particular had become rather vociferous. After all, their trip to the lake had been ruined now. And although she didn't actually say it, she evidently held the appearance of the Masons just as much a fun-killer as whatever might have caused Jenny Kinley's fall.

Jamie was stood at the top of the steps banging on the locked reception building doors.

Vicky was sitting on the top step, Bobbi-Leigh and Billie-Jo were stretched out at the bottom, sunning themselves. All of them looked thoroughly dejected.

Lisa and Caine were standing in silence letting Jamie take the lead.

Warren had positioned himself near the two girls. He was pretending, not particularly convincingly, to examine a colourful poster pasted on the wall, but he was in fact taking the opportunity to furtively admire Billie-Jo's long, slender legs.

She lazily turned her head towards him and he hastily returned his attention to the poster. It showed what appeared to be a map of the resort, yet there was a boating lake, a pool area and various other attractions that, as far as he was aware, simply didn't exist. It didn't really resemble what they had seen of the resort first hand at all. Oh well, Warren reasoned, Hallam had said the place wasn't finished yet. He glanced back at Billie-Jo and was relieved to see she was no longer looking at him.

Finally accepting that banging on the doors was futile, Jamie turned around angrily. 'No-one. Fuckin' no-one.'

Warren looked up at him. 'What? No-one at all?'

'I just fuckin' said so, didn't I?' Jamie shot back at him angrily. 'I just don't get it.'

Warren twitched. He had taken a bit of a shine to Jamie and it stung him to be addressed so rudely by the younger man. He didn't respond, but he stored it away; he would get his own back later. He took off his spectacles, spat on the lenses and wiped them against the side of his shorts. 'So much for "If you need anything",' he said. 'What if there had been an emergency.'

'It *is* a fuckin' emergency,' Vicky said. 'I need a drink.' She chortled.

Despite his agitated state, Jamie joined in. 'You and me both, babe.'

Kirsty was fighting a losing battle with her better judgement. She knew that anything she had to say would be treated with derision, or in the very least come across as inflammatory. None of these people seemed to like her or Nick, but that was absolutely fine as far as she was concerned; she didn't care so much for any of them either. Yet given the gravity of the situation, how could they not be taking it seriously?

'Can we all just stop larking around, please?' she snapped. 'Someone just got seriously hurt for God's sake.'

Jamie glared down at her scornfully. 'Who the fuck asked for your opinion?' he said, walking down the steps towards her.

'Yeah,' Vicky chimed in. 'Shut yer face, ya snotty cow.'

Jamie stepped up close to Kirsty, but as intimidated as she felt she stood her ground. In fact, she actually took a step towards him, but only to position herself between Jamie and Charlie. She clutched her son's hand tightly.

'You fink you're so much better than the rest of us, don't ya,' he sneered. 'You and that rat-fuck husband of yours. This is all his fault, ya know.'

'Sorry, *what*'s his fault?' Kirsty replied, hoping that the tremor in her voice wasn't as obvious as she thought it was.

'The fact we're all standin' round here like fuckin' twats instead of havin' a laugh at the lake.' His tone was spiked with vitriol.

Everyone was standing watching Jamie and Kirsty in silence. Even Vicky had gone quiet.

Kirsty could feel the blood rushing to her face. 'You can't be serious!'

Jamie was standing just a couple of feet in front of her. He leaned in conspiratorially and said, 'I don't reckon you're getting any, are ya?'

Kirsty frowned. What the hell was he talking about now? '*What*?!'

'You know, a good seeing to.' There was a wicked smile on his lips. He was now just inches away from her face and she could feel the heat of his breath on her cheek.

'I have no idea what you're talking about,' Kirsty said. She took a step back. 'And haven't you heard of personal space?'

Jamie stayed put. 'You need a good shag to loosen you up.' His dark brown eyes stared at her menacingly for a moment, then his face cracked into a smile and he burst out laughing.

He looked round, delighted to see that everyone had joined in on his joke.

Crimson-faced, Kirsty stared at him. 'How *dare* you insinuate…?'

'Your face!' Jamie cackled.

'Nice one, babe,' Vicky cried through tears of laughter. 'A good fuck would sort her out. Or maybe not!'

Before Kirsty could react, there was a shout and Nick appeared at the tree line.

Jamie quickly took a few steps back away from Kirsty and moved over to stand near Vicky.

Kirsty held Charlie close as Nick came running over.

'There's no sign of anyone at the Kinley chalet,' he said, trying to catch his breath. 'It's deserted. The back door was open, but there's no sign of him or the kids. There's breakfast stuff still on the table though. It felt a bit like the Marie Celeste.'

'What's some French bird gotta do with anyfing?' Jamie piped up.

Nick looked at him. Surely he wasn't being serious. 'Excuse me?'

'You just said Mary somethin'-or-other, whoever the fuck she is.'

'I said Marie Celeste. *She* was a famous ship, not "some French bird"!' He couldn't help the note of derision in his voice.

'There it is,' Jamie said heatedly, looking at Vicky. 'Tryin' to make me look thick.'

'That's not difficult,' Nick muttered.

Caine guffawed and Jamie flared up. 'What did you just say to me, you arrogant cunt?'

'For Christ's sake. What *is* your problem exactly?' Nick said angrily.

'You! *You're* my fuckin' problem.' Jamie jabbed a finger at Nick. 'You and yer wife and yer kid too. Ever since we met you've been lookin' down yer noses at the rest of us.'

'It's true,' Warren said, itching to get a dig in. 'Interfering with things that have nothing to do with him too.'

Lisa looked at Warren questioningly, but he waved a hand dismissively. 'I'll tell you later,' he said, without the least intention of doing so. 'Like I already told you, you need to mind your own business, mate,' he said to Nick.

Nick held up his hands. 'Okay, okay, time out. Let's just everyone calm down.'

'Don't you tell me to calm down!' Jamie growled.

'We need to stay focused,' Nick continued. 'Jenny Kinley's dead. It may or may not have been an accident…'

'Hang on…' Jamie said. 'You said she'd had a fall, you didn't say anything about dead.'

Nick sighed. 'Okay, well yes, she *is* dead. And now her husband and two little boys have gone AWOL.'

Jamie was about to ask what AWOL meant but thought better of it. 'So what's the plan then, Mr Smartarse?'

'I'll let that go,' Nick said. 'But that's the last one you're getting. Something's clearly very wrong on this island. We've got to stop sniping at each other and start working together.'

'Fair dos,' Warren said. 'But like he just said…' – he motioned to Jamie – '…what's the plan?'

'There isn't a plan. But first thing we need to do is find Hallam and let him know what's happened.'

'Yeah, well, good luck with that,' Jamie said peevishly, pointing at the reception building. 'The lights are off and no-one's home.'

'A bit like you then,' Kirsty said, still bristling at the way Jamie had intimidated her.

It might have been the way Vicky sniggered. Or maybe the thin smile he saw appear on Lisa's lips. Perhaps even the fact he heard Warren snigger. Whatever it was, Jamie charged at Kirsty with his hand raised. 'I'll slap that shit-don't-stink attitude right out of ya!' he exploded.

He got within two feet of her and was sent reeling backwards by Nick's fist. With a look of surprise, he staggered, almost fell, but managed to stay on his feet.

'That's enough!' Nick shouted furiously.

Jamie put a hand to his mouth and felt the trickle of blood. 'No it fuckin' ain't!' he yelled and lunged angrily at Nick.

The two men grappled for a moment and then pitched onto the ground, a ball of flailing arms and legs.

'Fiiiiight!' Caine hollered excitedly.

Kirsty turned away and tried to shield Charlie from the sight of his father brawling in the dirt.

By complete contrast Bobbi-Leigh and Billie-Jo jumped to their feet and along with Vicky clustered round, jeering and laughing like hyenas.

'Fuck's sake, come on,' Vicky shrieked. 'You can take that cunt easy!'

'Come on, Dad,' Bobbi-Leigh shouted. 'Knee him in the bollocks!'

'Fuck him up!' Billie-Jo chimed in. Grinning mischievously, she nudged her sister. 'Fuck him up, fuck him up, fuck him up!' she chanted over and over, and Bobbi-Leigh joined in, the pair of them jumping up and down elatedly.

Warren and Lisa had decided to take neutral ground and were stood well back watching the drama unfold with nervous interest.

Caine came over and leaned in close to Warren. 'Just look at those pretty little titties bouncing, Dad!'

'Hmmmm.' Warren had already noticed. His tongue flicked across his lips as he ogled the two girls jumping around excitedly. Then, as if it had taken a moment for Caine's words to sink in, he turned sharply and smacked the boy across the back of his head. 'I warned you once already today,' he growled. 'I'll not do so again. Now keep your eyes off those two girls and go stand with your Ma!'

Nick and Jamie were still thrashing around on the ground. Nick had landed several decent punches, but Jamie was putting up a good fight and they were showing no sign of tiring. Then, just as it started to look as if Jamie might be getting the upper hand, a tinny screeching sound akin to the feedback on a microphone filled the air.

Warren winced and cupped his hands over his ears.

The tannoy speaker on the roof of the reception block – which until that moment nobody had even noticed – crackled into life and Hallam's voice boomed out.

'Hi-de-hi, campers!'

CHAPTER 19

Nick and Jamie disentangled themselves and sat up. They were filthy and although neither of them would have admitted it, they were glad to have an excuse for a breather.

'What's all this then?' Hallam's voice continued jovially. 'You're breaking our unspoken rule, people. It's far too early to be turning on each other.'

Brushing the dirt off his clothes, Nick stood up and walked over to join Kirsty and Charlie.

'Are you alright?' she whispered. Her eyes were filled with tears.

He nodded.

'I'm sorry,' she said. 'That was my fault.'

'Forget it. He had it coming.' Nick looked over at Jamie, who was being helped up off the ground by Vicky. His nose was bleeding.

'You alright, babe? You so nearly had him!'

'No hard feelings?' Nick called out.

Billie-Jo and Bobbi-Leigh were staring at him, their eyes burning with hatred. Jamie just ignored him.

Hallam's voice roared from the speaker: 'Silence when I'm talking!'

Everyone stopped still.

'He must be looking at us right now,' Lisa said with dismay.

'Now then,' Hallam's voice boomed. 'As you may have gathered by now, this isn't quite the lovely little break you might have been expecting. There's a very specific reason you were all chosen to be Hallam Holidays' guinea pigs. I told you yesterday that people don't always get what they deserve. You probably thought that meant you were deserving of something nice to brighten up your pathetic little lives. The truth of the matter is quite the opposite. What I discerned all too clearly from your applications is that you are all a greedy blight on society. In your own way you have each helped to turn our once great country into – to use your vernacular – a shithole. You're whingers, whiners, spongers. The absolute scum of society...'

He faltered for a moment. He'd noticed something that had somehow eluded until now.

He cleared his throat and continued. 'You demand *everything*, yet you contribute *nothing*. And so it's now my immense pleasure to treat you to what you *really* deserve. You think you're deprived and hard done by? Well, you haven't seen anything yet. You sniveling scroungers have no idea of true hardship. But rest assured you're about to find out.'

Nick was looking at Kirsty in disbelief. His eyes said it all: Why did this guy choose us?

'We're getting the hell out of here as soon as possible,' he whispered.

'Now, before you go thinking I'm a completely unreasonable fellow,' the voice continued, 'I must say this: Whereas my raison d'être is to facilitate your deaths...'

Jamie frowned and looked at Vicky. 'Raisins what?' She shrugged; she hadn't a clue.

Hallam broke off mid-flow. 'Don't be so insolent!' he exclaimed angrily. 'I may not be able to hear you, but I can damned well see you and you're *still* talking! I think you'll find it's in your best interests to shut up and pay attention to what I have to say.'

He paused and waited until he was satisfied that everyone had ceased their ill-mannered behavior. In a blink, as if someone had flicked a switch, the ire was gone and the jovial tone returned.

'As I was saying, my raison d'être is to facilitate your deaths. However there *is* a chance for you. A slim one I'll admit, but a chance nevertheless. If you're able to put aside the fallacious belief that the world owes you a living, shelve that pig-headed self-righteousness that brought you to my door in the first place, collaborate to survive, *prove* you're actually capable of caring about someone other than yourselves... well, who knows? Maybe – just maybe – you'll get to leave Mástiga alive.' Hallam chuckled. 'But let's be honest. Given the criteria involved, you really haven't got much of a chance, have you? And alas, for the dearly departed Mr and Mrs Kinley it's too late anyway. Oh, and those two little lads of theirs. So sweet. So *dead*.'

The tannoy crackled again and then fell silent.

Everyone stared at each other in dumbfounded silence. Was this some sort of sick joke? Were Grant and Jenny Kinley suddenly going to come strolling out of the reception block laughing at them all, their two little boys cheekily giggling away behind them? Those ridiculous teatime television shows... *Game for a Laugh... Candid Camera... Beadle's About...* each of them designed to trick unwitting participants into a state of rage by pretending to drive a bulldozer over their car, or turning their lovingly toiled-over vegetable allotment into a parking lot; as incredibly elaborate as this whole prank must have been to set up, surely the Hallam Holidays' contest *had* to be one of those. But if it really was a joke, it was far from funny.

His face black as thunder, Hallam's fist crashed down on the desk. 'God *damn it*!'

Caroline physically jumped. She thought the speech had gone really well. 'What's wrong, sir?'

Hallam looked angrily over his shoulder at her. 'You've been looking at the screens, haven't you? You have a grasp of basic mathematics I assume?'

'Er... yes, of course,' Caroline replied hesitantly. Her mind was racing. What hadn't she noticed?

'Then I'm sure you observed that there was an absentee.' He swung his chair round to face her. 'Well?'

Caroline stood in front of him, lost for words. Her eyes flicked up to the screens, on which she could see the CCTV images of the group gathered around outside the recption building. 'Obviously the Kinley family aren't there...'

'Obviously,' Hallam replied. 'And?'

Then she realised. 'Hollie Page!' she exclaimed. 'She's not there.'

'Precisely.' Hallam spun his chair back to face the monitors.

Caroline breathed a silent sigh of relief.

'But what do you see up here?' Hallam continued. He pointed to the tracking monitor.

Caroline's eyelids flickered nervously as she tried to count the flashing red lights. 'Eleven, I think,' she said.

'You *think*?'

'Eleven. Definitely.'

'Correct. And yet there are only ten people out there.' He pointed to two of the flashing lights that were practically overlapping. 'Which means that one of them has Hollie Page's wristband.' He frowned. 'The question is, how did I not notice this before?'

'There are so many of them,' Caroline said, trying to be helpful. 'Remember, there aren't as many cameras installed as projected on the original manifesto either. It's impossible to keep watch all the time. And you've been *so* busy, sir.'

'Of course I've been busy,' Hallam snapped. 'But I took my eye off the ball. It won't happen again.'

'I have to ask, sir...those little boys...'

'Not now.'

'But...'

'I said *not now*!'

Caroline fell silent as Hallam started punching buttons. All except for one– which continued to display the families assembled outside of reception – the remaining screens changed to show a myriad of images from the cameras scattered around the resort; the woods, the gully, the lake, inside and outside the chalets. There was no visible movement in any of the locations.

He leaned forward in his chair, his eyes studying the screens. 'Now' he said quietly. 'Where are you?'

CHAPTER 20

'This has got to be a joke.'

Vicky Hazelwood was standing with her children and in an almost unheard of display of affection she actually had one arm around each of them. Her face was pale and for the first time since they'd all arrived on the island she seemed to have had the wind knocked out of her sails.

'It's fuckin' bullshit is what it is,' Jamie exclaimed furiously, banging on the reception block doors. 'Come on out and try telling that shit to my face, you fat nonce!' Exasperated, he turned to face everyone. 'He can't do this to us!'

Nick shook his head. 'In case you hadn't noticed, he *is* doing it to us!'

Jamie scowled at him. 'You tryin' to start another fight? I'll rip your…'

'For Christ's sake, just calm down, will you?' Nick moved so that he was standing between his family and Jamie. 'If what we just heard *is* true, it's not going to do us any good constantly going for each other's throats. We need to set aside our differences and put our heads together. I can't say what may or may not have happened to Grant Kinley or his kids, but I saw Jenny Kinley's body first hand – up close – and trust me, she was dead. And Hallam already knows about it, so I think it's safe to say that it wasn't an accident and no, what he just said *isn't* a joke.'

'Okay. Suppose you're right. What do we do?' Jamie said, seeming to have finally accepted they might be in serious trouble.

'He made a mistake,' Nick said thoughtfully.

'He made a fuckin' mistake threatenin' me, that's for sure!' Jamie exclaimed emphatically.

'No,' Nick began. 'He said…'

'He said he couldn't hear us,' a small voice whispered.

Everyone turned to face Charlie. The lad hadn't uttered a word since everyone had met up in the woods. Nick smiled at his son and felt a little glow of pride. '*Exactly*, buddy.'

Jamie rolled his eyes. Like father, like son, he thought. But just for once he kept his mouth shut.

Nick winked at Charlie and returned his attention to the others. 'He said he couldn't hear us.'

'So?' Warren said curtly.

'I'd suggest he didn't intend for that to slip out. And it could actually work in our favour.'

'What if he's lying?' Kirsty said. 'He could be listening to us right now.'

'Sure, he *could* be,' Nick mused. 'And yes, he might have been lying too, but to what end? He's played his hand now, why would he lie about not being able to hear us? He said he can *see* us, and we've all seen the cameras all over the place.'

'Cameras?' Warren said with a note of concern. 'I haven't seen any cameras.'

'Well, they're everywhere,' Nick said slightly dismissively. 'Hallam was angry that we weren't listening to him,' he continued. 'Remember? He said he couldn't *hear* us, but he could *see* us talking. I'd wager that was unintentional.'

'So what if you're right?' Vicky said dejectedly. 'How the fuck does that help us?'

'I've no idea,' Nick admitted. 'But it has to be a point in our favour. Unless he can lip-read, he'll have no idea what we're planning.'

'So what *are* we planning?' Warren said. He actually looked a little frightened and he too had his arms around his family, even though Caine looked distinctly uncomfortable in his father's embrace. Had Nick not witnessed Warren's dark side he might have felt sorry for him.

'We need to get the hell off this island,' Nick said bluntly. 'And you need to go get your daughter fast. Where is she?'

'We had a little squabble this morning,' Warren began. 'She went off in a sulk...' He trailed off as he saw the expression on Nick's face. 'Well, you were there, you know,' he muttered sheepishly.

Was that a trace of shame on the man's face? There damned well ought to be, Nick thought. 'Yeah,' he said through gritted teeth. 'I know.'

'She'll show up later,' Warren said breezily. 'She always does.'

'That's not good enough,' Nick said, trying to control his temper. 'In case you've not been listening properly, this holiday just went south real fast. One person is dead and three others are *probably* dead. You need to find her right now.' He looked at Caine. 'I suggest you go too. And make sure you stay with him, I wouldn't trust him as far as I could throw him looking for her on his own.'

'Look here,' Warren said indignantly. 'It's not my fault the silly girl has gone off in a strop.'

'We both know what happened,' Nick said. 'But we haven't got time for this now. Just make sure you bring her back.'

Lisa had been listening intently to the exchange between her husband and Nick. Now her face filled with rage. 'I knew it!' she declared. 'What have you done to my daughter, you bastard?'

Caine burst out laughing. 'Busted!' he exclaimed.

Warren lashed out and slapped Lisa hard across her face. Kirsty gasped and even Vicky looked shocked at the ferociousness of the act.

Curiously, the man immediately looked contrite. 'I'm sorry,' he said as Lisa put a hand up to her stinging face. 'You made me do that.'

Jamie laughed. 'Fuck's sake, don't say sorry mate. You need to keep the little wifey in check, show her who's boss.' He saw the expression on Vicky's face and trailed off.

Warren apologetically reached out a hand to Lisa, but she shrugged him away. 'How could you? If you've hurt her, I swear to God…'

'I never hurt her, honestly I didn't,' Warren muttered. 'I love her.'

Lisa's eyes were filled with anger and hurt, but not because of the slap. She was looking with disgust at her son. How long had Caine known for certain what she herself had only ever suspected? And why in God's name hadn't he said anything. In her heart she knew the answer to that, and it made her feel sick.

Vicky had been listening as the drama played out and finally she spoke up. 'Fuck me!' She laughed and looked at Jamie. 'And I thought *we* had problems.'

Jamie ignored her. 'Shouldn't we be trying to find Hallam?' he said, addressing Nick.

Good, Nick thought. He's starting to think. It was the most sensible thing that had come out of the man's mouth. 'Good question,' he replied. 'I don't think we can waste any time on that. It's possible he's not even on the island any more.'

Jamie nodded. 'Yeah, I had actually thought that,' he lied. 'What about the fences?'

'It's pretty clear now that they weren't intended to keep things out so much as keep us *in*. But where there's a will there's a way. And I'm in no doubt Hallam will be expecting us to try.'

'Come on,' Warren said, grabbing Lisa by her arm. 'We're going to get Hollie, then we're leaving.'

'Good,' Nick said. 'Here...' He pulled Hollie's baseball cap from his rucksack. 'I think this is hers.'

Lisa stared at Nick suspiciously: why did he have Hollie's cap?

Nick noticed her concerned expression. 'I found it hanging off a tree in the woods,' he said.

Warren let go of Lisa's arm and took it from him.

'Soon as you find her, get back here as fast as you can,' Nick said.

'We'll take care of ourselves,' Warren snapped back.

'You really don't get it, do you?' Nick said, the rising ire in his voice undisguised.

Kirsty squeezed his arm.

'Okay, look,' Nick said. 'I honestly think our best chance of getting out of here is if we stick together.'

'You can do what you like,' Warren replied. 'Count us out.' He grabbed Lisa's arm again, motioned to Caine to follow, and they set off across the forecourt towards the pathway up to the chalets.

'Dead meat,' Jamie called after them cockily. He looked at Nick. 'D'ya fink they'll change their minds?'

'I'd like to think so, but somehow I doubt it. If they want to strike out on their own, that's their business, we can't worry about them. Can I assume those of us that are here now are going to stick together?'

Jamie looked at Vicky for approval. She nodded at him.

He shrugged his shoulders. 'Sure.'

'Right,' Nick said, as he watched Warren, Lisa and Caine recede up the path towards their chalet. 'In that case what I suggest is…'

'Woah, woah, hang on a sec,' Jamie said. 'Who the fuck put you in charge?'

'Nobody's "in charge",' Nick sighed. 'But somebody has to come up with a plan of action. I'll make a suggestion, which you can either agree with or, alternatively, if you have one, you're perfectly at liberty to offer up a better idea.'

Jamie stood there for a moment as if he was processing what Nick had said. 'Fair enough,' he said eventually. He held up his hands. 'I ain't got nothin'.'

'Okay then, what I…'

'But just so as we're clear,' Jamie added, 'this workin' together shit, it don't mean we're suddenly fuckin' mates.'

Nick exchanged glances with Kirsty. 'I assure you, I never thought for one moment that it would,' he said.

'Good. Alright then, smart guy. What was you about to "suggest"?'

'I think we should head that way.' Nick pointed to the track leading off the forecourt that they'd come in on the previous afternoon. 'That'll take us to the gates and we can assess what our options are then.'

'Wait a minute!' Vicky exclaimed. 'We ain't leavin' without our stuff.'

Nick shook his head. 'No. Whatever Hallam might have planned for us, he isn't just going to sit there drinking tea, waiting for us to pack our things first. We need to go now.'

'Not till we get our stuff!' Vicky said adamantly.

Exasperated, Nick looked at her. She clearly wasn't going to budge. 'Okay, okay,' he said. 'Go get your stuff. But nothing more than you can carry easily. No suitcases.'

He looked as Kirsty. 'Is there anything we *really* need?'

She thought for a moment.

'It's just stuff,' he added. 'It's not important. It can be replaced.'

Kirsty nodded her agreement. 'There's nothing we can't live without.'

'Good,' Nick said. He turned to Jamie. 'Be back here in 15 minutes, or we're taking off without you.'

Vicky, Bobbi-Leigh and Billie-Jo all started to make a move, but Jamie slumped down on the bottom step in front of the reception block. 'You go, babe. I'm gonna wait here with these guys.'

Vicky stared at him '*Really*? You lazy bastard!'

'It's not that, babe. I just don't trust them not to go off without us.' He saw Nick glaring at him. 'What? Like you wouldn't!' he said.

Nick frowned. 'Wait a moment,' he called to Vicky. 'Something has just occurred to me too. We can't get too cocky about this whole can-he-or-can't-he hear us business. I'm pretty confident he can't, but we still have to assume he *might* be able to, if not outside then it's not beyond reason that the chalets could be wired. So no talking about anything we might be planning until we're out in the open. Just get your stuff and get back here fast as you can.'

'Okay,' Vicky replied.

CHAPTER 21

Red-faced and breathing heavily, Lisa grabbed handfuls of clothing from the closet and shoved them chaotically into the suitcase on the bed. 'What are we going to do?'

Warren was sitting at the foot of the bed watching her. 'Nothing until you've got the bags packed.'

'We're leaving though?'

'Of course we're leaving. Just shut up and keep packing, I need time to think.' He wiped the sweat from his brow with the palm of his hand.

Lisa stopped what she was doing and glared at him angrily. 'It'd be a lot quicker if you'd give me a hand.'

'It'd be a lot quicker if you weren't so fucking overweight!' Warren snapped back. Standing up, he crossed to the bedroom door.

'Just help me would you?' she said irritably.

He paused and looked at her. She was staring at him as if she actually expected him to help. 'You're going to waste time standing there arguing the toss? Take a look at yourself, woman. You're a heart attack waiting to happen!' He turned his back on her and crossed to the front door. 'I'll be back in a minute.'

Lisa hurried over and watched him from the bedroom doorway. 'Where are you going?'

'Don't worry, I'm not deserting you. If we're leaving I've got to check on something first.'

'Check on what?' Lisa said.

'Something.'

'*What*?'

Warren's face was flushed and dripping with sweat. He turned back to face her. 'I'm going to find Hollie, alright? Is that okay with you? Or were you planning on leaving without our daughter?'

'You know where she is, don't you?' Lisa said. She was on the verge of tears.

He ignored her and opened the door. 'Caine!' he shouted.

The boy appeared in the doorway of the second bedroom. 'I've lost my knife,' he said.

'What do you mean, you've lost your knife?' Lisa said in dismay. 'Why the hell did you bring it with you? For that matter, how did you even get it through the airport?'

'I carry it everywhere. I had it this morning, but I must've dropped it somewhere.'

'Too bad,' Warren said angrily. 'Help your Ma pack.'

'But…'

'I said help your Ma. Just do as you're fucking well told or you'll see the back of my hand! I won't be long.'

And with that he walked out.

*

In the Hazelwood cabin, the scene was pretty much the same as it was in the Page's: Vicky was busily cramming various unnecessary fripperies into carrier bags.

'Hurry up, girls,' she called. 'I'm nearly done. Do as I said and get yerselves dressed proper and we can get out of this hellhole.'

In their bedroom, Bobbi-Leigh and Billie-Jo were stripping off their bikinis.

'Why exactly do we have to get dressed again?' Bobbi-Leigh bleated. Two pairs of jeans and a couple of T-shirts were laid out on the bed.

'Cos ya can't fly home on a plane wearing fuckin' bikinis!' Vicky shouted. 'Now stop yer whingin' and get on with it.'

'Twat,' Billie-Jo said to her sister and stuck out her tongue at her.

Both girls had their backs to the window and didn't see Warren's face appear.

Gazing in at them from the corner of the glass, he was standing on tiptoe leering at the two naked teenagers. This couldn't have worked out better if he'd planned it, Warren thought.

He had genuinely set out five minutes earlier with the intention of finding Hollie. But when he'd heard Vicky's voice drifting up from the trees he'd sidestepped and concealed himself behind some bushes. As they passed by without noticing him, he had heard Vicky saying something about the girls needing to get changed. Feeling the familiar pulse of warmth through his loins, he had waited for them to pass and then stealthily taken pursuit.

He'd watched them go into the chalet and, making sure he wasn't observed, he had slipped around the side of the building and now here he was, the zip of his swimming shorts open and a hand thrust inside, rubbing gently.

As Billie-Jo picked up her underpants, she turned. Warren ducked down just that moment too late. She'd seen him. Letting out a cry, Billie-Jo dropped her underwear and threw up an arm to hide her breasts, as her other hand flew downwards to cover her crotch. 'Mum!' she screamed.

Outside, Warren turned away and started to run. He only got a few yards before tripping over a rut in the ground. There was an audible crack and, squealing with pain, he pitched headlong into the leaves.

Back inside, Vicky appeared at the girls' bedroom door. 'What the fuck is it now?'

Clutching a T-shirt to cover her chest, Billie-Jo was standing at the window. Bobbi-Leigh was behind her looking confused.

'That man was there!' Billie-Jo exclaimed.

'What man?'

'That creepy fat weirdo Warren. He's been fuckin' starin' at me and Bob all day. He was lookin' through the window watchin' us undress.'

'I didn't see nothin',' Bobbi-Leigh said.

'I don't give a shit. He was there. Honest, Mum, he was!'

'Right!' Vicky turned and ran across the chalet, grabbing the first thing to hand; an empty bottle of vodka from the coffee table. She raced out of the front door, across the veranda and hurtled down the steps, her feet barely touching them as she went.

At the rear of the chalet, a few metres from the girls' bedroom window, Warren had managed to get to his feet. It had been a struggle, but the moment he had put weight on the twisted ankle the pain coursed up through his leg and he had collapsed back into the dirt. His glasses had fallen off and as he'd attempted to get up again he'd knelt on them. The frames had snapped and one of the thick coke-bottle lenses had popped out.

As he was examining the lens, which now had a deep scratch on it, Vicky rounded the corner and came to a halt.

Warren looked up at her. 'Oh, Mrs Hazelwood… Er, I mean Vicky, I er…' He saw the bottle gripped in her hand.

'You dirty cunt!' Vicky took a step towards him.

Warren flinched and shuffled his bottom back away from her. 'No, wait a moment, I can explain.'

'You *dirty* fuckin' paedo cunt!' She took another step closer.

'I can explain, honestly.' Warren's mind was racing. 'I, er… I came over to, er…'

Vicky was incensed. She wasn't even listening properly. 'I've met your sort before,' she snarled.

She smashed the vodka bottle against the wall and it shattered, leaving just the neck and a long, vicious-looking shard clutched in her hand.

'No, no, wait. You don't want to do anything rash. I only came over to tell you we'd changed our minds.' He'd finally found an excuse; it was a pitifully insubstantial one, but it was all he had. 'Yes, that's it,' he blathered. 'We'd changed our minds and we've decided it'd be best to join forces with you folks.'

'What do ya take me for, a complete fuckin' idiot?' Vicky was only a couple of yards away from him now.

'Of course not. I... I mean you just don't understand. *Please.*'

She looked down at him and saw that the top of his shorts were gaping open. 'Oh I understand alright,' she said, advancing closer.

'Then just let me explain, please...'

'Shut the fuck up.' She stepped right up close and stared down at him. Her voice suddenly became calm. 'So you like lookin' at little girls, do you?'

Warren was laid on his back staring up at her. He was visibly quaking and his eyes were wide and filled with terror.. 'No... er, yes... er, I mean no. Of course not! That's horrible. Please, *please* Vicky, help me up and I'll explain.' He was wasting his breath and deep down inside he knew it.

Vicky bent over him. 'Get's your little cock hard, does it?' she said.

'Please...'

'Let's take a look, shall we?' She lowered the shard of glass towards his crotch.

With a moan, Warren screwed his eyes tightly shut and waited for the inevitable screaming pain.

Using the pointed end of the glass, Vicky gingerly pushed open the top of his shorts a little further. She peered down inquisitively at the flaccid, shriveled brown flap of flesh with a long thread of pre-ejaculate dribbling out of the end and down across his scrotum. 'Fuckin' hell, it's a bit small, ain't it?'

Warren opened his eyes and looked up at her. Maybe she wasn't going to hurt him after all. 'Yes. Yes it is. Now please, will you give me a chance to explain?'

Without taking her eyes off him, Vicky stood upright. The hand holding the remains of the bottle dropped to her side.

Warren stared up at her, then he chuckled nervously, 'I have to admit, I thought you were going to do something silly there for a moment.' He held out a hand. 'Do you think you could help me up please?'

'My old man was just like you,' Vicky said softly.

Warren frowned. 'I'm sorry?'

Without any sign of a forewarning, the glass flashed out and carved a gaping wound across the palm of Warren's outstretched hand. He screamed and withdrew it, grabbing hold of it with his other hand, blubbering like a child.

Before he could say anything coherent, Vicky had stepped astride him and with unfeasible force she bent over and plunged the broken bottle into his groin.

The noise that came out of Warren's mouth was barely human. He screamed so loudly that most of the birds in the branches overhead took flight and disappeared off among the trees. Only the brave and curious remained, gazing down dispassionately at the gruesome sight below.

His eyes wide and with sputum spraying from his lips, Warren thrashed on the ground as Vicky jabbed the bottle down again and again and again. 'You. Filthy. Disgusting. Piece. Of perverted. Shit!' she roared with every jab.

The long, thin shard of glass caught on Warren's pubic symphysis bone and the pointed end broke off. But still Vicky continued thrusting.

Warren jerked sideways and his head struck a rock on the ground.

The glass then punctured one of the two femoral arteries and blood fountained up all over Vicky's hand.

Warren had stopped screaming and, accompanied by a final gurgle, his body spasmed a couple of times and fell still.

Vicky stood up straight, breathing hard, trying to regain control.

'Mum?...'

The quiet voice came from behind her.

Vicky turned her head. Bobbi-Leigh and Billie-Jo – both of them now dressed in T-shirts and jeans – were standing at the corner of the chalet watching her. Their faces were ashen.

Bobbi-Leigh was clutching her older sister's arm and looked as if she was about to throw up. 'What have you done?'

Vicky flicked back her hair, which had fallen across her face, inadvertently smearing her cheek with Warren Page's blood as she did so.

'Go back inside,' she said calmly. 'Get yer stuff together.'

'But...' Billie-Jo began.

Then the anger came. 'I said get the fuck back inside and finish packin'!'

The girls hesitated, then turned away and disappeared round the corner.

When they had gone, Vicky squatted down on her haunches and the fetid stench of shit assailed her. She almost gagged as the source of the smell became apparent. As well as the blood that was pooling beneath the lower half of Warren's prone body, Vicky could see that in the throes of death he had messed himself; a viscous fecal sludge was leaking out from one of the legs of his shorts.

'You filthy cunt,' she muttered.

She reached into the wide open fly and feeling around she took hold of his penis – barely two-inches in length – and eased it free of the bloody pulp. Pinching the glans firmly between her thumb and forefinger, she pulled it out as far as she could until it was stretched taut, then with one swift cutting motion she used the jagged edge of the bottle to shear through it. But it failed to come away completely; one sinewy fibril kept it attached.

Vicky yanked it hard, the skin tore through and Warren's penis came off in her hand.

She stood up and tossed the severed chunk of flesh as far as she could into the undergrowth.

A small buzzard, which had been perched on one of the lower branches of a nearby tree preening its feathers – keeping one beady eye on the carnage taking place below – saw precisely where the discarded piece of meat fell. Swooping down, it snatched it up in its talons and, without pause, flew back into the tree to find a spot where it could settle and quietly feast on its impromptu meal.

Affording Warren's dead body a final look of revulsion, Vicky dropped the bottle and walked back along the side of the chalet.

CHAPTER 22

When Vicky entered the chalet, Bobbi-Leigh and Billie-Jo were standing waiting for her.

They watched in silence as their mother, spattered with blood, stepped calmly across the room to the bathroom, where she paused in the doorway.

'Have you finished packin'?' she asked matter-of-factly.

'Mum,' Billie-Jo said. 'We…'

'I won't be a moment,' Vicky said quietly. 'I have to clean up. Then we'll get goin'.'

She stepped into the bathroom and closed the door, sliding the bolt to lock it behind her.

Billie-Jo looked at her sister, her face etched with concern. 'What's the matter with her? How can she be so fuckin' calm?'

In the bathroom, Vicky rested both her hands on the sink and inhaled slowly and deeply. She felt a weird sense of euphoria, the sort of buzz she only ever got when she had been drinking, except that she hadn't had a drop yet.

She hadn't been exaggerating when she'd said Warren was just like her father. She had been only 12-years-old when it started. She was an early developer and her usually remote father had become increasingly more affectionate towards her, giving her a cuddle more often, ensuring he kissed her goodnight at bedtime *every* night and playing with her long hair when she sat next to him talking about her day at school. She had loved the attention at first, but even at that young age she had felt uncomfortable when he would playfully slip his hand beneath her clothing while they were talking – only ever when there was no-one else around to see, although that didn't really register with Vicky until years after the fact – and all the while chuckling and joking with her as if it was all an innocent game.

Even now, on those happily scarce occasions when she caught the smell of Irish whiskey, it triggered memories of the suffocating reek of his breath that first night he'd come into her room. It had been the night of her 14th birthday. She would never forget how dark it had been, the feel of his weight pressing down on her, the way he had slobbered over her – repeating again and again that he loved her – and how much it had hurt when…

Vicky shook the thoughts from her head and for a moment she thought her legs were going to buckle beneath her. She grabbed for the towel rail and steadied herself. Feeling her gorge rising, she lurched forward and threw up in the sink. Twice.

She wiped a streak of vomit from her chin and stared at herself in the mirror. Her father was six years in the ground, and until just now she had never told a soul what sort of man he really was. Warren had been the only person to ever hear her say the words. But that didn't matter; he wasn't going to be repeating anything to anyone this side of the gates of Hell.

Almost as if she'd been in a trance, for the first time she registered the blood; she appeared to be covered in it from head to toe. She unclipped her bikini top –

somehow blood had managed to get *inside* – then dropped the panties to the floor and stepped out of them.

There was a light tapping sound on the door. 'Mum, are you okay?' It was Bobbi-Leigh.

'I've just got to clean up. I'll be two-minutes. Just be ready to go.'

Copious shower gel and the hot needle-spray of the showerhead did the trick and no more than two-minutes later Vicky was out and standing in front of the mirror again with a towel wrapped tightly around her waist.

She breathed into the palm of her hand and smelt it. The acrid scent of bile nipped at her nostrils.

Opening the cabinet above the sink, she pulled out the bottle of mouthwash. She unscrewed the cap and sniffed it. To her slight surprise the odour was peppermint; the liquid was pink and for some reason she always associated green with peppermint. She poured a measure into the cap and tipped it into her mouth. Swooshing it round her teeth and gums, she gargled and spat.

As she put the bottle back into the cabinet, the little white box caught her eye: Hallam's gift.

She pulled the atomiser out of the package and looked at it scornfully. There was no label and it couldn't have contained more than 25ml, 30 at most. 'Tight-fisted fucker,' she muttered.

Pressing the little button on the top, she wafted the atomiser back and forth across her breasts a couple of times, then liberally sprayed it around her neck.

Some of the fine mist drifted into her eye. She winced at the sting and set down the bottle on the edge of the sink. She spun the cold tap and ran some water, but as she splashed it in her eye, the stinging got worse; it started to burn. She let out a little cry of pain, cupped her hands beneath the flowing water and urgently splashed it onto her face.

But now the fiery sensation was creeping through her chest and neck. She looked down and saw the ugly red welts across her breasts, and the peppering of pustules, which were swelling up and bursting like bubbles rising to the surface in a glass of lemonade. Her eyes widened in horror as her left nipple began to shrivel and split away from the breast. And the hideous burning... she had never known pain like it.

Screaming, she scooped up handfuls of water and threw it over her chest, crying out in pain as the cold water doused her burning flesh; it only seemed to exacerbate the agony.

She glanced in the mirror. Her whole neck had turned a vivid shade of burgundy. And then she saw something running down her cheek.

'Fuuuuuckk!'

The sallow skin beneath her right eye was drooping... no, not drooping... melting. Then the whole structure of her cheek began to malform. It sagged away from the bone and rivulets of blood began to appear, trickling like ice cream down a wafer cone on a scorching summer's day, and dripping from her chin.

Shrieking, she staggered across to the shower cubicle and the towel came loose and fell to the floor. She felt desperately for the water nozzle as the flesh around her neck slipped down in glutinous folds and spread out across the curvature of her collarbone.

She slumped sideways against the wall and sunk down in a heap as the water cascaded down upon her.

Bobbi-Leigh screamed. 'Muuum!' She hammered on the door.

'Stand back,' Billie-Jo cried. She ran at the door, putting her full weight on it. It burst open and shards of wood splintered from the frame.

The two girls stood in the open doorway gazing in abject terror at their mother – or something barely resembling their mother – writhing around on the tiles in the shower unit and making a noise that fell somewhere between sobbing and screaming.

Bobbi-Leigh turned away and promptly vomited.

Billie-Jo stepped into the bathroom with the futile thought in her head that she could do something to help. But it was immediately obvious that wasn't going to happen and she too turned away as Vicky began to convulse violently, repeatedly cracking her head against the wall. Her upper torso was pooled around her in the shower basin, a hideous amalgam of subcutaneous fat, blood and flesh. Her collarbone, along with the cheekbone and jawbone of her skull, had been stripped clean.

Vicky's legs twitched a couple of times and then she lay still.

For Terence Hallam, who had gleefully witnessed Vicky Hazelwood's psychotic assault on Warren Page, and then watched as the woman melted before his eyes, it felt as if all of his Christmases were coming at once. Things were going better than he could possibly have imagined.

He chuckled – a manic, throaty sound born of part of his brain that was no longer entirely sane – and turned his attention to one of the other screens.

'Six down, nine to go.'

If only I'd been able to locate Hollie Page, he thought.

To all intents and purposes the girl had vanished into thin air. Hallam knew she had to be out there somewhere; there was no way out of the resort, of that he was confident. So far none of the cameras had located her, but it could only be a matter of time.

Right now he had other fish to fry.

He watched as the panic-stricken Bobbi-Leigh and Billie-Jo fled from the chalet. Unexpectedly, they turned right and scarpered up the side, averting their eyes as they passed Warren's mangled corpse – that made Hallam smile – and took off into the woods.

How curious, Hallam thought. Where were they going? Rather than taking the path that would have led them back to the reception building where their father was waiting, they'd gone off in completely the opposite direction. Blind panic? Possibly. He frowned. He would have to monitor their movements carefully.

*

A harmony of birdsong from somewhere overhead bestowed an spontaneous and unwitting requiem upon Warren.

His unceremoniously disembowelled body lay in the undergrowth, the head laying at an unnaturally skewed angle against the rock.

Suddenly there came a scuffling sound and a small, furry, elongated creature snaked round the trunk. It paused to sniff the air and cocked it's head curiously at the bloody mess.

Had Warren been alive he might have pontificated that Hallam's fences – which, according to the man himself, had been erected specifically to keep out the indigenous wildlife – were clearly proving ineffective. But his cold, lifeless eyes stared vacantly at the sky.

Not entirely sure if it was safe, yet irresistibly drawn like the proverbial moth to the flame to investigate further, the beech marten moved cautiously forward and placed one of its tiny paws on Warren's leg. It hesitated for an instant, again sniffing the air in all directions. Then, in a single quick hop, the creature was on Warren's leg. It scurried up past his knee and settled itself down on his left thigh.

A squeak sounded from somewhere behind and the marten turned to see a similar creature, watching it with interest from behind the trunk. It was a female; its mate. Satisfied that it was safe to do so, she hopped up and joined the male on Warren's prone body, watching her mate as he stretched out his neck towards the tantalisingly moist shreds of tattered flesh, all that remained of Warren's lacerated scrotum. He gripped the tender sweetmeat in his tiny jaws and shook it vigorously. The flesh tore away and, placing one paw on Warren's midriff, the marten started pulling apart the prize, eagerly devouring it.

The female scampered forward and thrust her nose into the hole where Warren's private parts used to be. As she did so, a Chukar fluttered down from the roof of the chalet and landed next to the body.

The female marten squeaked at it angrily and the bird scuttered back. Possibly deciding it would be safer if it returned later to feed on whatever remained, the Chukar flew off.

Together the hungry beech martens began to feast, their tiny heads returning to the succulent wounds again and again, until eventually they slunk off back into the woods, their hunger satiated and their tiny silver muzzles stained scarlet.

CHAPTER 23

Lisa huffed and stood up. 'That's it, we're not waiting any longer.'

She picked up the two carrier bags – each packed to capacity – and handed one to Caine. 'Here, carry one of these.'

The boy looked up from the magazine he was browsing through and turned down the music that was blaring out of the mini speaker hooked up to his phone. 'Give us a minute.'

Lisa shook the bag. 'Never mind that, come on, take it.'

She thrust it towards him and knocked the magazine out of his hands. It fell open on the floor and Lisa saw the centrefold picture of a naked girl wearing nothing but kneesocks, with her hair done up in schoolgirl bunches. 'The apple hasn't fallen very far from the tree,' she said, scowling.

Caine looked at her quizically. 'Huh?'

'Just put that filth in the bin, we're going.'

'Don't we need to wait for Dad?' Caine argued.

'No, we don't.' Lisa spat back at him. 'Now come on!'

Caine still didn't budge. 'What about Hollie?' he protested. 'I thought he was going to find her and bring her back.'

'If he does they'll catch us up.'

'Are we gonna go back and join the others?'

'No,' Lisa said. 'There's not a lot I'd give your father credit for these days, but he was right about one thing – we can look after ourselves. There has to be a way out of this damned place and we're going to find it.'

Caine wasn't giving in. 'But what if they come back and we're not here? Won't they automatically think we've hooked up with the others?'

'Jesus Christ, boy,' Lisa snapped. 'Will you stop arguing with me, get off your lazy arse and come on!' Dropping the bags, she grabbed him by the arm and dragged him to his feet.

'Owwww, that hurt,' he whined pettishly.

'You're 17, not 7,' Lisa said angrily. She picked up one of the carrier bags and pushed it into his hand. 'Now stop whinging, take this and *come on*!'

As Lisa turned away and walked to the door, Caine swiftly bent down and retrieved his magazine. He folded it vertically and, checking his mother wasn't looking, hastily tucked it down among the clothes in the carrier bag.

*

While Lisa had been attempting to get Caine moving, Nick was pacing impatiently up and down in front of the reception block.

Jamie was sitting watching him, while Kirsty and Charlie had planted themselves at the far end of the steps, putting as much distance between them and the loathsome man as they could.

'Calm down,' Jamie said as he saw Nick glance at his watch. 'They'll be here.'

'Maybe if you'd gone with them it would have sped things up a bit,' Nick said, more to himself than in response to Jamie.

'And *what*? She can pack a couple of bags without assistance. Fuck's sake.' He shook his head.

Nick's patience was again dwindling rapidly. 'Okay, look, I'd suggest you need to go and find them and…'

Jamie abruptly stood up. 'You "suggest", do ya? He said truculently. 'Maybe you ought to stop suggestin' stuff. Who made you boss anyway?'

'Can we please not start all that nonsense again? We need to work together if we stand any chance at all of getting out of here.'

'Well then stop telling me what I "need" to do.'

Nick shrugged. 'Fine. But here's how it is. You can sit here waiting for them and if they don't show up in five minutes we're going – with or without you. Or, you can go and get them, but if you're not *all* back here in five minutes, we're still going. Now, which would you say is the better option?'

Jamie appeared to consider the question.

'Okay,' Nick sighed. 'You stand there and waste time having a little think about it. But I suggest you make up your mind quickly, because one way or the other,' – he tapped his watch – '*we* are leaving in five minutes.'

'You're always suggestin' stuff,' Jamie grumbled.

Nick shrugged again. 'Your choice.'

Jamie raised a conceding hand. 'Okay, okay, you win.' He turned away and, dragging his feet like a spoilt child that couldn't have its own way, he set off towards the path up to the chalets.

Nick watched him retreat. 'Five minutes,' he shouted.

Jamie didn't look back. He waved a dismissive hand in the air. 'Yeah, yeah, I hear ya. Five minutes.'

'Then pick your damned feet up!'

Jamie stopped and turned round. 'What are you, my fuckin' mother?'

Why was this man so damned exasperating? Glaring at him, Nick tapped his watch again. 'Four minutes!'

*

His face buried in his phone, willing it to find a signal, Caine tripped over an exposed tree root and almost took a tumble. 'Shit!'

He and his mother were making their way through a particularly dense stretch of woodland.

Caine was setting the pace, and Lisa, trailing a short distance behind him, was beginning to struggle. The temperature had risen noticeably since earlier that morning, midges were eating her alive, she kept having to dodge branches, her face was bright pink and her chest was beginning to hurt when she breathed in.

She saw Caine trip and rolled her eyes. 'Just get your head out of that stupid phone and pay attention to where you're walking.' She set the bag down to catch her breath.

Caine stopped and turned back to face her. 'I was hoping we might be able to get a signal.'

Lisa's expression of annoyance faded. 'Okay, I'm sorry.'

'Apology accepted.' Caine grinned.

'Okay,' she said. 'No luck I suppose?'

'Nope. No internet and no phone signal. If I try to access anything, a picture of a palm tree keeps popping up.'

Lisa sighed. She bent to pick up the carrier bag and it split down one side, spilling half the contents onto the ground. 'Balls,' she muttered, bending to retrieve her favourite top. 'Bag for life, my arse!'

Caine stifled a guffaw at the sight of his mother cramming a pair of her underpants back into the bag, the result of which being that something else fell out of the split in the side.

She stood upright and glared at him. 'Don't just stand there like a lemon, come and give me a hand,' she said breathlessly.

Caine sauntered back, picked up the pieces of clothing and carefully added them to his own bag.

'I was thinking,' he said. 'I really do reckon we should go back and join the others. We've no idea where we're going, or what we're going to do when we get there.'

'Will you please not keep on? It's like your father said, we can look after ourselves.'

Caine was becoming less and less sure about that. 'But Dad might be with them. Hollie too. We're stumbling around out here on our own and…'

'Enough!' Lisa snapped. 'Your father is a complete waste of space. You think I don't know what sort of man he is? You think I was born yesterday?'

'No, I...'

'No! You just shut up and listen. I should have done something about it years ago. But when he started showing interest in Hollie...' She trailed off and wiped away a tear that was running down her cheek. 'Well, I *didn't* do anything and, God forgive me, I've got to live with that. But I was trying so hard to keep us all together as a family.'

Her nose had started to run and she wiped away the mucus with her hand.

'But if something was going on, I just wish Hollie had come to me,' Lisa continued. 'She could have told me, confided in me. How do you think it makes me feel that my own daughter won't talk to me? Have you the vaguest notion of how much that hurts?'

Caine silently shook his head.

Her tone softened a little. 'You do know you can talk to me if there was ever anything bothering you, don't you?'

'The only thing bothering me right now is how we're gonna get off this island,' Caine replied.

'Okay, well look, we'll all sit down together and talk about this when we get back home. Right now, I've no idea what happened between her and your father today, but I know *something* did.'

Caine looked at her sullenly.

'I can't imagine him giving up until he finds her,' Lisa continued. 'And once he does, despite his protestations, he's a bloody wimp and I reckon he'll go and join the others. If we can get to that sodding jetty, we'll wait for them. Assuming they're not already there.'

'Maybe...' Caine started.

The irritable tone returned. 'But in the meantime we're on our own. You and me. Get it?'

Caine nodded.

'Good. So no more arguing, okay? We just keep moving.'

*

Charlie let out a little sigh. 'We could have gone and got some of our own things.'

'I know, buddy,' Nick replied. 'But I think we're safer out here in the open. And like I said before, it's just stuff.'

'So how long are we going to sit here waiting for those degenerates?' Kirsty said irritably.

Both she and Charlie were tiring of watching Nick pacing back and forth in front of them.

He stopped and glanced at his watch. 'Time was up two minutes ago.'

Kirsty frowned. 'Then why are we still here? Five minutes you gave him. You couldn't have made it any clearer if you'd tried.'

Nick sighed. 'I know. I honestly thought that would light a fire under his backside.'

'But why are we waiting at all?'

'Because one thing Hallam said made sense to me. I think we stand more chance of getting out of here if we stick together.'

'How do you know he's even coming back?' Kirsty said. 'I wouldn't trust him for one second.'

Nick looked at his watch again. 'Okay. I said five, it's now closer to ten. Come on, we're going.'

No sooner had Kirsty and Charlie stood up than a cry echoed across the forecourt.

Nick squinted against the sunlight and saw Jamie step out from the trees. Something immediately didn't seem right.

He came towards them and, as he got closer, Nick saw his face clearly. He was crying.

Jamie stumbled up and dropped to his knees a few yards away from them. 'She's dead,' he blubbered. 'Vik's dead.'

Kirsty put a hand to her mouth. 'What?!'

Jamie buried his face in his hands. 'My beautiful Vik. She's all… all melted.' The last word was accompanied by a sob.

Nick was lost for words. He looked to Kirsty for help and she nodded at him. Stepping forward, he placed a comforting hand on Jamie's shoulder.

His head shot up and he batted Nick away. 'Don't fuckin' touch me,' he exploded.

Nick raised his hands and took a pace back. The last thing they needed now was to start fighting again. 'Okay, it's cool,' he said. 'I just…'

'And Warren Page is dead too,' Jamie said, wiping a hand across his eyes. 'He was at the back of our chalet. There's bits of him everywhere, it looks like he's been torn apart by some wild animal.'

'Jesus,' Nick said. Again he looked to Kirsty to back him up.

'What about your girls?' she asked.

'I dunno,' Jamie said, clambering to his feet. 'There was no sign of them. What the fuck am I gonna do?'

'I'm sure they're fine,' Nick said.

'Are you? Are you *really* sure, Mr fuckin' know-it-all?'

'They're smart kids...' – Nick exchanged a glance with Kirsty – '...and if they weren't at the chalet, I'm pretty sure they'll be looking for a way out of here. As far as we know, there's only one road back to the coast and if they're heading to the jetty – which is what *I* would be doing – we'll find them sooner or later.'

'Why don't you just admit it? You don't give a shit.'

'Look, I'm sorry, but we can't hang about here any longer. We have to move.'

As the words left his mouth there was a loud tinny screeching sound and Hallam's voice boomed from the speaker. 'Decisions, decisions. What *are* you going to do?' He chuckled. 'I must say, I'm singularly unimpressed with your progress so far. Sitting around on your backsides as if you've got *allllllll* the time in the world. Two more of your party have met their maker while you've been arguing amongst yourselves and wrestling with indecision.'

Nick leant towards Jamie and spoke through the corner of his mouth. 'Which means your daughters are still alive.'

Hallam leant forward and peered at the screen. Had Mason just said something to Trot? Uncertain, he let it go. 'Perhaps I didn't impress upon you strongly enough your predicament,' he continued. 'You do realise that you're in a life or death situation, don't you?'

He shot a glance back at Caroline who was, as always, standing compliantly at his side. 'The way things are shaping up at the moment, your chances of preserving your lives are getting slimmer by the minute, eh what?'

Caroline afforded him a smile.

Hallam shifted in his chair. 'What you need to understand is this: my role is nothing more than that of puppet-master, the architect if you will. I merely light the blue touch paper and then I stand well back. The poor decisions your dearly departed have made are what led to their demise.' His index finger hovered over a button. 'So come along. Tick-tock. Time's running out.'

Switching off the tannoy, Hallam pointed to one of the screens; one of the CCTV cameras had picked up Bobbi-Leigh and Billie-Jo, who were hurrying through the woodland terrain.

'Go get them,' he said to Caroline. 'I have something special arranged for them.'

'I was thinking, sir,' Caroline began.

Hallam spun in his chair to look at her, an expression of mild amusement on his face. 'You were *thinking* Mrs Smart? I don't believe there's anything in your job description that indicates I pay you to think.'

Caroline looked slightly awkward. 'It's just... er...'

'Just *what*?' Hallam said tersely.

'Well... it's just... well, they're children, Mr Hallam.'

'Your point being?'

'My point...' Caroline's voice trailed off as she saw Hallam's face darken. 'My point... I... I... you said the children wouldn't be harmed. Those two little boys...'

'I hope I don't need to remind you of what we're doing here, Mrs Smart.' Hallam sat forward. 'They may be children now, but it won't be long before they're adults. And what will they have learned from their pitiful upbringing? Shout loud, stamp your foot hard, treat others like shit, only ever concern yourself with number one. Do you see? Do you *understand*?'

Caroline stared at him. Had he been planning to kill them all along? He had told her that the children would be well taken care of and had put over a very persuasive argument for separating them from their selfish and irresponsible parents, and gifting them with the opportunity of a better life. And it was certainly preferable to seeing them follow their mothers and fathers into an early grave. Yet now, as much as she hated admitting it to herself, it was becoming apparent he'd deceived her.

'But your plans to give them a better life, sir. You said they would be taken care of.'

'And they will be,' he said bluntly. 'But evidently not in the way you thought. If you fail to ask specific questions, I can hardly be held responsible for your naïve misinterpretation of the answers now, can I?' He peered at her oddly. Was that a trace of mockery in his eyes? 'Why are you here?'

The question threw her. 'I'm your PA.'

Hallam stared at her as if he was waiting for something more.

'I'm sorry, I don't understand,' she said.

Hallam ran a hand through his hair. 'It's a straight forward enough question. Why are you here?'

''You mean working for you?' she said nervously. Where was this leading?

'At all,' he said.

'Well, to earn money.'

Hallam frowned. 'To provide for a wastrel husband who should be out working himself, providing for you.' He couldn't have provoked a more startled reaction if he'd struck her with an open hand.

Horrified, Caroline's jaw dropped and she stared at him. 'He's ill! He has motor neurone disease.'

'You say that as if it's a valid excuse. Just one more blight on society.'

Caroline continued to stare at him. She didn't know what to say. Not only was he completely devoid of compassion and a remorseless liar, he was almost certainly insane.

'Forgive me for saying so, sir,' she started timidly. 'I disagree.'

Hallam held up a hand to silence her.

'There *are* nice people out there. Decent people. And their lives are being made a misery by people like *these*.' He gestured at the screens. 'What we're doing – and what we shall continue to do – is not only decreasing the surplus proletariat populace of today, but eradicating tomorrow's before they become a problem too. We're merely giving natural selection a little nudge. Do you see?'

Caroline nodded. She wished she had kept her mouth shut.

Hallam squinted up at her. 'Hmm. I'm not sure you do. Now is not the time to develop a misplaced conscience, Mrs Smart. Our work here is *so* important. We're doing our country an immeasurable service. You must *never* doubt that. *Never*. So I'll ask you again. Do you understand?'

Caroline forced an unconvincing smile. 'Yes, sir.'

He deliberated for a moment.

'Good.'

Hallam turned his chair back towards the screens. 'Now, the Hazelwood girls are heading in the direction of the ice cream parlour. So do as you're told and go get them. There's a good girl.'

CHAPTER 24

Bobbi-Leigh and Billie-Jo were lost. There was no question about it. Bobbi-Leigh was just articulating as much when she tripped and only just managed to avoid plunging headfirst into the leaves. 'Why didn't we just go and find Dad?' she whined.

'Stop fuckin' bitchin', will ya?' Billie-Jo snapped. 'We *will* find him.'

Bobbi-Leigh stopped and bent down. Rubbing her ankle, she looked up at her older sister. 'How? We don't even know where the fuck we are. And that tree over there…' – she pointed to an unremarkable olive tree – '…we've passed it before.'

'How can you say that? They all look the fuckin' same!'

'Er, they don't actually,' Bobbi-Leigh replied, adopting the slightly superior tone she knew rankled with her older sister. 'I recognise that spindly branch.'

Billie-Jo shook her head. 'Fuckwit.'

The whiny tone returned. 'We *have* passed it before. We're goin' in circles.'

'Christ, all you do is whinge,' Billie-Jo said wearily. 'Like *all* the time. Why did I have to get stuck with you as a sister?'

'Well you ain't exactly the best sister in the world neither,' Bobbi-Leigh retorted. 'Big sisters are supposed to look out for their little sisters, not be constantly mean to them.'

'If you was a sister actually worth looking out for then I would,' Billie-Jo shot back at her. 'But you're so fuckin' *not*. You're a whiny, bleating little slapper and I'm so sick to death of havin' to look after ya.'

'Slapper?' Bobbi-Leigh exclaimed angrily. 'That's rich comin' from someone incapable of closing her legs for more than five minutes.'

Billie-Jo stopped and turned. 'What's that supposed to mean?'

'Oh, look at you, acting all innocent.' Bobbi-Leigh glared at her sister heatedly. 'You might fink it's a big secret, but I know you're screwin' Tyler.'

'Oh really? What the fuck do you know about it?'

'I just know, okay?'

'You know fuck all!' Billie-Jo shouted.

Bobbi-Leigh screamed at her: 'I know exactly what you and Tyler are doin' cos he told me a few weeks ago when I gave him a blowy for his birthday!'

There was a fleeting moment of silence as Billie-Jo tried to process what her sister had just said and Bobbi-Leigh wished that she *hadn't* said it.

Then Billie-Jo slapped her hard across the face. 'Liar! Take that back!'

Bobbi-Leigh put a hand to her stinging face and looked at her penitently. 'I'm sorry, Bill. It's true.'

'I fuckin' *hate* you! I wish you was dead!' As she turned her face away to hide the tears of rage brimming in her eyes, a twig cracked away to the left and they looked up to see Hollie emerging from behind a tree.

'There's that cunty perv's daughter,' Bobbi-Leigh said dropping her hand from her face. 'D'ya fink she knows he's dead?' she whispered.

'Like I give two shits,' Billie-Jo snapped.

'Hi,' Hollie said nervously as she approached them.

'What the fuck do *you* want?' Billie-Jo said aggressively.

'I'm sorry,' Hollie said, although even as the words left her mouth she knew she had nothing to apologise for. She really needed to stop doing that. 'I'm kinda lost and I heard your voices. Something terrible's happening in this place and…'

'No shit, Sherlock,' Bobbi-Leigh said mockingly.

'I don't know what to do,' Hollie said quietly. 'Could I maybe tag along with you?'

Billie-Jo glared at her. 'I've already got this annoyin' slapper draggin' around behind me…' – she motioned her head towards her sister – '…I ain't lookin' after *two* whiny little cunts. You're on yer own.'

Bobbi-Leigh glanced at her sister sullenly.

Taken aback by the vitriol, Hollie looked at her tearfully. 'I'm sorry,' she said, mentally kicking herself for apologising again. "I…'

'Aww, look, she's gonna have a likkle cry,' Bobbi-Leigh said gloatingly.

Hollie felt her face flush, but she held back the tears. 'Why are you being so horrid? I haven't done anything to you.'

Billie-Jo was about to lay the Warren bombshell on her, but as she opened her mouth she thought better of it. Their mother had murdered him right in front of their eyes and even though Vicky was dead herself now, Billie-Jo had learned years ago that grassing someone up was a huge no-no, especially not if they were family. 'Jog on,' she said instead. 'And if ya come near me again I'll rip yer tits off.' She looked at Hollie's chest with derision. 'Not that anyone would notice the difference.'

Without another word, with tears streaming down her cheeks Hollie turned and ran off among the trees, the sound of raucous laughter reverberating in her ears.

Bobbi-Leigh looked at her sister. 'I really am sorry about Tyler,' she said. 'I didn't mean for you ever to find out. It just kinda slipped out.'

Smiling at her, Billie-Jo put a hand on her shoulder in a half-hearted show of forgiveness. 'Yeah, whatever. But just fink twice next time you're hangin' round the chicken shop lookin' for a cock to suck, eh?'

*

Lisa and Caine finally seemed to have broken away from the thicker part of the woods and the going had eased up considerably.

However, Lisa was still struggling. She was sweating heavily and reaching the point she would need to stop for a few minutes. Her knee was playing up too and she was limping badly.

In a rare display of empathy, Caine had offered to carry both bags and Lisa had gratefully handed hers over. Nevertheless, she was still finding the terrain exhausting.

'I'm going to have to rest and catch my breath in a minute,' she called out.

Seeing a break in the woods over to his left, Caine stopped and pointed. 'It looks like the trees are thinning out a bit over there. We'll find somewhere to sit down.'

Emerging from the treeline some fifty yards or more ahead of his mother, the boy stopped and hooted with laughter. 'It's the bloody lake!' he shouted.

'Seriously?' Lisa panted as she limped up alongside him.

'Yeah. Pretty cool, huh?'

The lake was situated in a gently ridged concave encircled by trees. Though serene and picturesque, it wasn't as large as Lisa had imagined it would be when they set out to find it earlier in the day. God, she thought, was that really only this morning? It feels like ages ago now.

The water was blue as sapphire flame and the early afternoon sun was sparkling on the gentle ripples. As she surveyed the almost overwhelming beauty, Lisa saw a fish with brightly maculated scales jump suddenly up out of the water a few feet from the shore. Catching a fly in its mouth, it plunged back beneath the surface and darted away.

Perhaps most pleasurable of all, the proximity of water was accompanied by a blissfully cooling freshness in the air.

Lisa carefully made her way down the short slope to the water's edge, bent over and splashed some over her face. The sensation was heavenly.

She stood up and looked out across the lake. 'If only we'd found this place earlier. Isn't it beautiful?'

Caine stepped up beside her and setting down the carrier bags he started fiddling with the zip on his shorts. At the last moment Lisa realised what he was doing, but before she could say anything he'd unfastened them, eased himself out and started to pee.

He let out a sigh as the pressure in his bladder ebbed. 'Aw, man, I've been busting for a slash for the last 10 minutes.'

'You're revolting!' Lisa snapped. 'Why the hell didn't you just go back in the woods? This place is beautiful and you've just callously ruined it.'

Caine laughed. 'Give over, Ma. It's way more fun pissing into the water.' He gyrated his hips, making small circles on the surface with his urine.

Shooting him a look of abject disgust, Lisa turned away. As she did so she caught sight of something glinting between the Cypress trees on the far side of the lake. 'What's that?'

'What?'

Lisa pointed. 'Over there beyond those trees.'

Caine squinted. He finished urinating, tucked himself back in and zipped up the fly on his shorts.

'I can't see anythi…' He stopped short as suddenly he saw what Lisa was pointing at. 'Hey, I reckon that's the fence!' he exclaimed.

It took them ten minutes to circumvent the lake and climb back up into the trees – the ridge was far steeper on the other side – but having made the effort they were both elated to discover it was indeed the resort's perimeter fence.

Lisa stared up at the steel mesh structure – almost 20-feet high and topped with razor wire – and let out an exasperated sigh. 'We'll never get over that.'

'I can,' Caine replied.

Lisa grimaced. 'Well I *can't*, so what are we going to do?'

Caine looked to the left and then the right. The fence stretched away into the distance in both directions.

'I'm strong,' he ventured. 'I can pull you up.'

'Don't be so bloody daft. You couldn't lift me an inch, let alone up and over that fence.'

Caine laughed. 'Of course I can't lift you. But surely you can climb a bit, can't you? Then if you take my hand I can help you up.'

Lisa peered up at the top of the fence, then looked at her son doubtfully. She was having visions of getting half way up and falling – or even the fence giving way.

'Honest, Mum' Caine said confidently. 'We can do it, it'll be a piece of piss.'

Lisa looked hopefully off to the right, where several hundred yards along the fence curved away out of sight among the trees. 'Maybe it'd be best if we just followed it. Eventually it has to lead to the entrance gates.'

'But which way?' Caine said. 'I don't know about you, but I've lost all sense of direction. Following the fence could lead us *away* from the gates.'

'But it will circle back round eventually.'

Caine shook his head. 'The gates might be a few hundred metres that way…' – he pointed to the left – 'or a few hundred metres that way.' He waved a hand off to the right. If we make the wrong choice we'd end up walking miles. How big did that Hallam guy say this place was? 200 acres?' It would take us ages to walk right the way round the enclosure.'

Lisa looked back up at the fence. 'Okay,' she said. 'I'll give it a try. But if I can't manage it, we'll just have to follow the damned fence, agreed? There's a 50-50 chance we'll pick the right way.'

'You can do it, Mum. And I'll help you.'

Caine stepped over to the fence, took a breath and hesitantly placed a finger against the wire. He looked back at Lisa and grinned. 'Just checking she ain't all electricityfied.'

Lisa rolled her eyes. 'The word is electrifed. And it'd be a bit bloody late now if it was!'

Caine guffawed and hoisted himself up onto the mesh. 'Kentucky Fried Caine, eh? LOL!'

'It's not funny.'

'Yeah.' Caine shimmied up a few feet. 'It really is though.'

'Just be careful,' Lisa said, watching him apprehensively.

Hanging off the mesh, Caine turned and extended a hand towards Lisa. 'Come on.'

Lisa stepped forward and took his hand. 'I can't see this is going to work.'

'Just trust me will you?'

Lisa managed to get a foot into the mesh, but as Caine tried to pull her up she felt her shoulder click. 'No!' she exclaimed. She stepped back down. 'I can't manage it, I'll fall. Come on, we're going to follow the line of the fence.'

'I can do it,' Caine said, swiftly ascending a few more feet.

'Get back down here!' Lisa said angrily.

'See ya,' Caine chuckled maliciously. 'Wouldn't wanna be ya.'

Lisa looked at him in disbelief as, in a matter of seconds, he'd reached the top.

Carefully worming through the coils of razor wire, he perched himself triumphantly on the top and grinned down at her. 'Told you. A cinch.'

'Please Caine, don't leave me here on my own,' Lisa said tearfully.

'Awww, come on, Mum, you didn't honestly think I'd abandon you, did you? I just wanted you to see how easy it is.'

'It might be for you,' she replied. 'I'm probably three times the size of you!'

'But I'll help you,' he said.

As he scooched back through the razor wire, there was a sudden loud crackling sound.

Spasming violently, Caine lurched downwards, but the expanding stainless steel bracelet on his watch caught on the razor wire, almost tearing his hand off.

Lisa, who still had her hand on the mesh, was hurled backwards by the shock. Letting out a cry, she hit the ground hard and rolled over onto her back.

Dangling helplessly some 20-feet up on the fence, Caine screamed and convulsed as the electricity surged through him.

Lisa could do nothing but lay there watching in horror as her son was fried alive in front of her. Sparks were flying in all directions as Caine lit up like a firework. He was still screaming and jerking around like a deranged marionette. His face contorted into a hideous rictus as blood began to seep from his eyes.

Then one of his eyeballs exploded and his hair caught fire. With a final gurgling noise, his body went limp.

Sobbing uncontrollably, Lisa sat herself up. As she struggled to get to her feet, she became aware that the crackling sound was intensifying. Although there could be no doubt he was dead, Caine's body began to shudder again. The sound got louder and louder and his flesh began to boil and blister.

And then his body suddenly exploded, showering Lisa with viscera. She rolled over onto her side, and was violently sick.

After a moment, she composed herself and sat up again. Although every fibre of her being was screaming at her not to look at Caine, she couldn't help it. She turned her head.

What remained of her son – and there wasn't very much – was barely identifiable as human in shape. The remains were splayed out on the fence like a hideous exhibit in the London Dungeon, a dubious attraction Lisa had visited on a dare with a group of friends when she was only just in her teens, and the source of nightmares for months afterwards.

Lisa tried to get up. She managed to manoeuvre herself onto her knees when a puzzled expression crossed her face. She clutched at her left arm and inhaled through gritted teeth. 'Oh God,' she mumbled, 'Not now, please…'

The puzzled expression turned to one of frightened acceptance and with a little moan and an abrupt jerk she keeled over.

Laying on the ground feeling the life draining from her, it occurred to Lisa that it would have been wiser to go back join the others after all, to follow the road they'd arrived on down to the gates. How bloody ridiculous it was to worry about that now, she thought.

It was the last thought she had.

*

In fact, the road down to the gates wouldn't have provided her with a swift exit at all, as Nick, Kirsty, Charlie and Jamie had found out when they got there.

Upon reaching them it had immediately become obvious that the way out which they had pinned their hopes on was no way out at all. The gates appeared to be much sturdier than Nick had remembered from when they arrived. Jamie bragged that he could easily shimmy up and over the top, but Nick had heard the almost unnoticeable humming sound coming from the small junction box on the ground to the left of the gates; when Nick suggested to him that the fence might be electrified, and he for one wasn't prepared to put it to the test, Jamie's bravado had quickly dissipated.

Thus, in stark contrast to Lisa's redundant plan of following the fence to locate the gates, they had decided to track the perimeter away from the entrance in the hope of finding part of the fence that might be breeched. Or maybe even another set of gates.

Kirsty and Charlie were following several yards back behind Nick and Jamie, who seemed to have put aside their differences and were engaged in a relatively civil conversation. Kirsty couldn't hear everything they were saying, but given some of the incendiary stuff that she *had* caught coming out of Jamie's mouth, she thought Nick – who was listening more than talking – was conducting himself impeccably. Quite an achievement, Kirsty thought.

Jamie was chattering away as if he didn't have a care in the world; the death of Vicky and the disappearance of Bobbi-Leigh and Billie-Jo seemed to be no longer a concern to him. Or maybe his overly loquacious state was a subconscious distraction from his grief.

'So I ain't done a day's work in years,' Jamie was saying, evidently proud of the fact.

'Don't you feel that's wrong though?' Nick said. He was genuinely interested in hearing Jamie's answer.

'Why would I?' Jamie replied, frowning. 'I'm tellin' ya, it's fuckin' ace. We pull in more from the state than if we was both workin'. Sure, as you'd expect from a woman, Vik always wants a bit more...' He trailed off at the mention of her name. 'Well, always *wanted* more. You know, before…'

'I've worked hard since I was a kid,' Nick said. 'Got my first part-time job helping to fix PCs when I was just 14. It's very rewarding to be paid for a hard day's graft.'

'It's even more rewarding to hold out ya hand and get it for nuffin'. Mind you, I don't say I wouldn't like a bit more too. Providin' for five kids tears holes in the old bank account.'

'Five?'

Jamie grinned. 'Yep. With three different mums. I was a dirty little bugger in my yoof, I don't mind tellin' ya. Shove it anywhere, I would.' He guffawed. 'And I did. Sure, the downside was a few accidents, if you know what I mean. I never planned on bein' a father five times.' He winked at Nick. 'I can't even remember all their names!'

'How can you not know their names?'

'Well, one of them was the result of a one-night stand, never saw the mother again. Didn't even know I'd got her preggers till later on when a letter came through the door from the CSA demanding money.'

'So are your two girls the last of your progeny?' Nick asked.

Jamie frowned. 'My *what*?'

'Your offspring.'

'Oh, yeah, okay. No, Bill and Bob ain't mine. Vik had them with her last bloke.' He paused and thought for a moment. 'Or was it the one before him? Can't remember. Don't matter. Anyway, a right fucker he was. Used to smack the kids about. She was well outta that relationship, I tell ya.'

'So including the two girls that's seven children you're supporting.'

'Yeah, I s'pose. I never really planned on havin' kids at all to be honest. But I could never resist me a bit of gash, ya know? Getting the old end away two or three times a night.' He thrust his hips back and forth. 'You guys never thought about havin' another one?'

Nick didn't answer. Jamie glanced back at Kirsty, blithely unaware he was touching a nerve. She turned her face away.

'No?' Jamie continued. 'Ah well, one's enough for some people, I s'pose. I tell ya, I…'

'We had a daughter,' Kirsty blurted out.

Jamie stopped walking and turned to face her. 'Yeah?'

'But we lost her.'

Nick shot Kirsty a glance. Please, don't discuss our precious Daisy with this halfwit, he thought.

'Never mind our children, just you worry about your own,' Nick snapped, adding under his breath, 'God help them.'

Jamie was delighted by the idea that he'd got under Nick's skin again. 'Alright, alright, don't go startin' ag. I was just makin' conversation.'

'Well don't,' Nick said firmly. 'Chit-chat stops right now, capiche? We need to focus, keep moving and find a way off this wretched island.'

CHAPTER 25

'Bloody spectacular, eh what?!'

The room erupted in a round of enthusiastic applause.

The screens in front of Hallam were replaying Caine's death on a loop. 'It's hard to say which was the more enjoyable, that one or the melting Hazelwood woman. Moving forward I think we need to focus on the more gratifying mode of retribution. I mean, quicksand and all that sort of nonsense, it obviously gets the job done of course, but once you've seen the results of toxic fragrance there's really no comparison, eh what?'

There was a mumble of approval.

'I have a wealth of ideas,' Hallam continued. ' You just keep the funding coming, my friends, and I'll provide the entertainment.' He chuckled. 'Who knows, however unorthodox it might seem at first – and there will always be dissenters – our program has the potential to earn us Knighthoods for services to Queen and country.'

'May I say something?' Despite the modulated distortion, it was clearly a woman's voice. 'Speaking for myself, I found the attack on the paedophile Page to be the most rewarding demise we have witnessed so far, primarily because it was the least expected. Not only was it satisfying for the obvious reasons – one less depraved and contemptible menace on the face of the planet – but for Hazelwood's display of sheer ferocity.

For all her myriad of faults, what Vicky Hazelwood showed us was the ultimate in unrepentant primeval instinct: a mother protecting her children. I found it fascinating to observe and I haven't enjoyed such eradication of vermin since the Boxing Day hunt at Wokingham.'

'Oh, I couldn't agree more,' Hallam said obsequiously. 'We always knew the rats would turn on each other, as indeed is the wont of all vermin. But I don't think any of us could have quite predicted a display of such feral magnitude. Blood sport for the modern age.'

Again there came a mumble of approval from the other investors.

'I do have one concern that we might need to look at. Cameras. I want to discuss the option of sound with you at some point, but I think as a priority we're going to need to install further surveillance equipment. We have coverage on a large part of the resort, but there are a number of black spots. It's too easy to lose track of someone. I...'

Another modulated voice interjected. 'Everyone must be accounted for.'

The corner of Hallam's mouth twitched slightly. He had just been considering putting forth the situation with Hollie Page to strengthen his request, but now he thought better of it. That little irritation would soon be dealt with anyway and he certainly didn't want to implant any doubt in the whole operation. 'Of course,' he said simply. 'That has never been in question, I assure you.'

Hallam quickly brought the discussion to a close. 'Thank you, my friends.' He touched a button and the screens changed from images of his investors back to CCTV footage of the resort.

Now, Hallam thought, where the hell has that Smart woman got to?

He switched through various screens until he found what he was looking for. He could see Caroline, Bobbi-Leigh and Billie-Jo standing near the pit of quicksand. They appeared to be talking.

'What the hell is that silly bint doing?' Hallam muttered irritably.

Caroline had in fact located the girls very quickly, intercepting them just as they had been about to walk out onto the quicksand.

'Wait!' she cried.

At the sound of the voice, Billie-Jo and Bobbi-Leigh stopped and spun around.

Caroline was standing a few yards away from them. 'Don't walk on that. It's quicksand.'

'Stay away from us, lady!' Billie-Jo exclaimed, looking at the sand inquisitively.

'I won't hurt you, you just need to listen to me.'

'Like fuck we do,' Bobbi-Leigh said.

Caroline held up her hands in front of her submissively. 'I understand how you feel, but if I meant you any harm why would I have stopped you walking into the quicksand?'

'We don't care,' Billie-Jo said. 'All we know is you're workin' with that fat fucker who brought us here.'

Caroline nodded. 'I am. Yes, I am. But I'm working *for* him, not *with* him.' She took a step towards them.

'Stay back!' Bobbi-Leigh shouted.

Caroline stopped. 'Okay, okay. But please just listen to what I have to say. That's all I'm asking you to do. Listen.'

The two girls exchanged glances.

'Go on then,' Billie-Jo said.

'The first thing you need to know is that we're probably being watched right now.'

'No shit,' Bobbi-Leigh said. 'We're not fick. We know there's cameras all over this place.'

Caroline nodded. 'Yes, there are. But the thing is they can only see us, they can't hear us. There's a camera in the tree behind me.'

Billie-Jo looked past Caroline's head directly into the camera. 'So fuckin' what?' she said, sticking up both her middle fingers indignantly.

'Please *don't* look at the cameras,' Caroline implored her. 'I'm going to help you. But it can't *appear* as if I am. It has to look like you've outwitted me. If for one second he suspects I'm helping you... well, let's not go there.'

'What the hell ya talkin' about, lady?' Billie-Jo snapped angrily.

Caroline knelt down. 'I know you're frightened, I understand. Really I do. But you *have* to trust me. This place... this whole plan... it should never have included children.'

Billie-Jo glared at her. '*Plan*? Our Mum's dead for fuck's sake!'

'Where's our Dad?' Bobbi-Leigh said.

'I don't know, darling,' Caroline said earnestly. 'Honestly I don't. But if you listen to me I can help you find him.'

'Like how?' Billie-Jo replied scornfully.

'He – Mr Hallam I mean – well, he sent me to bring you to him. I…'

'Then ya can fuck right off,' Bobbi-Leigh said angrily, putting her hands on her hips in a show of defiance.

'No, please just listen,' Caroline implored her. 'I've absolutely no intention of taking you to him. Please understand, I just want to *help* you.'

Billie-Jo looked at her warily. 'Come on then, how exactly are ya gonna do that?'

Caroline smiled. 'I'm going to tell him that for your safety I tried to talk you into coming with me.'

'We ain't goin' nowhere with you,' Billie-Jo said shaking her head.

'No, I know you aren't and I don't expect you to.'

Bobbi-Leigh frowned. 'So what the fuck *do* you want then?'

This was taking far too long. Caroline was certain Hallam would be watching and starting to get suspicious. 'If you just be quiet and listen to me, I'm trying to tell you,' she said with a manifest trace of impatience.

Billie-Jo picked up on her tone. 'Right, you listen to *me*, lady. I'm two seconds away from kickin' you in the cunt, so cut out the shitty 'tude and get to the point.'

Caroline raised an apologetic hand. 'I'm sorry. I'm going to tell him you wouldn't listen to me.' Not so far from the truth, she thought. 'Right, shake your heads at me.'

The girls looked at her blankly.

'Go on, shake your heads now.'

They complied.

'Good,' Caroline said. 'Now, in a moment I'm going to get up and try to take you by the hand...'

'I'm not holdin' yer fuckin' hand, lady,' Billie-Jo spat back, shooting her an angry look. 'How old do ya fink I am, five?!'

Caroline was beginning to struggle. She could understand their natural wariness and their hostility; they had witnessed some truly dreadful things. But why couldn't they see she was trying to help? 'I'm not *actually* going to take your hand,' she said trying to temper her ire. 'It just needs to appear that way. When I *try* to I want you both to turn and run.'

'Run where?' Bobbi-Leigh said.

'Not across the sandpit. Scoot around the outside. You need to go to the ice cream parlour over th...' – Bobbi-Leigh started to turn to look – 'Don't turn round!'

Billie-Jo glared at her. 'What did I say about the attitude, lady?'

'Sorry, but it can't appear as if I'm giving you instructions. Please, just keep your eyes on me for the moment. Now, there's a hidden trapdoor on the decking at the top of the steps, so you need to skirt round it to get to the door. Whatever you do don't step on it. Blink twice if you understand.'

Both girls did so.

'Good. Top step, jump, door, get inside fast as you can. Shutting the door behind you will activate an electronic lock.'

'Hang on,' Billie-Jo said suspiciously. 'So we'll be lockin' ourselves in? How exactly is that supposed to help us?'

'I'll be right behind you trying to get the door open. At least that's how it needs to appear. But it *will* be locked so I won't be able to. Then all you have to do is sit tight and wait. I'll come back for you as soon as I can.'

'And you'll find our Dad?' Bobbi-Leigh said.

Caroline looked her in the eye. 'I'm not going to lie to you, it might already be too late for that. But I *will* come back for you as soon as it's safe. I'll get you out of here, I promise.'

The girls looked at each other. What choice did they have? Keep running aimlessly or go along with what this woman was saying? Neither of them trusted her, but if she *was* being honest, right now she seemed to be offering them a chance.

'Right,' Caroline said. She smiled at Billie-Jo. 'Look after your sister.'

'Yeah, well, I can tell ya, my life would be far less of a shit show if I didn't have to babysit this little bitch all the time.'

Caroline looked a little confused. 'Okay. Well, on three I'm going to stand up and try to take your hand. That's when you both turn and run. One... two...three.'

She got to her feet and reached out towards Bobbi-Leigh.

Right on cue – with a cry of 'Fuck you!' from Billie-Jo – both girls took off, scarpering around the outskirts of the sandpit

Impressed at their speed, Caroline took chase.

Within 20-seconds they'd made it to the steps. Taking them two at a time, they launched themselves in unison from the top step and crashed through the swing door. As Caroline got to the top step they slammed the door behind them, activating the lock.

Caroline jumped forward and banged on the glass. On the other side, both girls were panting hard and looking at her. Bobbi-Leigh stuck up her middle finger.

Caroline made a show of rattling the door. 'Good,' she panted. 'Now just stay put.' She adopted a stern expression and deepened her voice in a pitiful attempt at impersonating Arnold Schwarzenegger. 'I'll come back,' she growled.

Billie-Jo stared at her. 'Fuck me, *seriously*? It's "I'll *be* back", ya stupid cow!'

Caroline smiled awkwardly. 'Yes, well, just stay here.' She was about to turn away when a thought flashed through her mind. 'Oh, and whatever else you do, stay away from the freezer and *don't* eat the ice cream!'

Hallam wasn't pleased. Not pleased at all. He had been watching Caroline and the girls attentively and something about what he'd seen just wasn't right.

There was no doubt in his mind that the girls would have resisted; it would have been odd if they hadn't. And on face value it had certainly looked as if she was trying to persuade them to go with her. Yet he had seen Bobbi-Leigh glance towards the parlour. Why had she done that? What had Smart said to them? His intuition had proved correct when the girls had vaulted across the trapdoor at the top of the steps. She was damned well helping them! In the very least she must have alerted them to the presence of the trapdoor.

'What a disappointment,' he said aloud. 'You really *don't* understand at all, do you Mrs Smart?' He sighed and stood up. 'Well, I'll make damned sure you're left in no doubt about the seriousness of your situation.'

CHAPTER 26

Nick was cautiously examining the wire barrier in front of them. They had been following the perimeter fence for almost half an hour with no sign of any way through. Then, a few minutes earlier, Jamie had noticed another stretch of fence off through the trees and they had veered off to check it out.

'What would be fenced off *within* the resort?' Nick pondered aloud.

Jamie shrugged. 'Search me.'

'Something Hallam doesn't want his guests seeing, obviously.' Nick glanced at Kirsty and Charlie. 'Stay back.'

He stepped up to the fence and peered through the mesh. All that there seemed to be on the other side was more woodland. The fence was about 10-feet high and ran more or less parallel to the far taller one. At regular intervals along its length – perhaps 50-yards apart – were small black placards bearing the words **PRIVATE: NO ENTRY**. Interspersed between them were much larger yellow ones, which stated in big bold letters: **DANGER ⚡ ELECTRICITY!**.

'Funny how this one is plastered with warnings, but the main fence – which I'm still pretty sure had to be electrified – wasn't. That suggests to me that there's something far more important to Hallam behind this one.'

'Even if we could get past it, I don't see how it would help,' Jamie said. 'We'll be going the wrong way. We need to get out of this cage and find the coastline.'

'Maybe,' Nick said thoughtfully. 'Or maybe not. But either way this fence looks just about as impenetrable as the other one anyway.'

'Hah!' Jamie exclaimed. 'Do not enter? Red rag to a bull. That's an open fuckin' invite in my manor.'

Nick shook his head. 'Be that as it may, getting through this isn't going to get us *out*. And if it's electrified like the main fence seemed to be…'

'Fuckin' wuss,' Jamie muttered. Reaching into his back pocket of his shorts, he withdrew a switchblade and stepped forward.

'Woah,' Nick said and stepped sharply away.

Jamie guffawed. 'Don't panic. There's nuffin this could do to ya that I couldn't do with my bare hands if I'd wanted to.'

'Hang on a sec,' Nick said. 'You've had that with you all this time?'

Jamie grinned and waved the knife in the air. 'Yep. Chawed it from that Caine kid when he fell over this mornin',' he said proudly. 'It fell out of his pocket. Dopey little fucker never even realised.' He flicked the knife and the blade shot out. 'Thought it might prove handy.'

He brushed past Nick and stepped up to the fence. Kissing the blade he hesitatingly reached out and, closing his eyes, touched it to the wire.

Nothing happened.

He breathed a sigh of relief. 'Someone up there loves me!' he exclaimed, closing the blade and slipping it back into his pocket. 'Looks like someone forgot to turn on the juice, don't it?'

Nick shook his head. 'Luck of the Devil,' he said. 'Though if you've had that thing with you all along, why didn't you pull the same stunt at the gates?'

Jamie thought for a moment. 'Good point,' he said. 'Didn't fink about it.'

Nick raised his eyebrows at Kirsty.

'Well, I'd rather it had been him than you.' She smiled.

Laughing, Jamie jumped up on the mesh and began to climb. Nick, Kirsty and Charlie all moved forward and followed suit.

*

When Caroline Smart was 12-years old and she was still plain little Caroline Jones, she had been caught smoking behind the music block at Saint Afra's Boarding School for Girls. She hadn't felt even remotely like the way she was feeling now since she had cowered before her headmistress, the permanently stern-faced Mrs Lisbeth Lowry, to receive her punishment.

It might be almost 28-years ago now, but Caroline would never forget how she had stood shame-faced while Mrs Lowry – or 'Lezzie' Lowry as she was unaffectionately known around the halls – had lectured her on the evils of tobacco. Caroline had refused to name the girl who had given her the cigarette in the first place; having to later face Helena Stratford if she had grassed on her had been far more daunting a prospect. Having started to become aware of her body, she recalled the humiliation as Lowry had instructed her to pull down her underpants to her knees and bend over the desk. And how, as the bitch had administered five swift open-handed slaps to Caroline's buttocks, she had warned her not to scream, threatening a penalty of three additional slaps if she heard so much as a whimper. The sense of disgrace had been overwhelming. But as harrowing as the ordeal had been, something good had come out of it. When she finally worked up the courage to tell her parents what had happened, contrary to the rebuking she expected to receive for her misdemeanour experimenting with tobacco, they had taken legal action, and Lowry had been dragged across the coals and sacked. Better yet, Caroline had been transferred to a state-funded co-educational school.

She was now standing contritely in front of her employer, with that same sick feeling she had experienced all those years ago in Mrs Lowry's office gnawing away in the pit of her stomach. Nevertheless, she thought, if she had to drop her panties here and now for a caning... well, she had endured far worse during her time working for this repugnant man.

All the screens were switched off and Hallam was seated, looking up at her. He was speaking calmy enough, but Caroline could sense the restrained anger behind his words.

'Not-so-sweet Caroline, it turns out,' Hallam said, shaking his head sorrowfully. He rested his cigar on an ashtray on the desk. 'I'm bitterly disappointed in you, Mrs Smart. Bitterly.'

'I'm…'

'Hush, please.' Hallam held up a hand. 'I pulled you out of the gutter. For the first time in your worthless life you were given purpose. And, my word, you've given me great pleasure in return. But I thought we had an understanding.'

'Mr Hallam, I tried to get them to come with me, but they just wouldn't listen. They were frightened and…'

'Don't lie to me. Did you really think I wouldn't be able to see that you were flagrantly betraying me?' The anger was beginning to surface now. 'I thought there was trust between us. Trust is imperative. I have to be able to *trust* the people who work for me. And without trust…' He shrugged. 'Well, what *do* we have?'

'I'm so sorry, Mr Hallam,' Caroline began. 'I…'

Again he raised a hand to silence her. His face darkened. 'I'll tell you precisely what we have. We have *mis*trust.'

He picked up the cigar, stood up and took a step towards her. Caroline instinctively moved back a pace.

'And mistrust is something that simply won't be tolerated,' he continued. 'Mistrust festers, it wheedles its little fingers…' – he reached out his fat hands and wiggled his fingers at her, making her flinch – '…its nasty, *grubby* little fingers into the fabric of a relationship. And then do you know what happens?'

Caroline felt as if she was going to throw up. She timidly shook her head.

'No. No, of course you don't,' Hallam said, a thin smile appearing on his lips. 'I'll tell you what happens.

The *formerly* trusted have to be chastised. They must be brought immediately back into line.'

As he spoke, Hallam was slowly advancing on her. With each step he took, she matched him by taking one backwards.

'But then again,' he said. 'Sometimes broken trust is beyond all hope of retrieval. Decimated. Destroyed. Which sadly leaves only one option for he who once trusted.'

'What are you going to do?' Caroline asked, her voice trembling.

Hallam stopped. 'Well,' he said. The anger suddenly seemed to be gone. 'You know how that treacherous Banks fellow ended up?'

Caroline nodded.

Hallam looked down at the cigar pinched between his fingers. The end had been had been slowly burning away and almost an inch of ash had accumulated.

Suddenly, he flicked it at Caroline. The embers sparked as the ash hit her face. As she flinched, Hallam dropped the cigar and lunged forward with sudden ferocity. He made a grab for her, but she dodged to one side, stumbled and fell. Quick as lightning she was on her feet again, but just as swiftly Hallam was upon her, pushing her back against the wall.

His chubby hands closed around her throat. 'When I tell someone to do something, they do it!' he exploded. 'If I tell them to put their hands in a bacon slicer, they fucking well *do* it!'

Caroline's fingers clawed at his hands, trying to break free of the vice-like grip. As he squeezed harder, beads of sweat began to cluster on his brow and spittle was erupting from between his clenched teeth as he spoke.

'You think you saved those grotty little toe-rags? You may have put a fly in the ointment, but you've only delayed the inevitable.'

Caroline's face was beginning to turn scarlet. Gasping for air, her eyes bulging, she scrabbled ever more desperately to break free of him. It was pointless; the man's full weight was forced up against her, and to her horror she felt his excitement pressing against her thigh.

His hands closed even tighter around her slender neck and, as blackness descended upon her, his voice softened. 'I want you to know this makes me very unhappy, Mrs Smart, really it does. You've given me so much pleasure, but I simply cannot…' – he twisted his hands and Caroline's body sagged – 'and *will* not…' – he took a step away and her body dropped to the floor like a stone – '…tolerate mutiny.'

Panting heavily, he stood back, staring at her body for a few moments.

'What a waste,' he said calmly. 'But you really weren't a very good PA.'

His foot flashed out and he kicked her hard in the face. Twice.

He pulled out a handkerchief from his trouser pocket, bent down and wiped away the spatters of blood from the topside of his patent leather shoe.

Then he tossed the handkerchief to one side, loosened the belt on his trousers and lowered the zip.

CHAPTER 27

Squatted low, Nick and Jamie peered out cautiously at the deserted compound from either side of the broad trunk of an olive tree.

After scaling the fence they had walked for no more than 200 yards through woodland as dense as any they had encountered, when Jamie had spotted a building up ahead of them through the trees. The one thing they had all noticed was the apparent absence of cameras, but nevertheless Nick had instructed Kirsty and Charlie to stay back for a minute while he and Jamie went ahead and surveyed the situation.

There was no sign of any life.

'What d'ya reckon then?' Jamie whispered.

Nick looked across at the concrete building with its iron door. Except for the presence of several windows, it wasn't unlike a vast wartime bunker. 'The private retreat of our persecutor, I'd say,' he said quietly. 'And as for those,' he added, looking up at the wires extending from the building across to a lofty wooden telephone pole on the far side of the compound, 'they strongly suggest to me there's telephone communication in that place.'

Beside the pole was a ramshackle portico, beneath which there were three vehicles parked. The minibus in which they had arrived was there, sitting between a Rolls Royce Silver Cloud and a bright red, open-top Mazda MX-5 convertible.

'Are you seein' what I'm seein'?' Jamie said excitedly.

'Yeah, I am,' Nick replied. 'And look over there.' He pointed.

Beyond the telephone pole was a track leading off the compound and away into the trees. 'That could well be our way out of here. I'm just concerned this suddenly feels too easy.'

'Too *easy*?' Jamie exclaimed. 'Fuck me. You really need to wake up. This *is* our way out.' He pointed at the line of vehicles. 'And there's the ticket.'

'Maybe,' Nick said.

'Maybe? *Maybe*?!' Jamie exploded. 'I tell ya, I've had my fuckin' fill of you, ya twat. You're doin' my head in. What isn't obvious to ya about getting' in one of them cars and driving the fuck outta here?'

'For Christ's sake keep your voice down,' Nick hissed. 'Let's not start arguing again. We'll take a closer look, okay?'

'There's nobody here, for f…'

There was a sudden loud crash as the door of the building was flung wide open.

Jamie and Nick ducked back behind the tree. After a second, Nick cautiously peered back out.

The figure of a man appeared in the doorway. He was coming out backwards and pulling something with which he was evidently struggling.

Even from behind Nick instantly recognised Hallam's bulk. But only when the man had fully emerged – dragging what initially appeared to be a large bundle of rags down the short flight of steps outside the door – did Nick register to his horror that it was in fact a human body.

Although the top half was clothed, the bottom half had been stripped naked except for a pair of stiletto shoes, one of which was hanging loose from the left foot. Hallam had hold of the legs and, as he pulled the body along with clear indifference, the head cracked hard against the steps, trailing bright red blood across the concrete.

As Hallam got to the bottom, the left shoe dropped off the corpse. Cursing, he bent down, picked it up and wedged it into his capacious jacket pocket.

It took Nick a moment, but then he caught a glimpse of the face. It was covered in blood and the nose had been smashed in, but although he couldn't recall her name, he was still able to see it was the woman who had been assisting Hallam when they'd arrived.

Cheerfully whistling the unmistakable chorus from Neil Diamond's hit "Sweet Caroline", Hallam dragged the body across the compound to the portico. Stopping in front of the Rolls Royce, he opened the boot, hoisted her up and unceremoniously dumped her inside. Then, slamming the boot shut, he strolled nonchalantly back across the compound. Still whistling, he disappeared back inside.

Nick turned and beckoned towards Kirsty and Charlie. As they approached he put a finger to his lips. They crouched down beside him.

'Don't say anything, just listen,' he whispered. 'We may have just found a way out of here. We need to get across to those cars,' – he pointed – 'as quickly and quietly as possible. I'll go first, you two follow right behind me.' He looked at Jamie. 'You bring up the rear.'

Jamie glared at him. 'Why am I last?'

'Because I damned well say so!' Nick snapped back. 'When we get over there, take cover behind the minibus.' He looked at Kirsty and Charlie. 'Remember, fast and quietly as we can.' He winked at his son. 'Okay, buddy?'

Charlie nodded.

'Come on then.' Glancing over at the door and satisfied there was no further sign of Hallam, Nick moved out from behind the tree. He ran swiftly across the compound, with Charlie, then Kirsty and Jamie, hot on his heels.

They reached the minibus in less than 10 seconds and ducked down out of sight on the side facing away from the building.

Jamie chuckled. 'Fuck me, I'm sweatin' like a paedo on a schoolbus here!' He didn't notice the look of disgust on Kirsty's face. 'Which one are we takin'?' he said. 'I vote for the sporty number.' He stood up and peered over the door of the car. 'Hah! They only went and left the keys in the ignition!'

'We're taking the minibus,' Nick said firmly. 'But there's something I need to do first. You three wait here while I...'

'Fuck that,' Jamie said, crouching back down. 'I ain't waitin' for you or no-one.' With that he stood up again and opened the passenger side door of the Mazda. 'I'm off.'

Nick jumped up and grabbed Jamie by the shoulders and swung him hard against the side of the minibus.

'For Christ's sake, you clown. You're going to jeopardise this for all of us!'

Jamie glared at him. 'I told ya before, ya nonce, don't touch me!' He pushed Nick away. 'Now back off.'

'Or *what*?' Nick had hit breaking point. 'I've had my fill of your shitty attitude, you selfish ignoramus! Now get *down*.'

'Selfish what?'

'Ignoramus. Look it up!' He pushed Jamie back down. 'All I'm asking you to do is wait here with my family, just for a few minutes. Then I promise you we'll all get out of here together.'

'Alright.' Jamie held up a surrendering hand. 'A couple of minutes, yeah?'

Nick was a little taken aback by the man's sudden apparent willingness to yield, but he nodded appreciatively. 'Thank you.' And he meant it.

Kirsty was looking at him with concern. 'Where are you going?'

'It'll be fine,' Nick said. 'You and Charlie stay here with him. I'll be back as fast as I can.'

He peered out from behind the minibus. There was still no sign of any activity from within the compound. Aside from the distant chirruping of cicadas, it was deathly quiet.

'Whatever it is you're thinking of doing, it can't be more important than getting the heck out of here,' Kirsty said.

'I can't leave without…'

Kirsty looked at him imploringly. 'Nick, please, no. Let's just go.'

Nick looked into her eyes. 'I can't, love. I can't just walk away without getting some answers.' He planted a quick kiss on her nose and ruffled Charlie's hair. 'I'll be back in five, buddy, okay?'

Charlie tried to smile. He had never been so scared in all his life as he had been the past few hours. What could a couple more minutes hurt? He nodded.

Scanning the compound, Nick quickly stepped out into the open.

'I love you,' Kirsty whispered, choking back the tears.

Nick didn't hear her, but Jamie did. He scowled and shook his head. 'Fuck me.'

As fast as he could, Nick covered the 20-or-so-yards across the compound to the building and flattened himself, back to the wall, below one of the windows. With his heart pounding, he wiped the sweat from his brow and began to edge along the wall towards the steps.

It only took him a few seconds to get there, but as he peered round the corner up at the door the silence was shattered by the sound of an engine starting.

Almost simultaneously Kirsty's voice screamed out: 'Niiiiick!'

Nick turned and looked back towards the portico. He saw Kirsty come running out from behind the minibus dragging Charlie behind her. At the same moment there was a flash of red and the Mazda – with Jamie at the wheel – reversed out fast.

As Nick began to run towards them, there seemed to be a moment of confusion between Kirsty and Charlie as to where they were running; she lost her grip on the boy's arm and he reeled off to the right, bounced off the side of the Mazda and was propelled sprawling to the ground.

'Charlie!' Kirsty screamed. She ran over to her son and crouched down. Although he looked slightly stunned, Charlie appeared uninjured and was already picking himself up. She held him tight.

In a deft manoeuvre worthy of a stunt driver, Jamie spun the car 180-degrees and it skidded to a halt, spewing up a cloud of dust.

Seeing that Charlie was safe, Nick hurtled past them and reached the car as Jamie was struggling with the gearstick.

Nick appeared beside the driver's side door. 'Get out!' he shouted, grabbing at Jamie's shoulder.

Jamie shot him a glance. 'You wanna keep that fuckin' kid of yours on a leash.' He found the gear. 'You already lost one,' he added as he put his foot down.

As Nick let out an anguished scream, the car surged forward violently and stalled.

'Fuck!' Jamie shifted the gearstick into neutral and turned the key in the ignition. It bit straight away and the engine roared back into life.

Nick appeared at his side again and scrabbled to get a hold on him. At the same moment, Jamie found what he thought was first gear and stamped down hard on the accelerator. But in the melee he'd chosen reverse; Nick was thrown off as the Mazda shot backwards and with a sickening crunch hit one of the concrete pillars on the portico.

In an instant, Nick was on his feet and running. As he reached the driver's side door, Jamie had managed to find first gear correctly. Nick hooked his arms over the door and lifted his feet off the ground as the car jerked into motion. There was a teeth-grating screech of metal as the rear bumper broke away and the car was propelled forward.

Trying to keep hold of the steering wheel with his left hand, Jamie hammered at Nick with his right. Nick held on tight, grabbing hold of the inside door handle to give himself some purchase. Having freed up a hand, he clawed at Jamie. 'Stop the damned car!'

Jamie fought to keep control and the Mazda veered to the left, then the right, and then swung into a wide u-turn, shot to the right and with a thunderous, dull crack it rammed headlong into the wooden telephone pole.

On impact, Jamie felt his upper ribs smash against the steering wheel and his head butted the windscreen, cracking the glass.

Nick lost his grip on the door handle and was flung off into the dirt.

The front of the Mazda was staved in, but although the pole splintered and listed to one side it remained in an upright position.

Jamie sat in the driver's seat looking dazed. Blood dribbled from a gash above his left eyebrow and his chest felt as if it were trapped in a vice. Before he could quite comprehend what had happened, Nick had appeared beside the car door. Yanking it open, he hauled Jamie out and punched him hard in the face.

Disoriented, Jamie staggered back, seemingly incapable of defending himself. Nick kicked his legs away from beneath him and he went down.

In a blink Nick flew at him, grabbed him by the shoulders and shook him. 'What the hell do you think you're doing?!'

'Get the fuck off me!' Jamie shook himself free and took a swing.

Nick deftly sidestepped and Jamie's first attempt went wide, but he came in quickly with a second. Nick threw up his arm and blocked the punch, grabbed Jamie by the wrist and swung him round. He lost his footing and went down.

Nick stood looking at him for a moment. 'For Christ's sake, I thought we agreed no more of this nonsense.' Then he bent forward and reached out a hand. 'Come on.'

Jamie nodded and took his hand, but instead of allowing Nick to help him up, he pulled him down. They struggled for a few moments, and then Nick managed to land a punch squarely in Jamie's face. He went limp and Nick sat back, gasping for breath.

Jamie's bloodied face was staring at him in a state of utter bewilderment. 'Fuck me, ya don't half hit hard,' he mumbled, blood bubbling up in the corner of his mouth.

Suddenly his eyes darted to the right past Nick's shoulder and his jaw dropped in horror. At the same moment there was a loud splintering sound.

'Dad, look out!' Charlie cried.

Nick jerked his head round just in time to glimpse something plunging down at him. Instinct took over and he hurled himself to one side.

The telegraph pole came crashing down and hit the ground with an earth-shaking thud, missing him by inches and throwing up a swirl of dust. The twin wires via which it was connected to the roof of the building remained attached. One of them, however, was stretched to breaking point; the metal brace with which it was attached to the pole was hanging off, held in place by a solitary bent screw.

Nick sat up, choking on dust. It was in his eyes, his nose and coating the back of his throat.

Charlie and Kirsty appeared at his side. 'He wasn't going to wait for you,' she said breathlessly. 'The second you'd turned your back he pulled out that knife. He said if we made a sound he'd cut us.' She was crying now. 'There was nothing I could do. I'm so sorry.'

Nick waved a hand at her. 'It's okay,' he managed to croak. 'It's all okay.'

The dust was settling and as Kirsty helped Nick to his feet there was a spluttering sound and on the other side of the fallen pole Jamie sat up, shaking the dust from his hair.

Chuckling, he started to get to his feet. 'Wow! How fuckin' close was *that*?' He looked a bit wobbly, but managed to get himself upright. Dusting himself down he grinned at Nick, Kirsty and Charlie; one of his front teeth was broken and the others were smeared with dark red blood. 'I told ya someone up there loves me.'

With a sharp cracking sound the metal brace affixing the taut wire to the telephone pole snapped. The wire broke loose, whiplashed, and the end whistled past Nick's head, missing his ear by millimeters.

But Jamie didn't stand a chance. The wire cut clean through him at 30 degrees, bisecting him just below his rib cage.

Kirsty screamed and turned away, hugging Charlie close to her so that he couldn't see.

His eyes wide, the stupid grin still plastered on his face, the top half of Jamie Trot's body slid to the left and toppled, divorcing itself from the lower half. It hit the ground with a muffled whump, spitting up dust. His legs remained ghoulishly upright for a few moments and then the knees buckled and the lower half of his body dropped, spilling intestines all over the ground.

Hardly able to believe what he had just witnessed, Nick turned his face away.

CHAPTER 28

Nick got to his knees and circled his arms around Kirsty and Charlie, hugging them and burying his face in Kirsty's hair.

'It's okay, it's over,' Nick whispered, holding them to him even more tightly.

They remained that way for half a minute and, as Nick raised his head again, the sound of slow clapping drifted across the compound, and his eyes fell upon the figure of Hallam.

The man's bulk was filling the open doorway, where he was standing looking out at the gruesome sight before him: the three dusty figures crouched on the ground in front of Jamie Trot's rended body.

The expression on Hallam's face was a blend of surprise and pure elation. Jamie's demise couldn't have been more spectacular if he had planned it himself.

Nick locked eyes with Hallam and they stared at each other for a moment without moving. Then, as Nick jumped to his feet, Hallam turned and hurried back inside.

'Wait here,' Nick said.

'We're coming with you,' Kirsty said, standing up.

'No, please, just…'

Kirsty took hold of Charlie's hand, 'I said we're coming with you,' she repeated firmly.

'Please,' Nick said softly. 'I just need you to wait here for me. I won't be long.' He looked into Kirsty's eyes. 'Please.'

She nodded. 'Okay.'

Nick smiled at Charlie. 'Keep your Mum safe, buddy.' Ruffling the boy's hair, he turned and hurried across the compound to the steps, scooted swiftly up to the open doorway and peered inside.

In front of him was a long, poorly illuminated corridor peppered with a number of doors down either side. There was no sign of Hallam.

Nick stepped inside. As he did so, he was assailed by a waft of humid, musty air and a clattering sound came from somewhere off down the corridor.

Nick froze for an instant and then edged slowly forward.

He came to the first door on the left hand side. It was closed and there was a small push-button lock affixed to the frame. Nick tried the handle anyway, but as he expected it wouldn't shift.

He moved cautiously on to the next door, this one on the right hand side of the corridor. It too was locked. The story was the same with the next three doors, situated on alternate sides along the length of the corridor; each had a push-button lock on it and refused to open.

At its far end, the corridor concluded with a T-junction. All his senses on full alert, Nick peered warily round the corner and glanced both ways. To the left and the right there was a short, narrow passage which ran for about 15-feet in either direction, each side terminating with a door. The one to the right was closed, but the one at the opposite end was slightly ajar.

He moved swiftly across the linoleum and – with his right hand clenched into a fist, and holding his breath – he pushed the door wide open.

In spite of the poor light, it was immediately obvious that the room was deserted. Nick took a step inside.

The décor was minimally efficient. Several filing cabinets were standing to the left of the door. On the right there was a small table bearing a few bottles of alcohol – amongst them ouzo, brandy and retsina – and tea-making facilities, positioned below an open window, through which Nick could hear the distant sound of the cicadas working themselves into a frenzy. The wall opposite the door was covered in TV monitors – perhaps 20 – all of them displaying an **HH** screensaver; the now familiar logo was moving swiftly around the screens and bouncing off the edges like a wasp trapped in a jar. In front of the screens there was a desk, on which was a telephone and what looked like a small pile of folders.

Nick went to the window and looked out. Beneath the six-foot drop to the ground there was a slender gap of about 12-inches between the wall and the compound fence, which ran parallel all the way along the rear of the building. Away to the right at the far end, Nick could see the back end of the portico roof. There was no way Hallam could possibly have got out this way, he thought; given the man's size, it would have been impossible for him to squeeze down there.

Unless there's a back exit he hadn't seen, Hallam had to be in here somewhere.

He crossed over to the desk, rolled the swivel chair out of the way and, as quietly as possible checked through the twin drawers on either side. They were all empty. He picked up the folders to examine them and there on the top was one bearing the name **MASON**. His eyes widened as he leafed through the paperwork inside. There were several pages about his family.

Suddenly a clattering noise echoed down the passageway outside.

Folding the papers in half and tucking them into his back pocket, he dropped the folder on the desk and moved fast across the room. As he looked round the edge of the door, his eyes fell upon a smear of blood on the frame. At the far end of the passageway, he could see that the door, which had moments earlier been closed, was now slightly open.

He went back out into the passageway, crossed the T-junction and moved stealthily towards the room at the far end. The door was swinging gently back and forth and he could see there was no light inside.

Stepping in, Nick's eyes adjusted to the inky blackness, but he had barely registered he was in some sort of store room when there came a throaty growl from his left and Hallam, clutching a broom, lunged at him. He swung the makeshift weapon hard, but due to the darkness his assault was poorly judged and the broom clipped Nick's shoulder.

Grunting as a wave of pain seared through his upper arm, Nick peeled away to one side and ducked, narrowly avoiding Hallam's second swing, executed with such brute force that when the broom struck the wall the shaft snapped in two.

Hallam dropped the handle, and before Nick could react the big man was upon him, knocking him off his feet and bringing his full weight down on top of him.

Nick was struggling to breathe as Hallam's huge hands closed around his throat and began to exert incredible pressure on his windpipe, administering extra force on the Adam's apple with his thumbs. Nick was barely able to move and he felt his head begin to swim. Yet somehow, perhaps in a subconscious act of desperation, he managed to bring his right knee up hard, finding a bullseye in the big man's crotch.

Hallam screamed – a high-pitched girlish squeal – and immediately released his grip on Nick's throat. He pitched sideways and rolled onto his back, clawing at his crotch.

Nick twisted away to one side and, gasping for air, grabbed up the broken broom handle, its splintered end now tantamount to a lethal weapon. He got to his feet, straddled Hallam and pressed the sharp tip to his forehead. 'Enough!'

Hallam, still clutching his groin and his face twisted in pain, raised a hand of surrender. 'Please...' he started. 'Don't hurt me.'

'Sit up!' Nick demanded, holding the broom handle rock steady and gently massaging his throat with his other hand.

'Okay, okay.' Floundering, Hallam rolled on to his side. 'I... I don't think I can,' he puffed.

'Sit the fuck up!' Nick repeated angrily. He pressed the broom handle even more firmly against Hallam's forehead, making him cry out.

'Alright, give me a moment,' he said, and with difficulty managed to lever himself up into the sitting position. He shuffled back a little until his back was up against the wall.

Nick, still holding the shattered broom handle to the man's head, moved with him.

'Listen,' Hallam began. 'Can we...?'

'Why did you bring us here?' Nick said calmly.

Hallam looked genuinely surprised by the question. 'What?'

'Why did you bring us to this damned island?'

Hallam chuckled in disbelief. 'If you have to ask that question now – when everything I'm doing here, and the reasons *why* must be all too obvious by now – then I suggest that even if I were to furnish you with an answer, you're simply too stupid to understand.'

'I don't mean everyone,' Nick said angrily. 'I mean *us* specifically. Me and my family.'

'How very interesting,' Hallam said, peering up at him curiously. 'You differentiate yourself from the others?'

Nick pulled out the paperwork from his back pocket. 'Damned right I do. I... what I mean is *we*, we're not like the others.' He waved the papers in the air. 'It looks like you've done your homework. So how you can compare our lives to the feckless reprobates you brought here is beyond me.'

'I see,' Hallam said with a thin smile. 'Each of you believed your pitiful little sob stories would result in some sort of entitlement, didn't you? Where in fact all that your entries into my little contest did was tick boxes and identify you to me as ripe for expunging.' He reached up slowly and tapped the broom handle, which was still pressed against his brow. 'Would you mind terribly removing this thing please?' he said. 'It's most off-putting.'

Nick thought for a moment and then stepped back, but he kept the end of the broom hovering a few inches away from Hallam's face.

'Thank you,' Hallam said, rubbing at the small indentation on his forehead. He shifted slightly to make himself more comfortable and continued. 'You see, I've had to tolerate your kind my entire life.'

Nick frowned. 'My *kind*?'

'Sluggards, young man. Dullards. Each and every one of you a worthless blight on the face of the planet.'

'You got it wrong,' Nick said through clenched teeth. 'Maybe not the others, I don't know. But you got *us* wrong.'

'Did I?' Hallam said tauntingly. He reached out again, placed his index finger on the end of the broom handle and steered it completely away from his face. Nick allowed him to do it. 'You stand there all airs and graces, as if you're some sort of pillar of virtue, yet there you are judging the others. In that respect you're no different to me.'

'Don't even begin to compare me to you!' Nick said angrily. 'You know nothing about me.'

The thin smile appeared again. 'I know all I need to know.'

Nick closed his eyes and Kirsty's words echoed in his mind: 'You're a good man, Nick Mason.'

Opening his eyes again, he dropped the broom handle to the floor.

Hallam looked up at him, unsure of what was happening. Nevertheless, Nick's anger appeared to have subsided a little and he wasn't about to waste the opportunity. 'Now listen here,' he said amicably. 'We're grown men, not children brawling in the schoolyard. There's a deal to be made here and you should know that you could come out of this very nicely indeed.'

Nick wasn't even looking at him any more. 'I'm not here to make a deal,' he said.

'Then what *are* you here for?' Hallam said, surreptitiously moving his hand a few inches towards his jacket pocket. 'You were smart enough to break into my little enclave.'

'Well, that wasn't difficult,' Nick said, turning to face him again. 'Next time you want to keep people out make sure you turn on the electricity.'

Hallam nodded. 'A foolish oversight on my part,' he said. 'Regardless of which, you had the means of escape at your disposal, yet still you chose not to flee.' He chuckled. 'Mind you, that didn't play out too well for Mr Trot, did it?'

'I wanted to put you straight.'

Hallam looked at him mockingly. 'Put me straight?'

'My life hasn't been an easy road,' Nick said, squatting down. 'But I've worked damned hard to keep my head above water. To provide for my family. Things aren't too good right now, that's true. It's been a terrible year since... well, anyway, I never took a penny from anyone that I didn't earn through hard graft. And I never would.'

Hallam appeared to be listening to Nick intently, but he subtly moved his hand another inch towards his pocket.

'These people you brought here may not have been family of the year material, and I'd be lying if I said they haven't all seriously wound me up one way or another.'

'Precisely!' Hallam interjected enthusiastically. 'You didn't know any of them, not really. They say we shouldn't judge a book by it's cover... well, that's utter stuff and nonsense. They were all despicable. You're a shrewd fellow and any fool could see your campmates had all the attributes that made them perfect candidates for my initiative.'

Nick pondered Hallam's words for a few moments. 'Despicable or not, there's no justification for murdering innocent people and their children.'

'Says who?' Hallam raised his hand and scratched his head thoughtfully. 'Although I suppose that depends on one's interpretation of justification.' He dropped his hand back down and rested it against the flap of his jacket pocket, feeling the solidity of the contents beneath his palm. 'Nevertheless, I would argue there's every justification.'

'We're not living in the dark ages,' Nick said. 'You can't just go around killing people who don't fit your twisted utopian vision.'

Hallam smiled. 'I think you'll find I can. And I have.' The smile faded. 'But look here, dear boy, this debate isn't getting us anywhere.'

'It's not a debate,' Nick snapped.

'Chat then,' Hallam replied. 'I say black, you say white. We could talk all day, but we're never going to see eye to eye and that's that. However, I *will* concede that I may – just *may* – have misjudged you. So let's cut to the chase. What do you say we draw a veil over all this and I write you a cheque for… oh, I don't know, what would be fair?… shall we say £500,000? And you simply walk away.'

Nick shook his head in disbelief. 'I don't want your dirty money.'

'A cool million then. Think about it. A million pounds. Life changing, eh? A fresh start for you and that pretty little wife of yours? Not to mention that handsome young son. Speaking of which…' – Hallam raised his eyebrows and winked at him – '…he clearly got those good looks from his father.'

Hallam was squinting up at him hungrily now, like a predatory spider examining the helpless fly caught on the delicate substrate of its web. To his delight, Nick actually appeared to be considering his offer, 'That's right,' he said silkily. 'A *million* pounds.'

Nick shook his head and stood up. 'I told you, I don't want your money.' He turned away and walked to the door.

Hallam chuckled sardonically. 'So my judgement was sound after all. The man driven to despair and the verge of financial ruin by his inability to protect his own child has principles.' He lifted the flap of his jacket pocket and curled his hand tightly around the toe of Caroline's errant shoe.

Nick stopped and turned back. 'What?'

'That dead daughter of yours,' Hallam said. 'All your fault, of course. No doubt about that.'

Nick was staring at him, hardly able to believe what he was hearing.

'What?' Hallam said innocently. 'You think I didn't check you out before bringing you here? I know more about you and your family than you know about yourselves.' He tutted. 'Poor little Daisy Mason. What a senseless waste of life. If only you'd been paying attention.' He continued to needle Nick mercilessly. 'Negligence I'd call it, pure and simple. Very remiss indeed.'

With a cry of anguish, Nick took a single step forward.

And that was when Hallam made his move. Yanking the shoe from his pocket, in a swift, seamless manoeuvre that defied his size, Hallam rose nimbly to his feet and effortlessly buried the stiletto heel between Nick's ribs.

CHAPTER 29

For his tenth birthday Nick Mason had received a metallic green 10-speed Puch racing bicycle. He had been badgering his parents for it since the previous Christmas when his best friend Tony received a maroon version of the same model. The very next day, on a downhill race with Tony, Nick had come off, hit the ground hard and cracked a rib.

Back then, laying on an x-ray table in A&E, Nick had felt as if he was dying. But with the tip of the stiletto heel wedged firmly between his second and third rib, the pain now was unlike anything he had ever experienced in his life before.

Grasping at the shoe, Nick staggered back against the wall.

Hallam towered in front of him, glowering. 'Offer rescinded then,' he said contemptuously. 'You just blew off a million quid.' He shrugged. 'Although, in all honesty, you wouldn't have lived long enough to spend it anyway.'

With a scream, Nick wrenched the shoe out of his chest and without even thinking he swung it at Hallam. The heel slid into his neck like a knife through butter. As the man's face contorted in a blend of shock, surprise and agony, Nick forced the shoe in even deeper and twisted it hard. There was a snapping sound and the shoe broke away from the heel, bringing with it a chunk of flesh and a spurt of crimson.

Clutching at the disembodied piece of shoe lodged in the gaping wound in his neck, Hallam dropped to his knees, his lifeblood seeping out between his fat fingers. He began to choke and globs of bloody mucus spattered from his mouth. He looked as if he was trying to speak, but then with a jerk he slumped forwards and face planted the concrete floor.

A dark red stain was spreading across the front of Nick's shirt. He stepped away from Hallam's body, leant against the doorframe and put a hand to his chest. As he did so, his vision began to blur and he was vaguely aware that his legs were no longer capable of supporting him.

He said – or through a rush of blackness *thought* he said – 'Fuck.'

Then he collapsed in a heap on the floor.

Kirsty and Charlie had done exactly as Nick had instructed and while they waited for him beside the minibus, the skies ominously darkened and the clouds had opened. Through the lashing rain, they had watched the open door of the building. Both of them willing Nick to appear, they waited... and waited. After what seemed like hours – in fact it was only a matter of minutes – Kirsty had told Charlie to wait for her and not come inside under any circumstances.

She had just reached the T-junction in the passageway leading to the store room when she saw her husband crumple in the open doorway.

She ran to him and crouched down. As she did so, she caught sight of Hallam's prone body, illuminated by a shaft of dim light from the passageway, laying in a pool of blood.

Then she saw the blood on Nick's T-shirt. 'Christ!' She shook him hard. There was no movement. With tears brimming in her eyes, Kirsty leant forward and put her ear to his mouth. She could feel the soft warmth of his breath.

As she went to shake him again, Nick suddenly inhaled deeply and opened his eyes.

'Thank God!' Kirsty bent and kissed him hard on the mouth.

Nick responded by snaking his arms up around her neck and pulling her to him. 'Arrghhh!' He let out a little cry as a pain shot through his chest, and Kirsty reeled back.

'What?!' she said fearfully.

'It's okay.' He smiled up at her. 'But I think I might need a bit of assistance getting up,' he said. Suddenly he became aware of the wetness on his cheek. He looked up into her twinkling eyes. 'You're leaking,' he said jokily.

Almost swooning with relief, Kirsty burst out laughing and slapped his shoulder with the back of her hand. 'Well what do you expect? I thought for a moment I'd lost you.'

'No, you're not getting rid of me that easily.' Nick suddenly became aware that Charlie wasn't with her. 'Where's…?'

'He's waiting by the minibus.' Carefully helping Nick to his feet, she glanced at Hallam's body. 'What happened here?'

'He was insane. He tried to kill me.' Nick shook his head and made a snorting noise somewhere between laughter and a sob. 'With a bloody shoe.'

Kirsty circled her arm around his waist, helping to support him, and they made their way slowly back down the corridor.

'Hey, you remember that holiday at Camber Sands a few years ago?' Nick said, wincing with every step.

'Of course I do!' Kirsty rolled her eyes. 'I'm hardly likely to forget it, am I? You said it was the worst holiday camp you ever stayed on – like, *ever*.'

Through the pain, Nick just about managed a smile. 'Yeah, well, I've just changed my mind.' As they reached the open door, Nick saw the rain, now falling so heavily that it was bouncing off the steps. 'Definitely,' he added.

As they reached the bottom of the steps they came to an abrupt halt.

Coming quickly across the compound towards them were two people: Charlie and, behind him, a tall man wearing a black oilskin overcoat and a matching sowester that shadowed his face. The man had his hand on Charlie's shoulder.

Nick swiftly propelled Kirsty back behind him and raised his fists, but the man passively held up his hands in surrender.

As the cloudburst subsided, dwindling to a light drizzle, the man pushed the sowester back off his forehead and grinned at them. It took both of them a moment, but then almost simultaneously Nick and Kirsty recognised Dimitri, the minibus driver who'd transported them up from the jetty the previous day.

Dimitri was looking at Nick uncertainly; he'd spotted the blood all over his shirt. 'Are you alright, sir?' he said with convincingly genuine concern.

Nick dropped his fists. 'I'll live.'

Charlie ran over and hugged his mother.

'Why are you dressed up like that?' Nick said.

Dimitri let out a huge belly laugh and waved his hands at the sky. 'It rain! This is Greece, sir. You live here long as Dimitri, you learn to be checking the…' – he struggled to find the right word – '…the.. the weather. Yes. And in September always rain can come very fast.' He looked at Nick earnestly. 'But now I am for to take you away from here.'

'But you work for Hallam,' Nick said warily. His fists were still balled tightly at his sides in readiness.

'No, no, sir. Dimitri work for self. Work to provide for family. I come back this afternoon because Mr Hallam call. He say he have extra job for me. I need money, so I come. But now I not want to work for him no more.'

Nick eyed the man suspiciously. 'You expect me to believe you have no idea what's been going on here?'

'Dimitri not know, sir. Honestly. But girl, she tell me. It is place of the Devil. So much death.'

'What girl?' Nick asked warily. As much as he needed to believe what Dimitri was telling him, all his senses were screaming at him to stay alert.

Dimitri turned and pointed towards the portico. As Nick and Kirsty looked, a figure stepped out from behind the minibus.

It was Hollie Page. She was dripping wet, and her tangled hair was streaked across her face, but nevertheless Nick could clearly see it was her.

She raised a hand to Nick, then broke into a run. She rushed over and flung her arms around him. Nick let out a little cry of pain and she stepped quickly back. 'Sorry.'

Dimitri grinned. 'I find her on road.' He waved a hand in the air. She fight with Dimitri.' He rubbed his arm vigorously. 'She very strong.'

Hollie looked at him apologetically. 'Yeah,' she said. 'Sorry about that.'

Dimitri gave her a smile. 'It fine, it no hurt now.' He laughed. 'Much.'

'It's lucky for you that you ran into someone friendly,' Nick said.

'At first Dimitri thought she lie to him. Mr Hallam always good man to me. But we come back and I looking around and I see dead bodies with own eyes. So I come here now to get money owed and, how you say... retire?'

'Resign?' Nick said.

Dimitri shrugged.

Nick looked at Hollie. 'Where have you been all this time?'

Hollie turned back to face him. 'After you saw my Dad and me in the woods when he was trying to...' She trailed off.

Nick frowned. 'Hang on, I'm confused. This man just said you told him what was happening here. How did *you* know?'

'I was close by when you all met up in the woods.' Hollie looked a bit sheepish. 'I was kinda tagging along behind my family. They didn't know I was there. But I heard what you said to them about an accident. So I followed you back to that reception place. I was hiding in the trees, but I heard what that man said over the loudspeaker thingy. That everyone was going to die. So I just took off. I ran and ran. And eventually I came to a fence and I managed to get out.'

'How?' Nick said incredulously. 'The fences are electrified!'

Hollie's eyes widened. 'Are they?' she said. 'It's lucky I've always been crap at climbing then or I might've got electrocuted.' She laughed nervously.

'Well hang on then,' Nick said, 'How *did* you manage to get out?'

'There was a dip in the ground beneath the fence. I just dug it out a bit deeper...' – she made little clawing motions in the air with her hands – '...and scooched underneath.'

Nick smiled and shook his head. 'Unbelievable,' he said. 'We should have all come with you. But where did you think you were going?'

Hollie shrugged. 'I didn't think it through. Back to the jetty to wait for a boat I guess. I dunno. I just needed to get the hell away from my Dad.' Her face dropped. 'Oh God, my Dad,' she said blanching. 'He's going to kill me!'

Nick glanced at Kirsty. Should he tell her?

Kirsty read his thoughts. 'Not now,' she said quietly.

Nick turned back to face Hollie. 'No, he's not,' he said. 'I promise you.'

Dimitri smiled comfortingly at Hollie. 'It okay, what sir promise to you be right. Your father, he dead.'

Hollie blanched. '*Wha*t?!'

Nick glared at Dimitri. His attempts at tact had been scuppered by the man's hamfisted revelation.

'Is true, is true' Dimitri continued, oblivious to his indiscretion. 'Your mother and brother too. Dimitri see bodies.' He winced. 'It terrible.'

Almost speechless, Hollie stared at him. Her eyes filled with tears. 'What am I going to do? How am I going to get home?'

'Don't worry,' Kirsty said. 'We'll make sure you get home safely, won't we?' She looked at Nick.

He smiled. 'Sure we will.' Turning to Dimitri, he said, 'What about the others? We can't leave without them.'

Dimitri shook his head. 'Dead.'

Kirsty looked aghast. '*All* of them?'

'What about Kinley and his boys?' Nick added.

Dimitri looked at him questioningly. 'Sorry, I not...'

'The black guy and his two little boys,' Nick said.

The man's face filled with sadness. 'Oh, I see teddy bear. I think ground it swallow them.'

Nick frowned. 'How do you mean "swallowed" them?'

'The ground it sand, but not solid sand. It very dangerous.' He thought for a second. 'Persons stand on it and they are sinking. I think man and boys sink in it.'

'He means quicksand, Dad!' Charlie said.

'I see many other bodies too. Everyone dead,' Dimitri continued.

'What about the two girls, the Hazelwood girls,' Kirsty said.

Dimitri shrugged. 'I not see them. Possibly they still live. But…'

'They're dead too.' Hollie was staring at the ground.

Nick looked at Dimitri, who shook his head. 'Dimitri no see. But if she say…'

'I saw their bodies in the woods near where I got out,' Hollie said adamantly. 'It was them and they were both dead.'

'So it's just us then,' Nick said, the gravity of his own words hitting home as he spoke them. He looked at Kirsty. 'Christ…' He motioned to Charlie. 'Come give your old man a hand getting to the minibus, would you buddy?'

Charlie came over and hooked an arm through his.

Nick shook his head and smiled at Kirsty. 'I think it's time to go home. Come on, let's get out of this rain and off this infernal island.'

CHAPTER 30

The ice cream parlour was shrouded in an eerie silence. A solitary Olive-tree Warbler was pecking at some small insect it had found on the decking.

Suddenly there was an almighty crash, the glass on one of the doors to the parlour shattered and a chair came flying out, bounced across the decking and spun to a halt in the dust.

As the startled bird took flight, Billie-Jo's face appeared on the other side of the hole.

'Hello?' she called out.

She waited for a few moments, then beckoned to Bobbi-Leigh, who stepped up behind her. 'What are we going to do now?'

Billie-Jo scowled. 'We're not waitin' here any longer. I told ya, that rancid bitch wasn't comin' back for us.'

'Maybe we shoulda shouted out to that guy after all. Maybe he was coming to help us.'

'Stop chattin' shit. What kind of person sneaks about in the woods in a long black coat with their face covered?' Billie-Jo shook her head. 'I fink we already had that conversation.'

As they carefully negotiated their way through the shards of glass still hanging on the door and stepped out onto the decking Bobbi-Leigh grabbed her sister's arm. 'Listen,' she said. 'What's that noise?'

'What ya chattin' about now? I can't hear nuffink. Come on.'

'No wait,' Bobbi-Leigh insisted. 'Listen.'

Billie-Jo strained her ears. At first she couldn't hear anything, but then it came again and this time she heard it: the muffled sound of banging.

'It's coming from underneath us!' Bobbi-Leigh exclaimed. She dropped to her knees and laid her ear to the floor. 'I think someone's down there.'

'Bollocks!' Billie-Jo said.

'No, really, listen,' Bobbi-Leigh implored her.

The sound came again. Louder this time. Billie-Jo squatted down and hammered her fist twice on the decking. Two muted banging noises reciprocated from over near the steps. 'Shit,' she said. 'You're right.' She moved over to the trapdoor and thumped the decking three times; after a moment she received the same pattern of knocks in return.

'This could be a trap,' Bobbi-Leigh said warily.

'It *is* a fuckin' trap you moron,' Billie-Jo scoffed. 'We know it is. And it sounds like someone's in it.'

'Maybe it's that perv's kid again.'

'Maybe we should fuckin' leave her there then.'

A thought flashed through Bobbi-Leigh's mind. 'Hey, what if it's Dad?!'

Billie-Jo's expression changed. 'Only one way to find out.' She got up and ducked back through the broken door into the parlour. A few moments later she reappeared with a strip of metal about two feet long in her hand.

'What's that?' Bobbi-Leigh said.

'I broke it off one of the tables.' She saw the look of her sister's face. 'So let 'em fuckin' sue me!'

She wedged the end of the metal between the edge of the decking and the side of the trap door. 'I dunno how anyone could fall for this,' she said. 'It's obvious it's a trapdoor, you'd have to be stupid to tread on it.'

'Which we probably would have done if that woman hadn't warned us,' Bobbi-Leigh mused. 'It's not *that* obvious, that's the point of a trapdoor, moron.'

'Says the traitorous bitch who can't keep her hands off other people's boyfriends,' Billie-Jo muttered without looking up. Using the strip of metal as a lever, she applied her full weight to the end. It started to bow, then slipped and came loose. 'Piece of shit!' she exclaimed, dropping it and clutching at her hand. 'Nearly broke my fuckin' wrist.'

'How about I *do* tread on it?' Bobbi-Leigh suggested. 'Just kinda stamp down really hard and fast. With some weight on it it's got to open, that's how trapdoors work ain't it?'

Billie-Jo looked at her doubtfully. 'I s'pose it's worth a try. Worst fing that could happen is ya die and I don't have to put up with ya no more.'

Bobbi-Leigh gave her sister a sarcastic smile. Then she bent down low alongside the trapdoor and banged on it. 'If ya can hear me, we're gonna try to get ya out. Stay away from the door, it's gonna open very suddenly. Bang twice if ya understand.'

Two muffled banging sounds came in response.

Bobbi-Leigh stood up and held out her hand to Billie-Jo. 'Hang on to me... just in case.'

Billie-Jo took her sister's hand. 'Just be fuckin' quick.'

Standing at the edge of the trapdoor, Bobbi-Leigh lifted her leg and brought her foot down hard. Nothing happened. She tried again, but with the same result. 'Fuck's sake.' She looked at Billie-Jo. 'You're holdin' tight as ya can aren't ya?'

'Course I am!'

Bobbi-Leigh brought down her foot again with all her might. There was a loud clang and as the hatchway yawned open beneath her, Billie-Jo yanked her hard and the two of them went sprawling back onto the decking, a tangle of flailing limbs.

They both sat up.

'Fuck me, that was intense, wasn't it?!' Bobbi-Leigh said, laughing. 'Thanks for pulling me back. I owe ya one.'

'Ya owe me for a shit ton more than that,' Billie-Jo said. She got onto her knees and crawled over to the edge of the trapdoor and peered into the gloom. 'Dad?'

A small voice echoed out of the darkness. 'Help us!'

Billie-Jo glanced at Bobbi-Leigh, who had crawled up beside her. 'Well it ain't Dad then.' She looked back down. 'Who's there?'

'It's Jordan and my brother Jack is with me. We're stuck down here inside some sort of metal box.'

Billie-Jo squinted and, as her eyes adjusted, she was able to make out two small, frightened faces gazing up at her. 'Fuck me, how long have ya been down there?'

'Ages.'

'Is there anything down there you can climb on?' Bobbi-Leigh said.

'No, nothing,' Jordan replied forlornly. Then his voice brightened. 'If I get down on all fours and Jack stands on my back, would you be able to reach him?'

'Probably,' Bobbi-Leigh replied.

Jack looked scared. 'I'm not sure I can get up there.'

Jordan smiled. 'Of course you can. I'll get you as high as I can, but then you're gonna have to stretch real far so they can get you.'

Billie-Jo looked at her sister. 'What d'ya reckon?'

'Sure. One arm each.'

Jack climbed carefully onto his brother's back and stretched up. The two girls, leaning as far as they could over the edge, took hold of one arm each and hoisted him out almost effortlessly.

'How are we gonna get the other one out?'

Jordan was back on his feet and fiddling with the belt on his cargo trousers. 'If I throw this up to you, can you dangle it?'

'We'll give it a try,' Bobbi-Leigh said.

Jordan flung it up and Billie-Jo caught it. She leaned over and stretched down as far as she could. At the bottom of the pit, standing on his tiptoes, the boy just managed to grab hold of the end. 'I've got it!'

As he dangled from the belt, scrabbling with his feet against the wall, the two girls managed to hoist him up and out.

'Thanks.' He smiled at the two girls. 'We'd never have got out without you.'

'No sweat,' Billie-Jo said. 'Now come on, we have to get out of here.'

As they made their way around the sandpit, Jack cast a last sad look at his abandoned teddy bear. 'Bye-bye, Mooch,' he said under his breath.

'Where are we going?' Jordan asked.

'We have to find a way back to the main gate,' Billie-Jo said. 'That's the only way out. There's fuckin' cameras everywhere, so we need to keep movin' as fast as we can.'

Jordan looked unsure. 'What about everyone else? Will they be there?'

'I don't know, but I don't actually give a shit about anyone else right now,' Billie-Jo snapped. 'If they're there they're there, if they ain't they ain't. You can either come with us or not, choice is yours.'

'Okay,' Jordan said. He took Jack's hand. 'What do we do if they aren't there?'

'We leave.'

'How?' Bobbi-Leigh said. 'There's a fuckin' big fence, or had ya kinda forgotten that little detail?'

'We find a way over the fence and we get our arses down to where that boat dropped us off and hope maybe Dad got there. And with luck there'll be a boat come along at some point.'

Bobbi-Leigh sighed. 'And what if it doesn't?'

'Fuck's sake, Bob, give it a rest with the questions! I just don't know, okay? If you've got a better idea let's hear it.'

A short time later, they had managed to find their way back through the undergrowth and out onto the track. They followed the line of the trees until they reached the entrance.

'Fuckin' hell, they're actually open!' Bobbi-Leigh exclaimed, staring in disbelief at the gates ahead.

Although he was pleased to see the exit, Jordan could barely disguise his disappointment that none of the adults were there.

'Come on!' Billie-Jo cried.

Jordan grabbed Jack's hand again and all four of them broke into a sprint. Moments later they were through the gates and out onto the road, tearing along at a frantic pace. A few minutes on, the road curved away and, as their last sight of the Hallam Holidays resort disappeared in the distance behind them, they slowed to a trot, and then finally stopped to catch their breath.

Bobbi-Leigh flopped down and stretched out on the grass at the side of the road. 'Shit, I'm absolutely knackered!'

The two boys sat down beside her.

'Don't get comfortable,' Billie-Jo said. 'We need to get to the sea as soon as we can.'

Bobbi-Leigh rolled her eyes at the two boys, but she kept silent.

A couple of minutes later they were on the move again. Billie-Jo set the pace with Jordan and Jack following closely in her wake.

Bobbi-Leigh was trailing behind a bit and she withdrew a bar of chunky chocolate from the back pocket of her jeans. Tearing off the end of the sparkly foil wrapper with her teeth and spitting it out, she winced at the sight of the partially melted contents, but then took a big bite anyway.

As she took a second large bite, Billie-Jo just happened to glance back. 'C'mon, Bob, keep up will ya, or we'll never…' Her eyes fell on the sweetie bar in her sister's hand and she saw her chewing. She stopped in her tracks. 'What the fuck's *that*?!'

'Calm down, it's only a bit of chocolate,' Bobbi-Leigh said. 'I was gonna share,' she added, hoping the fib wasn't too obvious.

'Where the fuck did it come from?!'

Bobbi-Leigh wiped a smear of chocolate from her lips and sucked it off her fingers. 'It was on the counter in the ice cream place.'

Billie-Jo could hardly believe what she was hearing. 'Are you fuckin' serious? That woman said not to touch anythin'!'

'No, she told us not to eat the ice cream, that's all. She didn't say anythin' about the sweets. This is really scrummy.' As the words left her mouth, Bobbi-Leigh let out a sudden cry, dropped the chocolate bar and doubled over, clutching at her stomach.

Billie-Jo ran past the boys, pushed Bobbi-Leigh to the ground, rolled her on to her side and forced open her mouth. 'Puke it up!' she shouted, thrusting her index and middle fingers down her sister's throat. The girl immediately gagged and brought up a mouthful of thick brown sludge. 'Again!' Billie-Jo cried, desperately forcing her fingers down Bobbi-Leigh's throat for a second time.

Rather than vomiting, Bobbi-Leigh jerked away, her eyes bugged out and she began to shake violently. As she tried to scream she wretched again, except this time the brown mess was speckled with bright red blood.

Jordan and Jack were watching, their eyes filled with terror, as Billie-Jo stood up and stared helplessly down at her sister. 'I don't know what to do!' she screamed.

Writhing around on the ground, Bobbi-Leigh was holding her stomach, which was convulsing. Her legs began to twitch and then, making a gurgling noise that Billie-Jo would never forget, her body gave a final shudder and fell still.

'Bob!' Billie-Jo screamed and knelt down beside her sister's body. She shook her vigorously. 'Wake up! This can't be fuckin' happenin'! No, no, no!' And then the futility of what she was doing struck home and the tears came.

Almost five minutes passed, during which Billie-Jo sat cradling Bobbi-Leigh's limp body in her arms, her face buried in her younger sister's soft hair, sobbing quietly to herself.

It was Jack who finally spoke. 'Can we go please?'

Billie-Jo looked up at him. Her face was streaked with tears. 'What?'

'Can we go?' the boy repeated.

Jordan stepped in to back up his little brother. 'I mean there's nothing more we can do, is there? We need to go.'

Billie-Jo looked down at Bobbi-Leigh and brushed the strands of hair away from her pretty face. 'I'm sorry,' she whispered and kissed her softly on her forehead. Then she eased her sister back onto the ground and stood up. She looked at Jordan. 'Give me a hand,' she said.

Together they carried Bobbi-Leigh's body over into the trees and set it gently down among the leaves.

'Go wait for me on the road,' Billie-Jo said.

When the boy had gone she scooped up several handfuls of foliage and carefully covered over the body. With a last look back – 'I love you, Bob.' – she walked back out onto the road where the two boys were waiting. Avoiding eye contact, she brushed past them and set off down the road. 'Come on then.'

The sun was low in the sky when the sea finally came into sight.

As Billie-Jo rounded the bend onto the final, quarter-mile stretch down to the jetty, her eyes widened. 'There's the bus!' she cried excitedly. 'And look – the boat!'

Jordan and Jack, who were tiring and had been lagging further and further behind, swiftly picked up the pace and ran up beside her.

They looked to where she was pointing and, sure enough, parked up at the top end of the jetty was the minibus and at the far end was a small motorboat. And although none of them could make out who exactly, they could clearly see people climbing aboard.

'Come on!' Billie-Jo shouted and took off. The two boys found their second wind and spurted after her.

The three of them ran as fast as their legs would carry them, yelling for all they were worth.

Suddenly Billie-Jo tripped and pitched forward onto the hot tarmac. Jordan and Jack were so close behind that they weren't able to stop. With a cry of surprise, both of them tripped over her and were sent sprawling.

'Motherfucker!' Billie-Jo exclaimed angrily, picking herself up. As she examined her bloody knees and hands, there was a sudden roaring sound and she looked up to see the motorboat move away from the end of the jetty. 'Wait!' she cried and started to run again, but her leg gave way beneath her and she hit the ground again.

Jack and Jordan were back on their feet too and they helped her up.

Jordan had tears in his eyes. 'They didn't see us.'

'They're leaving us behind,' Jack wailed.

Together they limped on down the road, waving and shouting, but each of them knew it was pointless. The boat was moving fast now and no-one on board would have been able to hear them over the loud whirring noise of the motor.

By the time Billie-Jo, Jordan and Jack reached the slatted walkway, the motorboat was at least half a mile out, receding into the distance.

The three youngsters sat themselves down on the end of the jetty and dangled their legs over the side. They watched in silence, silhouetted against the sun as it slowly dipped on the horizon. Its vibrant rays were defining the sporadic streaks of cottonwool cloud in the sky with radiant flares of orange and the gently undulating sea was dappled with shimmering light, which gradually darkened to crimson as the uppermost curve of the vast auburn sphere finally slipped sleepily out of sight.

Acknowledgements:
The authors would like to thank Sandra Watson and Sara Greaves.
Special thanks to John Sinclair-Thomas for the illustration
depicting the Hallam Holidays resort on Mástiga.

Rebecca Xibalba would especially like to thank Rik Mayall
for a lifetime of inspiraton, laughter and education.
Gone but never forgotten.

Cover photography and design by Rebecca Xibalba.

Also from Rebecca Xibalba and Tim Greaves:
Misdial (2020)
Available from Amazon, for Kindle and in paperback.
Also available in Audiobook format from Audible and iTunes.

Printed in Great Britain
by Amazon